HOLIDAY IN JULY

JULIET MADISON

To my miracle baby Zaki, who took just as long to come as this book took to write!

CHAPTER ONE

L acie Appleby was no stranger to keeping secrets. As a beauty therapist and make-up artist, clients often told her all about their lives; sometimes mundane, sometimes fascinating... but often with the odd secret slipping out during waxing, brow-shaping, or a foot spa. Whether it was something as innocent as pretending not to be home when an uninvited visitor turned up, or something not-so-innocent as a regretful fling with an ex after starting a promising new relationship, Lacie had heard it all. The lies, the confessions, the truth, the regrets, the marital dissatisfactions, and the wild dating adventures. But now, she had a secret of her own to keep.

Lacie stepped off the train and though she would normally walk the flight of stairs up to the crossbridge, even with luggage, she got in the elevator and rubbed her lower back. When she got out, the salty scent of the sea warmed her senses and woke her up from the travel fatigue.

Tarrin's Bay. Home. Well, the home she *used* to know.

She stood by the station entrance and scanned the drop-off zone and the lamp-lit street. A sedan drove in, and she sheltered her eyes from the glare. The lights switched off and Lacie squinted at the figure stepping out. 'Penny?'

'Lacie!'

Penny dashed towards her, arms outstretched, and Lacie flung her arms around the sister she hadn't seen in almost two years. 'Ohh,' she sighed. 'It's so good to see you.' She held on tightly for longer than a usual hug, and Penny sighed too.

'Can't believe you're here.' Penny pulled back but held Lacie at arm's length, her eyes slightly glossy. 'Wow, your hair is different again. Is that a touch of... pink?'

Lacie smiled and nodded. 'You know me. I get bored with the same do all the time.' She patted her tousled hair.

'Yep, and I have the same shoulder-length blonde bob I've had since high school.' She turned to the car and rubbed her hands together. 'Let's get in, I've got the heating on.' She popped open the boot and helped Lacie load her bright pink luggage; Lacie keeping hold of her small shoulder bag as she got into the passenger seat. 'The kids are so excited to see you, they wanted to come and greet you as well but it was too late for them, they fell asleep an hour ago.'

'Oh, can't I wake them up when I get to the house?' Lacie missed her niece and nephew and had brought them some surprises.

'Hmm, that could be a big mistake as then they'll be up half the night and grumpy tomorrow.'

'It's okay, they can wake *me* up bright and early... that's if I can get any sleep after snoozing on the plane, it's morning back in the States now.' She rubbed the back of her neck, sore from leaning against the window on the plane where she had propped her travel pillow.

'Ah, give it a few days and you'll be used to your native country's time zone again. It's in your DNA.'

'Hope so. Is everyone else still up?'

'Of course. Mum never sleeps as you know, and Chris and Matt were playing cards when I left. And my darling husband is on night shift.'

'And Ellie?'

'Earbuds in, tapping her foot to whatever ridiculous music she's listening to while using her laptop.'

Lacie smiled. She couldn't wait to see her siblings, even more so now, as they hadn't had their annual Christmas in July family reunion last year. *This year we'll make up for it*, her mum had said via text a week ago, when confirming flight details with Lacie. It would be different without Dad, but hopefully they'd be able to keep each other's spirits high this year, just as their father, ever the optimist, had always done in difficult times.

When Penny drove the car up the hill on the other side of the highway, through the rural landscape of one of the most prized locations in town that overlooked the distant but expansive ocean, an increasing swell of emotion rose higher with each breath that Lacie took. She sniffled.

'Hope you don't have a cold? Last thing we need is a bug to go around the family like that gastro catastrophe four years ago.'

Lacie flicked her hand. 'Nah, I'm fine. Just...' She sniffed again. 'It's just, good to be home, that's all.'

Penny turned her head a moment and smiled. And when her sister drove into the C-shaped driveway of South Haven, the Appleby family guest house, Lacie swallowed a large lump in her throat. She hadn't expected to feel this emotional, but apparently her body was responding with a mind of its own.

No tears, no tears.

'Here we are, home sweet home.' Penny stopped the engine.

Gravel crunched underneath Lacie's tan suede boots when she eagerly stepped out of the car, wanting to dash into the warmth of the grand sandstone house and sit around the fireplace with her mother's best hot cocoa.

Penny yawned. 'Bed is calling me, I've been up since the crack of dawn, but I'll stay up a while with you first.' She placed her arm around Lacie's waist as they walked to the front door together, each tugging a piece of luggage along the bumpy driveway until it reached the smoothness of the path.

The door opened before they got to it.

'Lacie!' Her mother, Martha, stood in the doorway with a soft but welcoming smile, and fluffy white dressing-gown-covered arms out to her sides like angel wings.

'Mum!' Lacie smiled and softened against her mother's embrace, another swell of emotion rising up. She was glad her flight had arrived at night, so she would have some time to settle in and think on her own for a while, before talking too much and catching up with everyone. She didn't know if she could even hold a proper conversation yet, with so much on her mind. So much she couldn't discuss.

'Now, how was the food on the plane? Do you need a proper home-cooked meal? What about a hot cocoa?' Martha got to work, checking on every little detail as they went into the house.

'I'm fine for now, Mum, thanks. Let me just see... Chris, hi! Good to see you.' Her oldest brother walked in, followed by Matt. 'Matt, you too.' She gave them each a hug, noticing that Chris felt more 'cuddlier' than usual.

'How was the flight?' they both asked at the same time, then chuckled.

'Not too bad,' she said first to Chris, then repeated her answer to Matt.

'Looking great, Lace.' Matt touched her pink-highlighted strawberry-blonde hair, the subtle curls of which had probably flattened out from the headrest on the plane.

'After a whole day of travel, yeah I bet!' She rolled her eyes.

When they resumed normal position, a flash of grey caught in her peripheral vision. 'Ellie, there you are! Come here, girl.'

Her youngest sister, perpetual student of literature and philosophy, seemed stuck to the door frame. Her grey hoodie loose and bulky over her petite frame, she ambled over slowly at Lacie's request and sunk into her embrace. 'You okay?'

'Just tired, too many late nights on the computer.'

'You should have some fun too, you know.'

'But there's so much to learn and so little time.'

'El, you're twenty-nine, you probably have a good sixty years in you yet.'

Her sister shrugged. 'Anyway, nice to see you, did you bring goodies?'

'Oh yeah, any more of that ready-to-eat cookie dough you got us last time?' Chris asked.

Lacie put her hands on her hips. 'Do you guys *only* care about the presents I may or may not have brought you?'

'What do you mean, *may not have*?' Matt nudged her.

'You can all wait until the present opening ceremony after our Christmas in July dinner,' Lacie instructed. 'Only the kids get an early gift now.'

'Okaaay,' Ellie said.

'Now, who's going to help Lacie take her luggage to her room while I make a batch of cocoa?' her mother asked.

'Me,' said Chris.

'That's only because you're losing at cards,' Matt teased.

'Again?' Lacie said.

'I may be *losing*,' he said in a dramatic voice, 'but I have not *lost*.' He picked up the handles of her two bags and rolled them behind him as he walked from the entry foyer into the living room.

Hadn't her dad said something like that before he died?

Martha paused in her busyness for a moment, her gaze distant, as though she wondered the same thing.

Every now and again, words he used to say would pop into Lacie's mind at weird moments. Or she would say them herself, as though he was watching over her, reminding her of things, and keeping her spirits up... *Oh well, there's always tomorrow...* and *Nonsense, there's no such thing as a 'bad day' if you're alive...* and the one that haunted her time and time again: *It's okay, Lace, I'll see you at the next reunion.*

But she never did.

His presence, though, was as much in her life, and in this house, as it ever was. Memories of his voice echoed through the rooms as she walked through the living room with Chris, expecting her dad to spring out of nowhere and say 'Boo!' as they entered the hallway, and then, wondering if he'd left a secret note on her pillow as she entered the ground-floor guest bedroom allocated to her for the next two weeks... *Always end your day with a happy thought*, or, *sweet dreams*, they would say. Her siblings would get them too, but hers always seemed so appropriate, as though her father always knew what was troubling her or what she was thinking on any given day.

She wished he had words of advice for her now, when she needed them the most.

Instead, she had her brother's more practical words of advice: 'If you get cold, just give the window a bit of a shove.' He demonstrated. 'It comes loose a bit from the side right here.' He pointed.

She nodded. 'Thanks.' But she was used to the cold, having lived in Chicago for so many years now.

They made their way back to the living room and sipped their warm beverages in front of the fireplace, while Penny yawned for the umpteenth time, Martha asked more questions, Chris ate muffins, Matt texted his girlfriend, and Ellie had one earbud in and one out; contributing occasionally to the conversation.

Lacie yawned too.

'Aren't you supposed to be wide awake at this time?' asked Penny.

Lacie shrugged. 'Guess I'm more tired than I thought.'

'Right, off to bed while you're feeling drowsy, then,' said her mother. 'Otherwise, when you try to sleep you won't be able to, and it'll be good to get into a routine as soon as possible.'

Lacie stood, grabbing hold of the armrest of the upholstered chair when a wave of dizziness surprised her.

Her mother held on to her arm. 'You look a bit pale, are you all right?'

'Yes, yes, totally fine. Just been a long day, Or night. Or whatever time it is.' She gave a wide 'I'm fine' smile and said her goodnights. 'Are we decorating the tree on Friday?' She turned to her mother.

Martha clasped her hands together. 'Indeedio.'

'Yay. Can't wait.' Lacie always looked forward to the family tree decorating tradition. And it was her turn to put the angel on the top this year.

She made her way to the bathroom adjacent to her room for a quick shower, then fell onto the soft and comforting bed. 'Ahhh...' She exhaled in relief, and that was the last thing she remembered before waking early to the sound of a lawnmower.

'Huh?' She sat half upright, not used to the sound as she lived in an apartment building with no grass in sight. *Why is Chris up so early mowing the lawn? Or is it Matt, or... no, it wouldn't be Ellie.*

She got up and put on a dressing gown, opened the French doors to her private patio and stepped outside. Sheltering her eyes from the morning sun with her hand, a lawnmower came into view, along with the broad back of a man.

As he turned around in readiness to do the next strip of grass, she caught his eye, at the same time as a twinge caught her stomach. Her mouth salivated suddenly and she gulped, her belly fluttering... but it wasn't from the sight of the man with the well-built frame and tanned face, it was...

Oh God.

Her stomach heaved. She held her hand over her mouth, looking side to side. The man stopped cutting the grass just as she turned to dash back inside to the bathroom, but she couldn't make it through the patio door in time. With an almighty heave and a loud retch, she leaned forward over the nearest pot plant and emptied her stomach contents.

Her legs wobbly and a headache forming, she wiped her mouth with her sleeve and tried to stand upright.

A hand gripped her arm. 'You okay?'

She turned her head and looked into the concerned eyes of the lawnmower man. She closed her eyes a moment and sighed. 'Oh, man.' She shook her head and covered her face with her free hand.

'Here, sit down.' He gestured to the wicker chair on the patio. 'I'll go get someone? And some water?'

Lacie straightened up suddenly, then grasped the armrest as she almost fell onto the chair. 'No!' She tucked a wet strand of hair behind her ear. 'I mean, thanks. But no, I'm okay.' She managed an embarrassed smile. 'It's just... jet lag, and... alcohol,' she lied. 'Never again.'

The man's posture loosened a bit and he put his hands in his pockets. 'Ahh, I see. In that case, maybe a shower, some water, B vitamins, and a big fat cheesy pizza?'

Lacie's stomach spasmed at the thought and she gulped down hard.

'Perhaps not,' he concluded. He turned and gestured to the front of the house. 'You sure you don't want me to get someone?'

'Definitely not. Don't want Mum to see me like this, I'll never hear the end of it.'

'You're Martha Appleby's daughter?'

'One of them, yes.'

'I know Penny and Ellie, but it appears I haven't met you.'

'You have now,' she said, 'and what a wonderful first impression I've made!' She managed a laugh and he let one out too.

'I'm Nathan, your mum hired me to do the gardens and odd jobs around the house.'

'I'm Lacie. And I'm usually only in the country once a year for our family reunion.'

He smiled and placed a finger over his lips. 'Well, your secret's safe with me. We've all been there, done that,' he said with a wink.

She nodded thanks, but he definitely did *not* know her secret, and he definitely had *not* been there and done that. And she definitely hoped that every morning for the next two weeks would *not* be exactly like this. Because then she would have a damn hard time keeping secret from her family the fact she was pregnant following a should-never-have-happened trip down memory lane with her ex-boyfriend, who just so happened to be one of Hollywood's rising stars. And with her successful life and career in Chicago, his in L.A., and the fact she had definitely *not* planned anything whatsoever to do with motherhood in the near future, she had absolutely no idea what to do.

CHAPTER TWO

A fter nibbling on salty crackers leftover from the flight and freshening up in the bathroom, Lacie went back to her bed. She tilted her head in the direction of the door as little footsteps padded down the hallway. She quickly pulled the covers up to her chin and closed her eyes, holding back a giggle.

'Shh, she might still be asleep!' her niece whispered outside the door.

A soft click sounded as the door opened, but Lacie stayed completely still as though fast asleep.

Muffled giggles from her sister's young kids made it hard for her not to laugh, but she kept her eyes tightly shut and waited.

The footsteps neared and when she sensed they were about to climb on her bed or tap her on the shoulder, she sat bolt upright.

'Raaa!' she roared, flicking the covers off and holding up her hands like claws.

'Agh!' The children jumped backwards in surprise, while Penny held a hand over her heart and laughed.

'You scared me!' seven-year-old Jessie exclaimed, before collapsing on the bed in a fit of giggles. Her younger brother

Dane jumped on the bed with hands like claws, copying Lacie's monster attempts.

Lacie growled further then pulled the boy into an embrace. 'Come here, little monster, how old are you now?'

'Five and a HALF.' He loudly emphasised the important bit.

She ruffled his scruffy, sandy-coloured hair. 'And what new skills do you have to tell me about, huh? Last time it was building a Lego mansion in under an hour.'

'I can eat a WHOLE pizza in one go.' He grinned and patted his belly.

'Oh, is that right? Well, I challenge you, mister. By the time I go back overseas, I want you to learn how to MAKE a whole pizza. How 'bout that?'

His eyes and mouth opened wide and he glanced at his mother, who raised her eyebrows and tried to appear confident, though Lacie knew she was thinking, 'yeah, nah, aint gonna happen'.

'I'll... THINK about it,' he decided.

'Do you have to go back overseas?' Jessie snuggled into Lacie's side. 'Can't you stay here all the time?'

'Ohh, sweetie, I'd love to but my work is in America. And it makes it extra special when I do come to visit you guys. And,' she clambered away from her niece's clingy grasp and rummaged in her bag, 'then I get to bring you... presents!' She held up a couple of wrapped gifts.

Their faces brightened and they jumped up and down. 'Yes!' Jessie said, sitting cross-legged on the bed and holding out her hands in readiness to receive.

Penny mouthed 'thank you' as the kids ripped open their presents.

Moments later Jessie was oohing and ahhing at her crystal

art kit and Dane was tipping out pieces from the box of his Lego pirate ship.

'Hey, hey, not in here. Let's take this to the lounge room, shall we?' Penny directed, and after an enthusiastic 'thanks, Aunty Lacie!' he dashed out the door to begin construction.

'Can you paint my nails again like last time too?' Jessie asked, hugging her present to her chest.

'I sure can.' She smiled. 'How about... rainbow colours this time?'

Jessie nodded rapidly.

'But first, Lacie needs to settle in and get a handle on her jet lag. C'mon, let's leave her to it and I'll help you get breakfast.' Penny smiled at her sister and left the room with her daughter.

Lacie shook her head in awe at how quickly the kids had grown.

Life moves so fast...

She lowered her gaze to her belly, and wondered how fast *this* life would grow. It wouldn't be obvious for a while yet, but she felt bigger than usual. And her emotions swelled too. She tipped her head back and sent a sharp exhale to the ceiling. There were important decisions to be made, and she would have to make them soon.

Lacie picked up her phone, checked the time difference in Los Angeles, and a moment later was greeted by Xavier's voicemail greeting. Her shoulders relaxed a little, relieved she didn't have to talk directly to him, but knowing she'd have to eventually.

'Hi, Xavier. It's me, Lacie. I, um, need to have a chat sometime, please. Thanks. Sometime soon, if possible. Call me, um, when you're free, thanks. Okay, thanks, bye. Oh wait, I'm in Australia by the way. Okay... thanks.'

Lacie rested her forehead on her palm and sighed. What was with all the pleasantries and excessive gratitude? She was always confident in dealing with people, but now she sounded like a nervous teenager calling her crush for the first time. And how was she going to tell him?

'Hi, Xavier, remember our great night together a few weeks ago? Well, surprise! Guess what?'

Anyway, he was always busy. It could be days, or even weeks before he returned her call. She knew he was due to start working on a new film this month, may have already started. He'd be 'in the zone' no doubt which would make having a serious discussion difficult. Still, it had to be done.

And so did something else...

'Hello, this is Lacie Appleby, Martha's daughter,' she said into the phone as she paced up and down the room. 'I'm in town for two weeks and was wondering if there are any appointments available soon?'

'Let me check for you. Who did you see last time you were here?' the receptionist said.

'Dr Greene. But it's been a while.'

She heard tapping. 'Dr Greene has a cancellation next Tuesday if you'd like to come at ten thirty?'

Lacie nibbled her lip. *Hmm, five more days.* But what if the morning sickness got worse? She wouldn't be able to keep it secret and put it down to a twenty-four-hour bug when it could go on for weeks. She couldn't tell anyone until she'd told the father and decided what to do. Besides, if her family knew, everyone would fuss over her and pester her with questions and she wouldn't be able to have a proper holiday.

'Okay, I'll take it, unless I can find something sooner elsewhere, in which case I'll call you back.'

'No problem, Lacie, and I'll let you know if there are any further cancellations.'

She ended the call and the bedroom door clicked open gently.

'Lace? Sorry, sweetheart, I was about to check on you and couldn't help but overhear. Are you okay?'

Lacie swiped a strand of hair from her temple. 'Yep. All good. Just jet lag and some bad airplane food, I think. Might need some melatonin or something.' She smiled. 'Anyway, good morning, Mumma dear.'

'Good morning.' Her mum kissed her cheek and gave her a hug. 'I have a doctor's appointment booked for tomorrow morning actually, but it's just a general check-up, no big deal. Would you like to take my slot and I'll reschedule?'

'Oh, are you sure? Unless you need it more than me.'

'Nonsense, I'm fit as a fiddle. Just due for my mammogram and ultrasound and a few blood tests soon. I'll change it to another time.' She held out her hand for Lacie's phone, and Lacie pressed the last number called.

A minute later Lacie was booked in to see Dr Greene at 9.45am tomorrow, her mother taking the Tuesday slot. *Phew!* She didn't know if much could be done but it was better to get everything checked out so she could try to relax for the next couple of weeks.

'Now, are you hungry? We've got some bacon and eggs cooking.' Martha's eyes widened and she ushered her daughter out the door. Lacie nodded but her stomach twinged, and her mouth salivated but not in the 'eager for food' way.

'I'll pop to the toilet and be out in a minute. Thanks, Mum!' Lacie closed the bathroom door behind her and took a deep breath.

Oh boy, this was going to be a challenge.

CHAPTER THREE

F riday was Nathan Sharp's favourite day of the week. He still got to work doing what he loved; gardening and landscaping, but also had the anticipation of the weekend when he could do his *own* gardening and landscaping, not that he had much room in his backyard. He would also make time for a surf if the weather was good for it, or fishing, or hanging out by the water or in nature. And when he wasn't experiencing it for himself, he was watching and learning about it through his documentary addiction.

Walking back home on Friday morning with a matcha latte in his hand after a jog around the harbour, he turned into his street. The sun shone brightly through the gaps between houses and trees, and it shimmered on a flash of pink up ahead. The pink highlights on strawberry blonde hair bounced as a woman walked along the pathway to the medical clinic. She stopped for a moment and took a swig from her water bottle, glancing around momentarily, and he realised it was Martha Appleby's daughter, Lacie. He quickened his pace in an attempt to call out to her and say hello, but she made her way briskly to the entrance and disappeared inside. A cheeky smile cornered its way onto his lips. She probably needed some help for her hangover and jet lag, poor woman. He'd had the odd female (and male) throw up around him in his early twenties when living in the Sydney suburbs and attending numerous parties, but it was a bit funny to see it happen to someone from a respectable family who looked like their drinking and partying days were a decade behind them.

He wasn't working at South Haven today, instead he'd be doing his fortnightly shift at the local primary school to weed and maintain the garden for a few hours this afternoon, as well as fixing up some seating that had come loose in the play area while the kids were on school holidays. He found himself curious about Lacie and looked forward to seeing her again on Monday when he returned to work on the property.

Nathan preferred to spend most of his time alone, only having the occasional catch-up with mates. Life was easier that way. Less conflicts to resolve. But he did miss female company, never having had more than a casual drink or lunch with a few dates here and there in the past couple of years or so, ever since... that time. That experience that had made his newly opened heart close up again like a heavy wooden door, with a few extra boards nailed across it for stronger protection. There had been a glimmer of something between him and Hannah Delaney a while back, but he hadn't felt enough of a spark, despite their shared love of nature. He'd wanted to feel something, but couldn't. The hurt was still too raw, so he'd resisted her flirting, and anyway, she'd ended up reuniting with her old school friend and his ex-roommate, Luca, who was no doubt the best man for her.

A couple of blocks past the clinic, Nathan unlocked the door to his townhouse, finished his latte and tossed the biodegradable cup into the kitchen bin, then switched on the TV. The documentary was still on pause from last night when he'd been too sleepy to finish watching it. He pressed play, then proceeded to make himself some brunch before he'd have to head off to work in an hour. As he arranged leftover roast lamb on four slices of bread, along with pickles and lettuce, the mesmerising voice of David Attenborough filled the room.

He was instantly transported to a world where all that mattered was living, surviving, and embracing the wonder of nature. As he cut his sandwiches into triangles, he mimicked the recognisable voice.

'This species evolved to survive in the harshest of habitats.'

He chuckled at his attempt and sat at the kitchen table to eat. He'd been used to amusing himself since he was a child, when often, he'd only had the company of himself. Being moved from foster home to foster home, he'd never found a true family to belong to. Or get close to. Solitude was his most trusted and reliable friend.

He paused mid bite as the close-up footage of the creatures captivated his curiosity. It always amazed him how animals were somehow designed to perfectly complement their environment, as though it had all been carefully planned out from the start of evolution.

When the documentary finished forty minutes later, he wondered if he should start his own YouTube channel, filming himself as he worked, and educating people about various plants, insects, birds, bees, and basic garden design tips. He shook his head.

Who would even watch?

He jumped in the shower then dressed, got into his Ute, and drove to the Tarrin's Bay hills where his favourite nursery and garden centre was. Using the funds the school had allocated to him, he purchased the plants and seeds they had wanted, based on his suggestions, to start preparing the new nature playground; mixing plants, herbs, and vegetables with an integrated playground for the kids to explore physical movement and health in a more natural way.

He would have to spend more time at the school come spring to keep everything maintained once students started to use the area, and would need to co-ordinate his work there with his work at South Haven. He loved both and didn't want to give up on one for the other, combined with the casual job as a lifeguard in the summer season that he did on weekends.

He paused for a moment to admire the surroundings of the nursery, eyeing a few plants he'd like for his own place. Before heading to the staff member to pay for the school's purchases, he added a couple of tea plants to his large plant trolley so he could take them home. He loved tea and thought it would be nice to grow his own.

He paid for them separately and loaded them into the Ute, then dropped the tea plants back home before heading to the school.

He parked in the reserved spot they had for him, close to the garden entry so he could easily bring the plants through, and signed in at the school office where a staff member was doing admin work. His phone beeped, and he glanced at it momentarily, expecting it to be an update from Martha about what was needed for next week's tasks, or perhaps one of his mates to see if he wanted to catch up for drinks tonight, but it was someone he hadn't heard from in a long time.

He furrowed his brow.

What the heck does she want?

He put his phone on silent and slid it into his pocket, wishing his ex-girlfriend's unexpected intrusion hadn't hijacked his favourite day.

'Lacie?' Dr Sylvia Greene called out as she emerged from her consulting room, smiling a greeting, her russet-red curls brightening the mostly white clinic.

'Hi,' Lacie said as she entered.

'It's been a long time. Your mother fills me in sometimes on your adventures in the States, how is everything going over there?'

Lacie wriggled a little to get comfortable on the firm chair. 'Good, I love it. So different to Tarrin's Bay but I really enjoy my work and have made some great friends.'

'Fantastic, are you still working in Hollywood as a make-up artist?'

'No, not much anymore. I've settled into my own beauty salon in Chicago, pampering people with scars, disabilities, and other issues; helping them feel confident about themselves.' Lacie smiled in satisfaction. She loved nothing more than to see a client leave her salon with a smile and a glow that wasn't there when they'd entered.

'How wonderful. Well, I hope you enjoy a well-earned break while you're here. How can I help you today?' Dr Greene clasped her hands on her lap and leaned slightly forward.

Lacie wriggled a bit more. 'Umm, the thing is.' She touched her belly. 'I'm pregnant.'

'Oh? Planned or unplanned?'

'Unplanned. I only just found out, the day I left to catch my flight. Took two tests to be sure. I'd been so busy tying up loose ends before my trip that I hadn't realised my period was late until I packed my toiletries bag.'

'How late is it? And what length are your cycles usually?'

'I'm fairly irregular, thanks to polycystic ovary syndrome… usually around thirty to thirty-five days. I was about a week late by the time I realised. I had bloating so I thought it was that time of the month coming on.'

Dr Greene asked some more questions including the date of her last period. 'Well, that would put you at about six weeks along,' she said. 'When do you fly back home?'

'July fifteenth.'

Dr Greene plucked a piece of paper from the wall shelf. 'I'll refer you for an ultrasound to check everything looks good and confirm how far along you are, and find out your estimated due date.' She started writing, then looked up. 'That is, if you'd like to?'

Lacie nodded, but scratched her head. 'I haven't even told the father. Or anyone else. I really don't know what to do.'

Dr Greene put down the pen. 'Do you want to have a baby?'

'I guess so. I mean, yes, eventually, but... oh, man.' She lowered her head.

'You weren't planning on it being so soon.'

'Exactly. And I'm not even in a relationship. It was just a brief... catch-up with my ex-boyfriend.'

'I see.' She nodded. 'Maybe you'll have some more clarity once you've told him. See what he thinks about it too.'

'Yeah. I left a message on his voicemail. Not sure when I'll hear back. Time differences and his busy schedule can make it difficult to get in touch.'

'Hopefully you get to speak soon and decide on your next steps. For now, though, it's my job to make sure you're healthy, so I do think a scan is a good idea, and some blood tests so I can confirm the pregnancy hormone levels and check on your thyroid, iron levels, immunity, and other things. Are you okay with that?'

'Sure.'

Dr Greene continued filling in the form then handed it to Lacie. 'Call them to make an appointment for late next week, probably Friday at the seven-week mark, so by then we should see a heartbeat.'

Heartbeat? Inside me? Was this really happening?

A wave of dizziness washed through her even though she was sitting, and she rubbed her forehead.

'How are you feeling?' the doctor asked.

'Tired and nauseous and a bit light-headed. I threw up yesterday in front of Mum's gardener.'

'Oh dear. Do you think you'll tell your mother, or other family members yet?'

'Not yet. I need to talk to my ex first, figure out what to do, then see. But for now, I want to try and enjoy my holiday without them knowing so I don't get fussed over and I can just relax.'

'Sounds like a plan. If you need some help with the nausea, try taking ginger tablets.' She wrote the suggestion down. 'Eat a small snack before getting out of bed, get plenty of rest, and here's the name of a medication you can take before bedtime if needed; it may make you drowsy but should help reduce the nausea quite a bit the next day. Just be sure to see a doctor when you return to America and have them reassess you, okay?'

'Will do.'

'Oh, and are you already taking a multivitamin? You'll need enough folic acid.'

'I take a women's multi,' Lacie said, searching on her phone for the brand to show her. 'Here, this one.'

Dr Greene looked at it. 'It's good, but I think you'll be better off with a specific pregnancy one.' She wrote down a name, then took Lacie's blood pressure and handed her the paper, a blood test request form, and also a fact sheet with a list of foods to avoid during pregnancy (no Brie? Damn!), along with links to various websites for advice.

'Acupuncture may also help, my husband does that here. Although it's best if it's done weekly, so as you're not staying long, see how you go and call us if you need any further help.'

'Thanks so much, Dr Greene. And do I come and see you after the ultrasound?'

'Only if you need to. I'll call you if there are any issues with your blood tests or scan results, and if you need to come in, I'll make sure we can squeeze you in before you fly back.'

'Sounds good. Thanks again.'

Lacie smiled and left the room, her gaze drawn to a young mother waiting in a nearby chair trying to read a book to her squirming toddler.

Was this really going to be her reality in a few years' time?

It was so far removed from the life she had pictured for herself for the next five years; running her business and working on the occasional movie, having free time to do as she pleased with her friends. But at thirty-one, maybe her biological clock was trying to tell her something different, in the most direct way:

Your time is now. Be grateful you have this opportunity when so many struggle with infertility.

Dr Greene was right, she needed to talk to Xavier sooner rather than later. It was his baby too, and he had a right to know, although she knew his reaction would be more than likely a negative one.

She stepped outside and walked along the path with her head down, deep in thought. She noticed a stem with leaves sprouting from between the cracks in the concrete. Amazing, and bizarre, how life could grow somewhere so unexpected. The persistence of nature.

Lacie stopped suddenly. She turned back toward the clinic, having forgotten to go to the attached pathology centre next door to have her blood taken. It must be the baby brain, or the sheer sense of being overwhelmed at her circumstances.

Ten minutes later she walked back along the pathway, a Band-Aid on her inner elbow. She pulled her sleeve back down to cover it and protect her from the slight chill in the air. Next stop: pharmacy.

She picked up the ginger tablets, multivitamin, and the 'just-in-case' medication which she'd already decided she'd try, so when she left the pharmacy, she bought a juice and packet of potato chips from the shop and swallowed two ginger tablets. Munching on the chips, she paused at the window display of Mrs May's Bookstore. A miniature red armchair with a teddy bear seated on it was facing the street, a fluffy blanket draped over it, and a teacup and saucer sat on the small round table next to it, along with a pile of three old-fashioned books. The cosiness invited her in. She shoved the half-eaten chip packet inside her bag and wiped her hands on a tissue, entering the store she remembered coming to as a child for Mrs May's reading sessions.

'How's your morning been? Oh, Lacie, is that you?' Mrs May's granddaughter, Olivia asked. Lacie remembered meeting her when Olivia had taken over the store along with her mother. They'd gone to the same school but Olivia was several years older.

'Hi, how've you been?' Lacie smiled.

'Great, thanks. And you? I saw your sister a couple of days ago, Ellie isn't it? She loves to browse.'

'I'm, ah, great too.' Suddenly self-conscious, she wondered if other people could tell she was pregnant somehow, as though a neon sign were flashing above her head. 'Yes, that's Ellie, always with a book, music, or something to keep her mind busy.'

'How long are you here for?'

'Couple of weeks,' she said.

'Nice, enjoy. Let me know if I can help you find anything.'

Thanks.' Lacie smiled and her face became warmer. *Oh, just books on pregnancy, motherhood, single motherhood, decision-making, that sort of thing.*

Unless she wanted to make her situation obvious, she probably couldn't buy a book from here, she'd have to order something online or get an e-book to hide her research. Anyway, she still had to decide what to do first. There was no doubt in her mind she was going to have this baby... but to keep it? Maybe it would be better off with someone ready and waiting to have a family, with a partner by their side, and a heart bursting with love and eagerness to become a mother. The thought made her feel guilty, but it presented itself nonetheless.

She browsed the fiction section mindlessly, then segued casually into the health section, scanning over the titles. There were several pregnancy related books gathered together just above eye level, photos of smiling mothers-to-be proudly cradling their baby bump with their hands, and others with perfect-looking little humans smiling with their rosy cheeks and button noses. Her heart leapt.

What would her baby look like?

Was it a boy or a girl?

What if it was twins?

The possibilities made her mind race. She took a deep breath. She needed to focus on the day ahead of her right now, not the next nine months. Still, she mentally recorded the titles of some of the books with the intention of looking them up later.

Before walking out, she stopped at the home and garden section. The most beautiful book cover caught her eye... bright, joyful flowers burst onto the page, as though alive and breathing with a mind of their own. *Wildflowers and Words.* She opened the large hardcover and carefully turned the pages. Stunning photographs combined with poetry, motivational quotes, and flower facts filled the pages.

I have to have it.

Lacie hugged the book to her chest and took it to the

counter. It would take her luggage weight up a notch for the trip back home but she'd allowed room.

'How nice is this?' Olivia admired the front and back cover. 'My daughter Mia has taken quite a liking to photographing flowers.'

'Oh, how lovely. Maybe she'll create her own book one day,' Lacie suggested.

'Probably. That girl of mine lets nothing get in her way of anything she wants to do! Motherhood is such a surprising journey; you never know what your child will become.'

Lacie tucked her hair behind her ear. 'True.'

'That's forty-nine ninety-five, thanks. You don't have kids, do you?' she asked, holding out the EFTPOS machine for Lacie to tap her card on.

That warmth from before rose a tad. 'Not yet,' she said, which was true.

'Maybe one day, hey? Sometimes I have to strain to remember my life pre-child, but I wouldn't change it for the world.'

Lacie wondered if somehow Olivia had spied on her through a security camera, looking at the pregnancy books. Or maybe she was a mind reader.

'Sometimes I have to strain to remember my life in Tarrin's Bay. It's so different to Chicago.'

'I can imagine! I bet it's nice to be back though.'

'Absolutely. It's going to go fast unfortunately. I miss my family so much sometimes.'

Olivia smiled a soft smile. 'Well, don't waste a single minute. Go, enjoy your time with them.' She flicked her hand toward the door. 'And enjoy the book.'

'Thanks! And tell Mia if she makes a book, I'll be the first to buy a copy.'

Olivia waved and Lacie left the store, the book in a paper

carry bag with the *Mrs May's* logo. She walked on with her head raised high, a surge of satisfaction with her new purchase. Apart from beauty, flowers were her other passion. But she'd forgone a career as a florist when her annoying adult acne had led her to try various skin treatments, and along with taking better care of her health, they'd given her great results. She wanted to do that for others; help them love the skin they were in and feel confident in themselves. And she'd done just that. She was happy with her life and career, but had no idea how a baby would fit into it.

'Can we do my rainbow nails now?' Jessie asked when Lacie opened the front door.

'Give her a minute, Jess,' Penny said. 'She's just come home.'

Dane also bounded towards her. 'Come and see my pirate ship, it's all finished!'

'I'd love to do your nails,' she glanced at Jessie, 'and look at your pirate ship,' she glanced at Dane. Olivia was right, she should enjoy every minute with them, especially after what happened to her dad. She could hardly forgive herself for not having been there. She shook the memory away as she admired Dane's Lego creation.

'That is even better than the *Pirates of the Caribbean* pirate ship!'

Dane glowed. 'Can I watch that movie yet?'

She eyed Penny.

'Absolutely not, young man. When you're older.'

'Ohh.' He pouted.

'These kids.' She shook her head. 'More work than my day job.' She chuckled. Penny worked part time as a primary school teacher, in a job-share arrangement. As it was now the school holidays, this was basically her 'holiday', and Lacie wondered how she managed, with barely a spare moment to herself. Lacie decided she would try to spend as much time with the kids as possible, not only because she loved them, but to give Penny some reprieve. She just hoped *she'd* have the energy.

'Now, before I do your nails, Miss Jessie, I'll just put my stuff in my room and freshen up. Back soon!'

Lacie walked down the hallway to the guest quarters and plonked her bag on the chair next to her bed. She felt like plonking herself onto the bed, but if she did that now she'd probably sleep all day and be up all night, besides, then she'd miss the afternoon tree decorating ceremony. She opted to sit for a minute, taking a few deep breaths. She checked her phone. No messages from Xavier. She put her new book on the bedside table and looked forward to flipping through it tonight, and she put her medications and a bottle of water into the drawer of the bedside table. All set.

Lacie freshened up and returned to the living room, an array of nail polish colours in her hands.

'Lunch in half an hour!' her mother called out from the kitchen. Lacie gave her a nod.

'I've got more nail polish than you've got fingers,' she said to Jessie.

The girl laughed. 'You'll have to do my toes too!'

'I will. Take off those socks then.'

Lacie sat at the dining table with Jessie, a paper napkin covering her knees as Jessie placed her feet on her aunt's lap.

'Feet first, then fingers. Which colours?'

'All of them!'

'As you wish, Miss Rainbow.'

Jessie giggled.

Soon after, Jessie was walking around the house awkwardly, her toes fanned out as far as she could spread them, and her hands like claws, blowing on her fingers as the polish dried. Penny took a photo. 'Going onto Facebook that is.' She laughed.

'Oh, Mum!' Jessie retorted.

By the time lunch was ready, Ellie came in, having been to a library talk, and her real estate agent brother Chris arrived, saying, 'I've got a few more appointments later this afternoon, so let's get this show on the road.' He took off his tie and sat at the table. 'And I've had yet another person ask if you want to sell the house, but as I keep telling them, it's not an option.'

Martha rolled her eyes. 'Why would I give up my beautiful home, even for a nice sum? And you kids will get it when I'm gone.'

Lacie tried not to think about that. It was enough that her dad was gone.

'Where's Matt? We all have to be here for the tree decorating ceremony. Oh, whoops, I missed his text,' Martha said, glancing at her phone. 'Running half an hour late, got caught up at work. Start without me, but don't let Chris eat my serving,' she read out the text and Lacie laughed. 'Oh well, let's get started, I am absolutely starving!'

'Mum, you had morning tea, like, ninety minutes ago,' said Penny.

'Exactly, ninety minutes without a boost to my blood sugar levels. That's cutting it fine.' She winked. 'You wait till you get to my age.'

Martha ladled pumpkin soup into bowls, and Penny placed a basket of crispy bread rolls onto the table. There were also mini sausage rolls for the kids, not to mention Chris who grabbed four. 'Anyone for a wine, or should I open it at dinner?'

Lacie was about to say 'me please' when she bit her tongue. Nine months with no wine, damn it.

'Can't drink on the job,' said Chris.

'Not for me,' said Ellie.

'Oh, well I was going to say bring it on but am I going to be the only one drinking?' Penny glanced at Lacie.

Lacie shook her head. 'Too early in the day.' But that excuse wouldn't save her later. 'Besides, I'm kind of... on a bit of a detox.'

'Detox?' Chris mumbled through a mouthful of sausage roll. 'I thought you loved everything in moderation.'

'Um, I've been hanging out with some healthy peeps in my hood, doing yoga and stuff. I'm on a bit of a health kick, that's all.'

Chris laughed. 'Detox? Hood? Where has our Lacie gone?'

'She's right here!' said Dane, seated next to her. He squeezed Lacie's cheeks. Lacie snuck a kiss on his forehead.

'Anyway, this soup looks delicious, Mum.' Lacie slid her spoon into the soup and tasted it. 'Yum.'

Everyone got on with eating and changed the subject from wine to which Christmas movie would be viewed tonight, and Matt finally arrived, catching up on lunch at record speed.

'Okay, guys, are we ready for the tree?' Matt stood when he'd finished.

The kids had already been chasing each other around the table, but they stopped. 'Yes, yes, yes!' Jessie jumped up and down.

'I get to put the first decoration on, because I'm the youngest!' said Dane.

'That's right, sweetheart,' Martha responded. 'And you'll probably be the youngest for quite a while.' She glanced at her grown-up children. 'Unless we get blessed with any new cousins in the near future.'

'Not on my radar right now, Mum,' said Matt, who was only a couple of months into a new relationship with a fellow chiropractor from the practice he worked at, though they'd been trying to keep that under the radar at work too, apparently.

'Pfft,' scoffed Ellie, as though it was the most preposterous thing she'd ever heard.

Chris just scratched his head.

Lacie gulped. Did her mother suspect something? Mother's intuition? 'So,' Lacie said brightly, clasping her hands together and standing. 'Are we going to put on some happy music to get us all in the festive mood?' She raised her eyebrows as far as they would go.

'You said it, sister,' said Matt, pressing his phone. The boppy sound of Pharrell Williams' song 'Happy' filled the room, and he moved his body to the rhythm. The kids laughed and copied him, Chris rolled his eyes but eventually joined in, though not with as much enthusiasm. Penny sang along, and Martha danced her own unique style, clapping her hands, smiling, and radiating joy. Ellie simply tapped her fingers on the table. She always took longer than everyone else to get excited about things. Lacie held her younger sister's hands and encouraged her to stand, then moved her arms up and down, side to side, until a reluctant but genuine smile formed. Lacie's heart warmed, both from the effort and the sight in front of her. Her family, bar one, being happy and silly and living in the moment.

At the end of the song, they all laughed and clapped, and Martha fanned her face.

Jessie started hopping on both feet towards the living room. 'Because I'm *hoppy*...' she sang, and they all laughed.

The corner for the Christmas tree was already cleared and ready. Matt and Chris lugged the large box into the room and began unpacking the branches, stand, and trunk. Martha insisted on a real Christmas tree each December, but for their Christmas in July reunion, the pretend kind would have to do.

When the tree was assembled, Dane rummaged through the box of ornaments and chose the coveted first decoration – a wooden sleigh with sparkly glitter paint on the edges, and a gold string to hang it. Penny picked up her phone and took pictures as he held it up to the highest branch he could reach by standing on tiptoes, and flashed a toothy smile. He threaded the branch through the string, then stepped back to admire his efforts. 'Ta-da!'

Matt gave him a high-five, and Jessie quickly chose the second decoration to hang; a glimmering pair of white doves, cut-out letters forming the word 'peace' above them. Martha put on Christmas music and together they brought the tree to life.

Lacie rested for a moment, observing. Tree decorating was her favourite thing as a child, and it brought her joy to see her niece and nephew enjoying it just as much. Thanks to her father and his British heritage, their family had started this tradition once all five children were born and Martha had decided they wouldn't have any more. Lacie's dad had missed the cold English Christmases, and decided to bring them to winter in Australia, minus the snow. As children, it was pretty exciting, having two Christmases a year. And with Lacie moving overseas, flights were cheaper in the middle of the year than at Christmas time, so they'd decided to make July the main event.

'I think that's about it,' said Martha. 'Where's the angel?' She looked in the near-empty box and pulled out a smaller box that encased the stunning gold-winged and white-gowned angel. She smiled at Lacie. 'Ready?'

Lacie nodded, and her mother carefully placed it in her hands, Penny taking another photo. Matt placed the step ladder near the tree, and Lacie wondered if it was wise to be standing on a ladder in her 'condition', but she did, cautiously, holding on to the nearby mantelpiece of the fireplace to steady her footing. She reached up, and placed the angel on the tallest branch in the centre, and glanced slightly to the side with a smile so Penny could capture the moment. There, done. She stepped down the ladder as a wave of light-headedness unsteadied her and she grasped the mantelpiece, knocking over a photo frame.

'Lace, you all right?' Her mother held on to her arm as she regained her balance.

Lacie exhaled in relief. 'Yep, all good. Whoops! Lucky I didn't grab hold of a branch and send the tree to the ground.'

Her mother eyed her with concern. 'You sure you're okay? What did the doctor say?'

'You went to the doctor? What's wrong?' asked Ellie. She seemed to have a phobia of anything medical since the death of her father.

'Nothing, nothing's wrong at all. A bit of jet lag,' said Lacie. 'Now can we all have a rest and enjoy our beautiful creation?' She sat on the couch and looked up at the sparkling tree.

'It's the bestest one ever,' said Dane, his eyes wide and innocent.

'It sure is.' Lacie's bottom lip trembled a little and her eyes stung with moisture. Surprised at her sudden emotion she clenched her lips together and held back tears.

When everyone had finished admiring the tree and busied themselves with various things, Lacie sunk deeper into the couch. Her eyes became heavy, and the next thing she knew, Jessie was waking her up telling her it was time for dinner.

Jet lag indeed.

The festivities continued into the evening with a lamb roast dinner, and a viewing of the movie *The Santa Clause*. As it neared the end, Lacie's phone rang from the coffee table.

'Sorry,' she said, leaning forward to pick it up. Her heart beat faster on seeing the caller ID.

It was Xavier.

CHAPTER FOUR

L acie walked out of the room and down the hall. 'Hi, Xavier.'

'Hey there, how's it going in Australia?'

'Fine, thanks. Great. Spending time with my family. It must be the middle of the night over there?'

'Early morning, sun's about to come up and I've only just got in after a marathon late-night shoot. Can't sleep yet, too wired, so thought I'd call and see what's up. You thinking about taking on that job I mentioned last time I saw you?'

'No, no job. Just a chat.'

'Oh. Cool. Okay. Maybe your voice will help me relax so I can sleep, had so much coffee.'

'Well, um,' she began, walking into her bedroom and closing the door behind her. 'About when I last saw you. You know, how, um...'

'It was a great night, wasn't it? Honestly, sometimes I feel like you're the only one who understands me, Lace. I know our relationship wasn't practical anymore, but I have to say, it was pretty awesome to end things on a high note. A mutual, clean break. No residual hard feelings.'

A high note? Clean break? Little did he know there was definitely something residual.

'I guess so,' replied Lacie. 'Except for one thing.'

'Oh? You don't want to continue it, you know, like a friends with benefits kinda thing. Is that it?'

Lacie rolled her eyes. Xavier had been sweet, attentive, and exuberant when they'd first met, but it seemed the more successful he became, the more over-confident he became too.

'Nope, that's not it.' She exhaled a short, sharp breath. 'I'm pregnant.' There, that was the only way to say it.

The line went silent.

'Xavier?'

'Uh-huh,' he mumbled. 'Did you say pregnant?'

'Yes.'

'And... you think I'm the father?'

Oh my God.

'Xavier, I *know* you're the father. Geez, who do you think I am?'

'But it can't be. We used...'

'I know, I know, I wondered how too, but we *had* had a few drinks, and maybe we failed to notice if something didn't quite... do the job.'

Xavier swore under his breath. 'So, you're sure?'

'Definitely sure. I'm having a scan next week, to check everything's okay.'

'Whoa, hang on. You're going to *have it*? It was an accident that shouldn't have happened.'

'Well, yes. I can't *not*. I just can't.'

Silence again.

'Look,' Lacie said, feeling both relief at having let the cat out of the bag and trepidation at knowing what was coming. 'I just wanted to let you know, since it is yours, you are entitled to have your say too, however, I *will* be having the baby, I just haven't decided yet if I'll keep it or give it up for adoption.' The last word sent a sharp jolt through her heart. 'But I think I'll... probably, um...' She sat on the bed.

Keep it.

Was she seriously leaning towards that option? Or was it hormones and maternal instinct making the decision for her?

'Okay, look.' Xavier exhaled loudly. 'To be completely honest, I think you should give it up. There are people who are desperate to have children. But you? Your career is on a high and you have so much more potential. Why let this get in the way?' By the sound of his breathy voice, Lacie was sure Xavier was now pacing his room and nowhere near relaxed enough to sleep. 'Anyway, either way, I can't be part of it. I'm sorry.'

Straight to the point.

'My current lifestyle doesn't allow for being a father,' he explained. 'And in no way am I ready for that! Nothing will get in the way of where I'm headed, I need you to understand that.'

'Oh, I do, believe me. I'm not asking for anything, just being courteous, in case, you know, you wanted to know that your blessed genetics were being passed on, and in case you ever wanted to meet your own child.'

'Meet? Lacie, you're getting way ahead with this. Please, don't bring me into it. I've made my decision, and I'm sorry if it seems callous but I can't and will not be a father, in any way, shape, or form.'

Lacie's jaw tightened. He was unbelievable. She didn't want to be in a relationship with him anymore anyway, but he could at least show a bit of compassion.

'Fine. I guess that's it then.'

'Guess it is.'

'Have a fabulous life, Xavier.' She ended the call.

Her tightened jaw slackened and her lip trembled again.

So much for a clean break.

Lacie managed to put the conversation out of her mind over the weekend, putting all her focus and energy on her family and taking time to relax. She had already read half of the flower book, and even though spring was two months away, she even took to picking whatever flowers and greenery she could find in the garden and arranging them into bouquets for various places in the house. Including a posy of bottlebrushes in a cute vintage vase beside her bed. She loved the red splash of colour, reminding her to get out of bed with enthusiasm and passion for this precious time she had to share with her loved ones, and hopefully without too much nausea. The medication the doctor suggested had worked a treat. She still felt a slight niggle here and there, a sudden urgency to sit down or to splash water on her face, but it was keeping things at bay for now, though Dr Greene had also said the effects may wear off slightly after time as the body got used to the medication.

On Monday morning while the rest of the family were busy and Chris was helping Martha assemble new bookcases, Lacie was left to her own devices. She took the opportunity to do some more flower picking, getting ideas for the grand table centrepiece of their Christmas in July dinner on Friday night. She was thinking a warm, comforting theme with reds, oranges, and earthy tones... grevilleas, clivias, fern branches, and pine cones. She smiled as she thought of getting Jessie to paint the tips of the cones with red nail polish. She gathered some of the flowers and plants into her basket to do a small practice run, then looked up as Nathan approached the area with a smile and a wheelbarrow full of pebbles.

'Hey,' he said, 'taking over my job, are you?' He winked.

Lacie grinned. 'Not quite. Picking flowers for a table centrepiece.'

'Nice.'

'At least I'm not throwing up into them this time.' Lacie chuckled.

'Oh, I don't know. That shrub on your patio has never looked so healthy since you showered it with organic fertiliser.'

Lacie's cheeks warmed and she lowered her face as she giggled.

'Sorry, I shouldn't joke. Seriously, I hope you're okay and feeling much better?'

'Much, thanks.' She eyed the pebbles. 'That looks heavy. What are you going to do with them?'

Nathan moved his hand in a 'follow me' gesture. He wheeled them a little further to the barbeque area beyond the fruit trees, where a cleared circle of earth surrounded by grass waited like a blank canvas for an artist to create something out of it.

'I know it looks like a crop circle at the moment, but I assure you by Friday it'll be a centrepiece of its own.' He let go of the wheelbarrow handles and exhaled.

'Water fountain?' Lacie mused.

Nathan shook his head. 'Nope. Do you like marshmallows?'

Lacie had to think twice. She usually did, but wasn't sure now if her stomach could handle the squishy texture, the thought made her feel squeamish. She just nodded. 'Oh, a firepit?'

Nathan smiled. 'You got it.'

'Awesome, that'll be so cool. I mean warm.' She walked to the circle. 'I'll have to make sure Mum adds marshmallows to the shopping list.'

'Once the firepit and pebbles are in, I'll create some edging around the circle, and then some seating.' He glanced around. 'Your mum and I figured this would be the perfect spot. Not too close to any trees or branches, but secluded enough in this little pocket of garden that the heat can be contained somewhat. Should be cosy.' He rubbed his hands together.

Lacie could imagine her family gathering around the firepit; toasting marshmallows, Matt playing a tune on his guitar, the kids running around in circles... and a spare seat where her dad should have been.

'I don't know why we didn't think of this earlier,' Lacie said.

'Your mum said the same thing. But she was more focused on establishing the gardens first, she said.'

'And we have a fireplace inside to keep warm in winter, so I guess we've just been used to that.'

'Must be nice. But there's nothing like being outside under the stars on a cool winter's night,' he glanced up at the sky, 'taking it easy and enjoying the moment.'

She noticed the stubble under his jaw had a subtle sparkle as the patchy sunlight sprinkled its glow onto his face. It reminded her a little of Xavier, but she quickly shook the memory from her mind. She had no room for the man who wanted nothing to do with her or their baby.

There was a strange silence, a moment of stillness, nothing but the gentle breeze wafting the scent of grass and winter blooms her way. Her sense of smell had been heightened, she'd noticed.

'Anyway, gotta do what I'm here to do.' He seemingly snapped out of his moment. 'I'll bring the firepit over from my Ute.' He turned slightly, but then turned back to face her. 'Those clivias,' he pointed to her basket, 'they match the orangey colours in your dress.' He smiled, and walked to his vehicle.

Lacie glanced down at the floaty dress she wore over leggings. Orange swirled and mixed with an earthy red, creating a pattern resembling an outback sunset. How bizarre of him, or a man, to notice such things. She hadn't even realised she was picking flowers that matched her choice of clothing. But he was a gardener, and apart from knowing what the flowers were called, clearly had an eye for detail and design.

Lacie put her basket down and wandered around the area, revelling in the peace, familiarity, and possibilities. With no garden of her own, she wanted to make the most of it here. She grabbed an orange from the tree and peeled off the skin, taking a wedge and biting into the juicy flesh. She had been craving a lot of citrus fruits lately, which Google had told her might indicate a need for more vitamin C.

She ate another one as Nathan returned, carrying the firepit in his bare hands, his rolled-up shirt sleeves tightening at his inner elbows.

'Orange?' she asked, holding it out.

'Sure. I'll just...' He placed the firepit down in the centre of the circle.

She tossed it his way and he caught it in his left hand. 'Thanks.' He peeled it and bit into it. 'You sure your mum won't mind me eating the produce?'

She waved away his hesitation. 'There's more than enough to go around. Help yourself when you like.'

Lacie sat on the edge of a bench near the inbuilt barbeque that her dad had cooked many a steak on. Nathan remained standing.

'How did you become interested in gardening?' she asked.

He finished his mouthful then replied, 'As a kid I used to play with my toy cars in the dirt. There wasn't any grass where I first lived. One day, I'd left them outside under a tree and when I went back to get them, a flower of some kind had fallen on one of them. I don't know what it was, but I looked up and realised I had never noticed the tree before. There was a bird going from branch to branch, and for some reason it captivated me. I'd had a rough day and, I dunno, I think somehow it gave me a moment of peace.' He took another bite of his orange. 'After that I started to notice things around me more. Trees, plants, insects... colours, sounds. I was kind of an introvert, trying to process so much of what was going on in my life at the time, that I never really noticed the world around me much, until then.'

'It sounds like you had a lot more to think about than any child should,' Lacie said, sensing some kind of memory simmering away in his mind.

He nodded. 'And then, at school they had us watching a nature documentary in science, and I was hooked. I wanted to immerse myself in the natural world, where things made sense and I felt at home.' He finished his orange and scooped pebbles from the wheelbarrow with a shovel and onto the bare circle around the firepit.

Lacie found that her body was leaning forward, eager to hear more of his story, her hands clasped together between her knees to balance herself and keep her fingers warm. Usually, she would listen to people's stories while lathering creams and lotions on their faces or bodies, having to be both present and attentive, but focused on what she was doing. But now all she had to do was sit and listen.

'It's so great you're doing what you love,' she said.

He smiled. 'I'm very lucky.'

'I've always loved flowers,' she blurted, thinking she should let him get on with his work but feeling the urge to balance out the conversation with some input of her own.

Nathan eyed the basket on the ground nearby. 'I can tell.'

'Since I was a child too. I used to pick flowers for Mum and leave them on her bedside table so she'd get a surprise when she went to bed. I didn't realise at the time I should have put them in water, most of them were shrivelled and wilted by the time she saw them!' Lacie laughed at her childhood naivety.

Nathan chuckled. 'That's how we learn, I guess, through our mistakes.'

'True. When Mum explained to me that flowers needed water, I started putting them into leftover jam jars filled with water, tying a ribbon around the top.'

'Sounds like you have a great relationship with your mum.' Nathan paused his pebble scooping.

'I do. I'm very lucky.' She mirrored his choice of words from before, and was about to ask him about his own family when he scooped another mound of pebbles quicker and louder than before and it made her lose her train of thought.

'So, flowers, eh? Tell me you've put your flowers-in-jam-jars and ribbon-tying skills to good use as a florist?'

Lacie's eyes widened. 'Good guess! But no. Well, I *almost* become a florist.'

'Almost? What changed?'

'I did.' Lacie stood and stretched her arms above her head, easing some muscle soreness from her back. 'Became more confident in myself. I loved flowers, still do, but when I received treatments for a skin condition and learned how to improve it, I wanted to help others feel better about themselves too. So I became a beauty therapist, and then a make-up artist.'

'Oh, cool. It's great you're doing what you love too. Did you say you lived overseas?'

'America. I run my own salon in Chicago. Used to work mostly as a freelance make-up artist but it got pretty hectic going from location to location, and I wanted a more consistent lifestyle.'

'Sounds fair. Did you have to travel far, to do your work? You must have seen way more places than I have!'

'Yes. I worked on set for various films and TV shows, some in Hollywood studios but many on location around the country.

I got used to flying at short notice, always had a bag packed and an extra suitcase filled with my make-up supplies!'

'Wow.' Nathan leaned on the shovel. 'What an amazing experience! A Hollywood star in your own right. Such a world away from little Tarrin's Bay.'

Lacie shielded her eyes from the sun's glare, or was it to try to hide her flushed cheeks? 'It sure is. Have you travelled much?'

Nathan pressed his lips together and shook his head. 'Never been out of the country. Never really had the chance.' He resumed scattering the pebbles. 'Besides, I think we're pretty lucky here in Australia, I've never felt the need to go anywhere else. Look at our amazing environment.' He moved his arm in an arc. 'Greenery, stunning coastline, farms, beaches, and the city's conveniences only a couple of hours away.'

'It does have its advantages, that's for sure.' Lacie had definitely missed the clean, fresh air of small-town living. Her environment smelled like car fumes and cigarette smoke and the icy cold wind, if that even had a smell, but still, she loved her little corner of the globe, her business, and her cosy apartment, even though her beloved cat, Lightning, had died a few months ago from a heart condition at only four years of age. She wanted to get another one, but now, well, maybe she should wait and see. A baby would be enough to look after.

'I didn't mean to discount your life in the States though, hope it didn't come out that way.'

Lacie hadn't sensed any hint of criticism, and was surprised he even mentioned it. This guy seemed such a thoughtful, aware human being. 'Not at all.' She smiled.

'Hey, Lace!' Chris called out from the open window in the upstairs sitting room that overlooked the garden. 'We need an extra set of hands to steady the bookcase with Mum while I attach the base. Nothing strenuous, don't worry.'

'Be right up!' She gave a thumbs up.

Damn, she was enjoying talking to Nathan and wanted to know more... how long had he lived in Tarrin's Bay, what happened in his childhood, was there another reason why a man in his thirties had not wanted to venture overseas at least once, and, and... what was his favourite flower? All the important stuff.

'I should let you get back to work without interruption,' she said. 'It was a *delight* chatting with you, Nathan.' She didn't know why she had put on a fake English voice. Like her dad used to do, except his accent was mostly real having grown up in England, but it had relaxed into a more Aussie intonation over time since he'd moved here as a young man.

'The delight was all mine,' he said in his own fake accent. 'Seriously, it was a nice interruption.' Back to his Aussie accent. 'I hope you'll consider interrupting me again tomorrow.'

The corner of Lacie's mouth inched up in an anticipatory half-smile. 'Somebody's gotta check on how this firepit's going, and make sure it's up to scratch.' She winked, and she didn't know if she'd ever winked at anyone before in her life. Maybe it felt okay because he'd winked at her when he'd first approached with the wheelbarrow.

'I better up my game then.' He picked up one pebble from the wheelbarrow and painstakingly placed it on the ground, then moved it slightly to one side as though it had to be perfect.

'Ha!' She laughed. 'That's gonna take you a while. Good luck.' She lifted up her basket of blooms, and walked back to the house to help her brother.

'Looks like you two were having quite the conversation,' Martha said when Lacie arrived upstairs in the rich burgundy wallpapered room, a chandelier dangling from the ceiling creating rainbows on the floor from the rays of sunlight streaming in.

'She was dilly-dallying at the window while I was hard at work getting all the bookcase pieces in order,' said Chris, kneeling on the floor getting all OCD with the wooden shelves.

'Just admiring my beautiful garden.' She winked at Lacie. 'And daughter.'

What was with all the winking? Was there some kind of substance in the water causing eye twitches?

'Well, Nathan wasn't slacking off if that's what you're wondering, he kept working the whole time. I did give him an orange though, told him to help himself when needed, hope that's okay, Mum. He'll do better work then.'

'Of course, Nath knows he's practically part of the family now.'

'Nath?' Chris said.

Her mother shrugged. 'He's such a nice man. Wish he was thirty years older.'

'Mum!' Chris stood. 'It's been less than two years since Dad went.'

Martha crossed her arms and gripped her elbows.

'Hey, it's perfectly within Mum's right to move on if and when she wishes.' Lacie placed an arm around her mother's shoulders. 'Just not with the young gardener, though, okay?' She gently nudged her mum then kissed her cheek.

'I was only joking anyway,' Martha said. 'I just...' She dabbed at the corner of her eyes. 'I just miss him, that's all.'

'Oh, Mum.' Chris put down the instructions and held his arms out, welcoming his mother into an embrace. 'I miss him too.'

Lacie turned it into a group hug, wrapping her arms around the pair and glad she didn't have a large belly getting in the way yet. 'We all do,' she said.

After Martha wiped her eyes and Lacie stayed to help them until the new bookcases were standing tall and proud in the grand sitting room, she went downstairs to her flower basket on the hall table.

She had an idea.

Lacie picked up one of the orange clivias, found an old jar from the kitchen and filled it with water, tied a bow around it with some twine, and popped the flower in it, before sneaking back upstairs to her mother's bedroom and placing it on her bedside table next to her reading glasses, and a pile of half-read books with tattered bookmarks poking out from between the pages.

She *was* lucky, indeed, to have her mum.

And she hoped that one day, she would be a good enough mother that someone would feel the same way about her.

CHAPTER FIVE

Lacie had found herself going outside via the guest bedroom patio a lot lately instead of the front door. Visits to town, walks along the beach, and enjoying the cool but pleasant weather. She would sometimes sit on the patio chair in the morning to read, where the winter sun landed and warmed her up. Except on Wednesday when she almost puked in the pot plant again, having forgotten to take the morning sickness medicine the night before. Then, when it was time to go out, she'd pick an orange along the way, toss one to Nathan who'd give a friendly wave, and make her way to the front of the house. They had enjoyed several interruptions in the last few days; snippets of conversation and laughter, but today, as she tossed the orange to him, she was mentally preoccupied and it landed a metre to his side.

'Hey, I'm over here,' he said, waving both arms across his body and out to the side as though he was flagging down a rescue helicopter.

Lacie laughed. 'Sorry, must still be half asleep!'

He picked up the orange and smiled. 'An orange a day keeps the doctor away.' He peeled it and took a bite.

Hmm, not in her case. No orange would have any impact on her situation. Today was the appointment for the ultrasound, and the pregnancy would become real.

'Have a good day, I'm out for a while.' She waved.

'Thanks, you too. If I don't see you later, I hope tonight's reunion dinner goes well and you guys enjoy the firepit.'

'It looks awesome, Nathan, thank you.' She took a quick look again at the circular display of pebbles around the firepit, the hem of mini bricks surrounding it, and the tree stump stools he had created. He'd also hung a large wrought-iron leaf design onto the dividing wall near the barbeque area, which sectioned off the yard from the neighbouring guest cottage her mother rented out to holiday goers. He'd lifted a new bench seat over to the area as well, so there'd be enough seating for everyone who was coming tonight.

She waved and smiled again as Nathan knelt down to continue weeding the flowerbeds, then made her way to the front where her mother's car was waiting for her to use. She had told her she was going to Welston for a haircut at a recommended salon, and that she might catch up with one of her old school friends who lived there. She had booked the hairdresser mostly as a diversion for where she was really going, but did need a trim, so it wasn't a complete waste of time, and the truth was she had tried to reach her friend but she was too busy with work. They had lost contact over the years and their visits when Lacie was in town had become less and less. Anyway, she would probably need some time to herself after the ultrasound appointment anyway.

Lacie got into her mother's sedan, familiarised herself with things being on the opposite side, and, having drunk two glasses of water as advised, was already wishing she could use the bathroom. She clenched and drove out of the arced driveway for the thirty-minute trip to see her baby for the first time.

'First pregnancy?' the sonographer asked as she squirted cold gel on her lower abdomen.

Lacie nodded.

'I'll take a quick look first and get some basic measurements, then you can duck to the bathroom before we do the internal scan which will give us a better view of the pregnancy.'

'Okay,' she whispered. *Doesn't she mean view of the baby? Or maybe they didn't like to use that word in case anything was wrong. Would something be wrong?* 'Um, I might close my eyes and look when you tell me to, is that okay?' Lacie was suddenly overwhelmed with nerves.

'Of course. I need to do the technical things first anyway and then I can show you what's what on the screen.'

She closed her eyes and breathed, as the transducer slid and pressed into various parts of her abdomen, some a little uncomfortably given her full bladder. Not long after, she was told she could go to the toilet.

'Phew!' She dashed into the attached cubicle then returned, ready for the main event.

When the procedure continued, she looked at the screen on the wall.

'This here,' the sonographer said, pointing the cursor to a grey area surrounding a big black spot, 'is your uterus.' She continued to move the transducer and tap at the computer.

'What's the white circle?' Lacie asked. 'Is that the baby?'

'That's the yolk sac,' she replied. 'But this,' she pointed to a small white patch next to it, 'is the embryo, or what we call the fetal pole.'

Lacie squinted to get a better look. 'So, it's really there? I haven't been imagining all this?'

'No, definitely not. You are one hundred per cent pregnant. And this... see the tiny flicker?'

Lacie could see what might be cells on the screen, but there was a tiny bit on the white patch, or embryo, that flickered bright and fast. 'Is that the...'

'Heartbeat. Yes.'

Lacie's own heart beat faster, as though trying to synchronise with the one on the screen, and an immense and unfamiliar emotion rose up within like a giant wave. She blinked a few times as moisture blurred her vision. That sight was simple perfection. Pure life, *new* life, living, beating, and glowing inside her.

'Oh my God.'

'It's a strong heartbeat. And,' she said as she did something on the computer, putting a couple of crosses near the embryo and drawing a line between the two, 'measurements are consistent with seven weeks. Your estimated due date is February twenty-fifth.'

'My due date? I hadn't even thought about that. An approximate birthday, wow. My dad was born in February.'

'Meant to be,' said the sonographer. She continued with the scan and typed into the computer. 'Your doctor will call if they need to see you, but all looks good at this stage. You can get dressed now, and I'll send the link to the images and video to your phone.'

Wow. 'Thank you so much.' Lacie smiled and got up when the sonographer left the room, put the bottom half of her clothes back on, and steadied herself against the chair. She placed her hand on her belly.

There was a living, growing being inside her.

Meant to be.

'Ooh, your hair looks lovely, sweetheart,' Martha exclaimed, as Lacie got out of the car at South Haven. Her mother stood near the garden entrance with Nathan. 'Love the little curls at the ends.'

'Thanks.' Lacie smiled, and she noticed Nathan observing her. 'Haircuts are so much cheaper here than where I live!'

'Lucky you could fit one in. Hey,' her mum said, 'I've invited Nathan to join us tonight. He's done such a great job with the firepit and garden, and he's going to put together some extra beehives and harvest honey in spring from our old beehives! I'm glad he's doing it, there's no way I'm getting in one of those white suits.'

'Can't wait,' he said. 'For both things.'

Lacie's skin tingled. She had a feeling her mother would sit her and Nathan next to each other at the table, though she had no idea why as there was no hope in setting the two of them up since she lived overseas, but she didn't mind. He was an interesting person, nice to talk to, and right now, that was a worthy distraction for her.

'Great. I hope you don't get overwhelmed with the Appleby family goings-on, we can be a rowdy bunch, especially when all in one room,' Martha said to Nathan.

'Sounds fantastic. I didn't grow up with that, so it'll be fun for me.'

She wondered what he *did* grow up with. He seemed so... alone. Not lonely, just by himself. Independent. Solitary. Like a lone tall tree growing strong and resilient in the dry Australian outback.

'Well, I better go get the centrepiece organised, and Mum, do you want me to arrange the place cards or will you?'

'I've got that all organised, don't you worry. And we've added an extra table to the end of the dining table, so the kids and teens can sit on that one. Maybe make a mini version of the centrepiece for them so they feel special. I'll be inside shortly to get back to my cooking.'

Lacie nodded and went inside. Chris's wife and her teenaged daughters would be coming tonight. It was rare to have them all together, since the girls stayed with their biological father every second weekend. And Matt would be bringing his new girlfriend for everyone to meet, so Nathan was in for an interesting night, as they all were.

'Hey,' she said to Chris when she entered the living room. 'How was your day?'

'Not bad.' He was piling kindling and logs into the fireplace so it'd be ready for later. He stood when he was finished and exhaled sharply.

'You okay?'

'Yep. I guess.'

'Something wrong?'

He waved his hand. 'Ah, nothing. Doesn't matter. Just life stuff. Anyway, how was yours?'

'It was... different.'

'Oh, you did something to your hair.'

'I did. I was at Welston, was nice to have a bit of a day to myself.'

'Can't remember having one of them for a long time,' he mumbled. 'Anyway, I've gotta pick up some drinks for tonight. Any requests? Oh wait, you still on that detox thing?'

'Um, yeah, pretty much. I'll have lemonade.'

'Living on the edge, huh? Okay, catch you a bit later.' He gave her a peck on the cheek as he walked past.

Chris had always been a bit of a grumpy pants, but he seemed more stressed than usual. Maybe it was grief too, with all the family being here, except for Dad. Everyone was feeling it in different ways.

Ellie appeared, ninja-like, at the bottom of the stairs, her black mohair jumper like a shadow.

'Oh, Ellie. You surprised me. Whatcha got there?'

'These old things? Apparently, they're called CDs.' She shrugged.

'Ah, vintage. Music for tonight?'

'Yep. Mum wanted some of the old stuff, so we've got Frank Sinatra, a Christmas compilation, some instrumental thingo, and Ella Fitzgerald. Now if only I can figure out how to work the CD player.'

Lacie smiled. Ellie didn't speak much, but when she did, she often cracked a bit of humour, which was nice to see, as she was usually so serious about everything.

'I'm sure you'll work it out. I'll be in the dining room if you have any tech trouble.' She gave her sister a rub on the back and went to the hall table where she had left the flowers and greenery. She smiled at the memory of her mother approaching her that morning at breakfast with arms outstretched, having received her surprise bedside gift the night before. She would have to surprise her more often, maybe a regular flower delivery once she went back to America. It may not be the same as handpicked blooms in a jam jar, but it was something.

The dining table had been extended to fit twelve to fourteen people (with two people squished at each end), but an extra, small table had been added so the kids could have their own section and everyone could have a bit more elbow room. Especially now that Nathan was coming.

Lacie placed the basket on the smaller table, and began arranging the flowers and foliage as she'd practised, the large fern leaves extending lengthways along the table and the flowers gathered in an oval in the centre. She placed a large three-wick candle in the middle, made sure the wicks were trimmed to a few millimetres so it didn't get smoky, and arranged some pine cones around the base. Jessie had indeed painted the tips with red and peach nail polish, and after that, was hooked on the fun of it; going to the garden each day to collect more to paint them all, creating a magical rainbow garden of pine cones. The grevilleas hemmed the pine cones with their elegance, and the clivias extended their exuberance toward each end over the fern leaves.

For the kids' table, she arranged some pine cones in a shallow round bowl, and placed grevilleas around it in a pretty circle. Smaller green leaves radiated out like spokes, creating a circular centrepiece she hoped Jessie would be proud of, having her own pine cone creations centre stage.

Lacie adjusted a few things, took some photos, then stepped back and admired her handiwork. She had missed working with flowers and nature, it gave her such a warm sense of accomplishment – enhancing beauty in another way. She always emphasised to her clients that she wasn't there to *make* them look beautiful, she was there to enhance the beauty already present. And help them see that it certainly did exist.

A gentle, old song wafted into the house, and Ellie entered the dining room quietly. Lacie glanced sideways, smiling. 'What do you think?'

'It's perfect,' Ellie replied.

Lacie slid an arm around Ellie's waist, and Ellie reciprocated with hers. They stood there silently, looking at the flowers, and drinking in the music that reminded her of times gone by. And a tiny tear slid down her cheek.

Like life, this holiday wouldn't last forever.

'I'll let you get back to Hannah and Jasmine,' Nathan said to Luca, having met his friend for a late-afternoon drink when he'd finished the lunch shift at his restaurant.

'Thanks, it's rare I have a Friday night off, but my new chef is fantastic so I can relax knowing the place is in good hands for our busiest night of the week.'

'Say hi to Hannah for me.'

'Will do. Have a good night with the Applebys.'

'I'm sure I will.' Nathan waved him off. Luca was a lucky man. His own dream restaurant, a wife, and now a daughter. As he'd said to Nathan, life was busy and sleep deprived, but blessed.

Nathan's was too, though in different ways. He was settled and happy, but still, part of him longed for more. He just didn't know how to open the door that had been closed for so long.

He ducked into the supermarket and bought a large, luxury box of Belgian chocolates to take to dinner and share with the family. Martha had insisted he didn't need to bring anything but himself, but he didn't feel right showing up empty-handed.

He was hungry and tempted to sneak one now, but that wouldn't leave a good impression, so he resisted. By the sounds of it, he'd have to save his appetite for tonight's feast anyway.

He arrived home, gave his plants a quick water, then finally looked at his text messages. He hadn't replied to the one he'd got last week from his ex, but now, there was another.

> Just checking you got my last message? No worries if you're busy. Just hoping to catch up sometime and hope all is well with you. Tess x

He thought he'd forgiven her and moved on, but he mustn't have because seeing her message sent ripples of discomfort through his veins. Like when he'd found out the truth. It wasn't that she was the world's worst person, but she *had* hurt him, and badly.

Did he want to catch up with her, give her a chance to say whatever was on her mind? He tapped his foot on the floor and thought.

No.

Why revisit the past when the present was so much better? He typed a reply:

> Hey, just on my way out. Glad you and yours are well. I am pretty busy actually, and don't think now is the right time. Sorry. Take care. N

He didn't know how else to put it. He certainly wouldn't have sent a reply that considerate just after their break-up, and he had texted some things he'd regretted when he was in the midst of the upheaval. But he didn't see the point in letting things get heated, it never solved anything. He preferred to cut his losses calmly and then walk away. He'd learned that at a young age. Getting angry or upset only brought him trouble as a child… it was safer to keep the peace. Even if the peace wasn't true peace, but more like resignation.

He left his phone on the kitchen counter near the chocolates and went to the bathroom, washing away the day under the hot shower. His stomach grumbled and his mind wandered with the curiosity of what would be on the menu for tonight, literally and figuratively.

CHAPTER SIX

'Not too many chips, kids, you don't want to spoil your appetite before dinner!' Penny shooed her offspring away from the bowl of salt and vinegar potato chips on the coffee table. Lacie had enjoyed some too as it was all she felt like eating lately; salty, crunchy food, but realised she too should wait for dinner as she couldn't handle big meals anymore and didn't want to waste their feast.

'But they taste better than dinner,' Dane objected with a pout.

'Hey, your grandma's dinner is going to be more delicious than you could imagine,' Penny defended. 'And if you eat too many chips you won't have any room for marshmallows by the new firepit later tonight... when it's *past* your bedtime.' She narrowed her eyes.

Dane's mouth went into an 'O' and he quickly moved away from the chip bowl.

'What are you doing, Jessie?' Penny asked her daughter who was standing near the Christmas tree making strange gestures.

'I'm... copying... the... Christmas... lights,' she said in between movements consisting of her hands opening and closing like flashes, and her body popping forwards and backwards, then jittering when the lights went into rapid flashing mode.

Lacie laughed. 'Can I join in?'

'Yes... you... can.'

Lacie did the hand flashes too, but refrained from any major jittering in fear of somehow hurting the baby. They laughed together and Jessie sat on the couch in a huff. 'Now I need a nap,' she said.

'Me too.' Lacie sat next to her and rested her head on her niece's.

The doorbell rang.

Lacie got up. 'We'll have to save our naps for later. Looks like our guests are here.'

Jessie got up too. 'I'll get it, I'll get it!' She dashed to the front door and opened it. 'It's Nathan the gardener,' she said. 'Hi, Nathan the gardener.'

'Hi, Jessie the lady of the house.' Nathan took her hand and gave it a gentle shake, and Jessie curtsied. Lacie wondered where she'd learnt that, or maybe Penny had introduced her to *Pride and Prejudice*.

'And Dane the man of the house.' Nathan shook Dane's hand.

'We're having marshmallows tonight,' Dane said.

'For dinner? Lucky, they are my *favourite*.' Nathan patted his belly.

Dane giggled. 'Not dinner, silly, dessert!'

'Oh. Right. Oops. Well, I look forward to dessert. And I brought these to share too.' He held out the box of chocolates.

Penny took hold of them before Dane could. 'I'll take those. Thank you, Nathan.'

'My pleasure.'

'Oh, Nathan, you shouldn't have, but thank you.' Martha

emerged from the kitchen wiping her hands on her apron. 'I will definitely save room in my stomach for at least one. Or two.' She smiled. 'Welcome. Come in, come in. Make yourself at home.'

He took off his jacket and hung it on the coat rack. 'This room feels so warm and cosy. Wow.' He looked at the log fire. 'There's nothing like a real fireplace.'

'Except maybe a firepit. I can't wait to test it out,' Penny said.

Lacie smiled a hello to Nathan and he did the same. 'Welcome to the madhouse,' she said.

'I spend more time here than at my own house,' he said.

'But always on the *outside*,' said Dane.

'True.'

'Do you want to see my Lego pirate ship?' Dane tugged on Nathan's hand. 'It's over here.'

'Sure.' Dane led him to the library under the staircase where his creation sat on a side table, and the front door opened again.

Steve, Penny's paramedic husband, walked through with Matt and his girlfriend, having been assigned the job of picking them up so the couple could enjoy a few drinks with dinner.

'Daddy!' Jessie ran toward him and clung to his legs like one of those rubber toys you throw at the wall and it sticks.

'Hey, my Jessie girl.'

'I was being a set of Christmas lights,' she said, quickly dashing to the tree and showing him her moves.

Her dad smiled. 'Bright and sparkly.'

Matt laughed at his niece, then turned to the woman beside him. 'This is Sophia.' He gestured to his rosy-cheeked partner, her dark curls falling softly around her woollen scarf.

Penny held out her hand to Matt's girlfriend. 'I'm the big sister, Penny. Nice to meet you.'

'Likewise.'

'I'm Lacie.' She smiled and shook her hand.

'I love your hair,' Sophia said in her French accent.

'Oh, thanks. I love your curls.'

'And mine?' Matt asked, patting his short dark crop.

'I love yours too.' Sophia giggled, running her hand over his head.

Oh, new love. If only relationships could stay that way, Lacie thought.

Sophia was also introduced to Dane and Nathan, and Martha who looked overjoyed to see Matt with what could be a serious girlfriend, finally. Ellie came out and said hello to everyone, just as the next lot arrived; Chris and his wife, Melina, and her teenaged daughters Anastasia and Allana.

'Memorised everyone's names yet?' Lacie nudged Nathan's side.

'Absolutely. I think. Um, what was yours again?' He feigned confusion.

She nudged him again.

'Do you need any help in the kitchen, Mrs Appleby?' Sophia asked. Apparently, her father was a chef in France.

'Call me Martha, please, and not at all, you go and settle in. Thank you so much for asking.' She gestured toward the dining room. 'If everyone would like to take their seats, dinner is just about ready.'

Chris sidled up next to Martha. 'I'll help you with the turkey, Mum.'

'Please. It's such a heavy thing.' She went back to the kitchen with him, and Lacie followed to see what she could do, even though her mother said she didn't need any help. Martha had always loved catering for family events, and used to cook breakfasts for guests staying in the cottage when she ran it as a B&B, though she'd decided to reduce her workload after her husband died and let it simply be a basic holiday rental.

Martha handed Lacie two bowls of sides – extra bread rolls,

and some gluten-free ones for Melina and her daughters who were coeliac.

Lacie took them to the dining room and explained what was what, keeping the regular bread rolls at the end of the table away from the kids. She returned to the kitchen and brought out some sides of vegetables and condiments, while Martha brought out a potato bake, and Chris carried the huge turkey that had already had half of it cut and sliced ready for serving onto plates. There was just enough room for the centrepiece and the food. It looked like a royal buffet. At least, that's what her dad used to say at just about every Christmas in July. And then he'd explain how there were some possible connections within his family history to the royal family, going way back. He always liked to mention that.

'This baby's been cooking most of the day,' Martha said, about the turkey. 'Hope you all enjoy it, and just to confirm, no one is vegetarian, right?' She mainly eyed Sophia and Nathan.

They shook their heads.

'I grew up with many varieties of meats, and butter on everything,' Sophia said. 'This looks absolutely wonderful. And the flowers, wow. Do you mind if I take a photo to show my father? He will be glad to know I am being well looked after over here!'

'Go ahead, my dear. It's not often my accomplishments get seen by a French chef.'

Lacie wondered if her mother might be feeling a bit self-conscious now, but she didn't appear to be. Martha had a way of keeping everything together during an event, no matter what was going on in life.

Lacie took her seat in between Ellie at the end of the table and Nathan to her left (yep, just as she'd thought), with Sophia directly opposite her. She adjusted her waistband slightly as it dug into her belly. Perhaps she should have worn a dress tonight to allow for more expansion. She hadn't even started eating yet, but her belly felt full.

Jessie was telling everyone how she painted the pine cone centrepiece while Matt stood and poured the drinks, and then Martha cleared her throat. 'I'm not a religious person myself, but my husband was, and I'd like to say a prayer on his behalf, in gratitude for this food we are blessed with.' Everyone lowered their heads as Martha said a few words, and Lacie wondered if somehow, her dad could hear or see all of this. He'd be proud of how her mother was coping, how she was still looking after everyone. 'Okay, let's eat! Enjoy.'

'Can we open these now?' Dane asked, holding up a Christmas cracker.

'Not till after we've eaten,' Steve said, 'otherwise it'll make a mess on the table.' He gently placed his hand on Dane's cracker to lower it.

They all put food on their plates, helped each other reach things, and drizzled gravy over the turkey and vegetables, while Lacie opted for the cranberry sauce instead. The potato bake looked enticing, but when she took a mouthful she changed her mind, instead focusing on eating the vegetables. It was funny how her eyes were hungry for something but then her stomach wouldn't let her eat it.

The usual conversations ensued about work, study, and what the kids had planned for the last weekend of the school holidays. As plates gradually emptied and stomachs became full, Penny piped up. 'Oh, before I forget, I have to get tables finalised by Monday for the school trivia night on Wednesday. Who's coming?' She got out her phone, ready to jot down names and table bookings.

'Me, of course. Wouldn't miss my trivia fix.' Martha nodded eagerly.

'Well, since Wednesday is my last night in the country, I better come too,' Lacie said.

'Oh, don't remind me,' Martha said in a sad voice, and Lacie blew her a kiss. 'Melina, Chris?'

Melina shook her head. 'Sorry, it's a school night for these two.' She pointed to the teenagers. 'And first week back, better not have a late night. But if you want to go, honey.' She glanced at Chris.

'Okay sure, I'll go then,' he said, looking quite relieved.

Matt and Sophia were whispering, checking their schedules on their phone. Then they high-fived each other.

'Looks like we'll both be there,' Matt said with a victorious fist pump.

'Great!' Penny jotted down names. 'Ellie?'

She shrugged. 'Not sure.'

'Go on, it won't be the same without you.' Penny put her hands in the prayer position.

'Oh, okay then.'

'Yes! And Nathan, would you like to come too?'

Nathan's eyebrows rose. 'You sure? If there's enough room on the table, then okay. Sounds fun.'

'There are two places left. I might have to allocate a stranger to sit with us too.'

'Aren't you joining us, Penny?' Ellie asked her sister.

'I'm the MC. Hopefully I can pop over for a chat in between question sessions though. But I'm not giving you *any* clues about the answers.'

'I hope they have lots of nature questions,' Lacie said. 'Then we're in with a good chance of winning with this expert right here.' She gestured to Nathan.

'Oh, stop. I'm sure there'll be lots of questions on other things too, and we'll have a good chance of winning either way, with this intelligent bunch.' He motioned to the others and then took a sip of wine.

After a dessert of pudding and ice cream, the kids exclaimed 'yes!' when it was time to pull the Christmas crackers. Loud pops and laughter ensued as fourteen of them were opened, their plastic novelty gifts spilling out all over the table, jokes being read out, and party hats being put on. Half the family was standing, pouring drinks or stretching their legs, the kids jumping around and playing with their new toys. Lacie glanced to the kids' table, and then to Melina who sat still, watching them play. Her eyes glossed over and she dabbed at the corners of them, then stood, sniffling, before dashing out of the room.

Lacie went to follow her, but Chris placed a hand on her arm. 'I'll go,' he said.

Martha noticed too, concern creasing the corners of her eyes.

'Who wants to play a quick game of cards?' Matt asked.

'Me! Me!' the kids yelled. 'But can we do presents first?'

'One game of cards, then presents. How about that?'

They smiled and jumped, then went to the living room, everyone following except for Martha, Nathan, and Lacie.

'Can I help bring some plates to the sink?' Nathan asked.

'If you insist,' Martha replied with a smile, as Chris walked back in the room.

'Sorry about that. Melina's in the bathroom freshening up.'

'Is she okay?' Martha asked.

Chris rubbed the back of his neck. 'Yeah. Sort of. It's just...' He stole a glance back towards the bathroom, then leaned forward and whispered, 'I haven't said anything because we wanted to wait, but we've been trying for a baby.'

'Oh, that's wonderful.' Martha grasped his hand.

'Not so much,' he replied. 'We haven't had any luck for the past year, and she's forty next month.'

'Oh.' Martha's hand went to her heart.

Lacie instinctively placed a hand subtly on her lower belly.

'She wants to do IVF, but… I don't think I want to. I'm having second thoughts about the whole thing, to be honest.'

'Oh, Chris, I'm sorry. I wish I'd known.'

'We thought we'd surprise you eventually with a pregnancy announcement, but looks like it's this instead.' He raised his hands in defeat. 'She's been pretty upset with me.' He stole another glance to see if she was coming or not. 'The girls, they're full on. A handful at times. Especially with all the dramas with their father. He lifts them up then drags them down, gets their hopes up but disappoints. We have to undo all the damage after they've stayed with him. It's a lot of work.' He exhaled. 'I love them and want to do the best for them. With a new baby, that'd become more difficult. Plus, with Melina's diabetes, I'd be worried a new pregnancy at her age would be a lot for her body to handle, not to mention going through IVF.' He ran a hand through his hair. 'I mean there's also surrogacy, or adoption as a last resort, but it's all so overwhelming.'

So that's why he'd seemed stressed, Lacie thought. And here she was, carrying a baby no one knew about, while Melina was just trying to get to the same position.

'Sweetheart, don't let the pressure get too much. I can always help with the girls when needed too. And take some time to listen to Melina's feelings and understand where she's coming from. Maternal instinct is a strong urge. It's not something you can talk a woman out of if that's what she wants.'

Lacie gulped.

'Tell her how you feel too, and why. Help her to see that your concern is for Anastasia and Allana. She'll respect that. And maybe let things settle for a month or two, take a break, and then reassess. If you want to take a holiday somewhere, let me know and I'll take care of the girls, don't you worry.'

'Great idea,' said Lacie.

'Oh, Mum, that's more than I'd expect, but thank you.'

'Be gentle with her, and yourself.' She rubbed his back. 'Now go see if she needs anything. And maybe some present opening will cheer her up. I got her something for her new reading corner she's going to love.'

'Okay, thanks, Mum.' He hugged her and left the room.

Martha picked up two bowls. 'Let's clear this table, shall we?'

'On it.' Nathan picked up the pile of dirty plates, and when Martha left the room, whispered to Lacie, 'Your mum is one special lady.'

'She sure is,' Lacie replied. 'She sure is.'

When the card games and present open ceremony was complete, and wrapping paper littered the living room, they all made their way outside, rugged up in coats and scarves, chocolates and marshmallows at the ready to christen the firepit.

Nathan did the honours, starting the fire and building it up till it warmed the area around them.

'This is so cool!' Jessie said. 'Oops, I mean hot.' She fanned her face.

'Looks amazing.' Penny gestured around. 'And those fairy lights.' She pointed to the hedging a couple of metres behind them. 'This is going to become my new favourite place.'

Mine too. Lacie wanted to imprint the scene into her mind and take it with her back to the States.

'Now, careful with those,' Steve said, as his kids held out their marshmallows on forks. 'Here, I'll do yours, mate,' he said to Dane. 'It can get hot.'

Soon, marshmallows were toasted and being enjoyed, and

chocolates were shared around the circle. Lacie was definitely too full now and couldn't fit a single extra thing in.

They all chit-chatted, laughed, reminisced, and Lacie's stomach fluttered at Nathan's warm glow and how much he seemed to be enjoying the evening. His down-to-earth nature and gratitude to her family was endearing.

'I have an activity for us all to do,' Penny said, already in MC mode, and always in school teacher mode. She picked up a basket nearby containing pens and paper, and handed them out. 'To celebrate the first firepit night ever, we're going to make some wishes.'

'Will they come true, Mummy?' Dane asked.

'They just might, you never know.' She winked.

'Write your wish on the paper, then when you're ready, toss it into the firepit.'

'But won't that destroy the wishes?' Jessie asked.

'No, darling. It'll send the energy of your wish out into the universe, where all things are decided and created. Sort of like magic.'

'Oh, wow. I'm writing one now. Can I do two?'

'You sure can. Just be careful when you throw it in, you have to do it very carefully with me helping you, okay?'

Jessie nodded. Anything for a wish to come true.

'Dad, how do you write Lego castle?' Dane asked, pen poised against the paper.

Steve spelled it out and helped his son to write the words.

Lacie grinned. If only her wishes were as simple as a Lego castle. She eyed Nathan who seemed equally perplexed by what to write. He tapped the pen against his chin, and she shrugged as if to say 'I don't know what to write either'.

Everyone turned quiet as wishes were decided and written. Then Penny said, 'Who wants to go first? Let's take turns around the circle.'

'Me!' Dane exclaimed.

Penny got him to scrunch up the paper into a ball so it'd be easier to toss in, made sure he was standing far enough away yet close enough for it to land in the fire, then with the confidence of a warrior, threw it in. He gave his mum and dad a high-five. Jessie made her wish next, holding the paper to her heart and closing her eyes, then tossing it in swiftly. Lacie wondered what it was but didn't ask.

Penny went next, followed by Steve, Matt and Sophia, and all the others. Nathan and Lacie were last. Nathan stood a metre away from the firepit and casually tossed it in as though it was the most natural thing to do. He didn't seem fussed, though, if it came true or not, Lacie thought he was just being polite by joining in, for the sake of the kids.

But for Lacie, she took it seriously. It was a chance for her to actually think about what was important, what she wanted.

She glanced at her paper one more time, glad that it was going to be burnt and no one could read it.

I wish that no matter what happens, this baby will be healthy and happy in life.

Simple, but important. She had more than herself to think about now, and this little life was counting on her.

She took a breath, glanced briefly up at the silver stars against the navy-blue backdrop of the night sky, and threw it in gently but purposefully.

Her family clapped, at her or at the whole ceremony she wasn't sure.

'That looked like it must be one hell of an important wish,' Nathan whispered in her ear when she sat back next to him.

'It was. It is.' She smiled. 'And yours?'

He shrugged. 'Ah, well let's just say I'll believe it when I see it.'

'Sounds like someone needs to learn to believe a bit more in the magic of the universe.' She gave him an encouraging glance.

'I believe in the magic of nature, and that's part of the universe.'

'Well, that's a start, I guess.'

Lacie glanced back up at the sky, mesmerised by the twinkling stars and realising she hadn't admired the night sky like this in a long while. She barely noticed that some of her family were filtering back inside, until her mum thanked Nathan again for the firepit, wrapped her pashmina more tightly around her, and followed the chattering bunch back into the house.

Matt and Sophia stayed a while longer, then they stood too. 'You guys coming back in?'

'A few more minutes,' Lacie said. 'It's been a long time since I've done this, I want to drink it in a bit more.'

Matt nodded, slid his arm around Sophia and wandered slowly back indoors, pausing for a loving kiss along the way.

'You're not cold?' Nathan asked.

She had been feeling warmer than usual since her pregnancy had started, but had rugged up well for tonight with long suede boots over her thick leggings, merino wool turtle neck top, red velvet tunic, cardigan and scarf. If she was back home in the States, she would need a few extra layers and a coat on a winter's night, plus a beanie and ear muffs. 'Chicago gets cold. This is pleasant.' She smiled.

'Oh yes, of course. I don't know how you handle it. I don't think I could take anything below 5 degrees Celsius.'

'Double glazed windows and ducted heating.' She gave a thumbs up.

They both stared at the fire a while, until Nathan asked, 'So, may I ask what you wished for?'

'Don't you know the rules?' she teased. 'It won't come true if I share.'

'Don't tell Dane that. Everyone knows he wants a Lego castle.'

'I didn't have the heart to inform him about the number one rule of making wishes,' she replied.

'Sometimes, rules can be broken,' Nathan said.

'What was yours then?' She nudged him with her elbow.

'Nothing much, just regular stuff.'

'Hmm, somehow I think yours was more important than you'd like to let on, Mr Sharp.'

He kept his gaze straight ahead. 'If it comes true, I'll tell you then. How about that?'

'Deal.' Before he could say 'and you can tell me yours', she added, 'Seems like you've enjoyed the night. I'm assuming you don't have any brothers or sisters?'

'How did you know?'

'Just a hunch.'

'None. Not even any cousins, that I know of.'

Lacie felt a pang of sadness for him. She couldn't imagine life without her siblings, and she had cousins located in various parts of the country. 'Your mum,' Lacie said. 'Is she... around?'

Nathan tossed a stray twig into the firepit. He shook his head.

'Oh, I'm sorry. I shouldn't have asked.'

'It's okay. She died when I was four.'

'Oh, Nathan.' She placed her hand on his forearm, and didn't dare ask what from, but she didn't have to, as he blurted it out.

'Drug overdose.'

That was *not* what she was expecting.

'I didn't understand it at the time, of course, they just told me she took too much medicine and it made her sick.'

'I can't even imagine…'

'Looking back, though my memories from that age are only flashes, I do remember her often "sleeping" longer than seemed normal, like when she was supposed to be looking after me. And sometimes she'd be all hyperactive and stuff, and other times really scared.' He crossed his ankles and leaned forward to rest on his elbows. 'My dad left when I was a baby, I tried to look him up once when I was a teen, but never found him. I think part of me didn't want to. Decided if he'd left, I'd be better off without him anyway.'

'I'm so sorry. That must have been so difficult to go through at such a young age.'

He nodded.

'Who looked after you after that?'

'Foster parents. But I was so traumatised by it all I must've acted out a lot, I was pretty naughty, and I don't think they coped, so I ended up going to another family. I'd gone through quite a few by the time I was eighteen, when I got a job organising plants at a nursery and moved into a share house.'

No wonder he seemed so independent and self-sufficient. 'And that's how you were playing with cars by yourself and discovering nature.'

'Yep, it brought me out of my shell somewhat, gave me a purpose, something to learn about each day and keep me going. When I started looking after my own plants, I was keeping them alive, but they kept me alive too.'

'Wow. I don't know what to say, I can't imagine how that must've been. I lost my dad eighteen months ago, but we had many good years with him.'

'So sorry for your loss,' he said. 'And no need to say anything, listening is good. I don't think I've told anyone this since…' He waved his hand as if to say 'it doesn't matter'. 'Anyway, enough about me.' He swivelled slightly to face her.

'So, you almost became a florist, then became a beauty therapist and make-up artist... what's your business name?'

Oh, that was easy. She thought he was going to ask her a personal question. 'I have two. My make-up services are called Looks by Lacie, and my salon in Chicago is YOU Beauty.'

'Ha, nice one. Bringing some good ol' Aussie slang to the States. Love it.' He held up his hand and she high-fived it.

'Thanks. It's also about embracing the YOU as in each individual and their own unique beauty. I do a lot of work with scarred people and those with disabilities. Everyone deserves to look and feel their best.'

'That's so awesome.'

'I also did a counselling course, because I found a lot of people came to me not only to pamper them, but to talk. I wanted to make sure I was saying the right things and helping them as much as possible.'

'That's really admirable. Do you have any photos of your salon or your make-up work?'

'Of course, I'll show you. Oops, I don't have my phone with me. I'll show you next time I interrupt you while you're working, shall I?'

'Sounds like a plan.' He nodded. 'Hey, so I've gotta ask... I'm not really into the entertainment world, but you must have met some celebrities through your work?'

'Uh-huh.'

'Anyone I'd know of?' He raised his eyebrows.

It was a question people always asked. 'Some well known and some not so well known.' She smiled. 'It was a big thrill at first, but then it wore off after a bit. Some of the bigger names are actually quite self-conscious. The ones you wouldn't think would be. They'd get me to hide certain imperfections that weren't even much of an issue, be indecisive about colours, and spend ages looking at themselves at different angles in the mirror, trying to gauge how others would see them.'

'Interesting. Both men and women?'

'Yep. Some don't interact with me at all, others tell me everything. The stories I've heard.' She shook her head. 'But we sign agreements not to spill the beans to the media, so I have to keep quiet.'

'Of course. So, did you become friends with any of them? Dated Chris Hemsworth?'

'Haha, nope. Not him.' She scratched her chin.

'Oh, but someone *else*, huh?'

Lacie's skin warmed despite the fire dying down somewhat, and she loosened her scarf. 'I was dating an actor for a while, but it didn't work out. Their schedules are crazy.'

'I can imagine. Well, I won't ask who, as that would be nosy.'

'Xavier Black.' The name came out before she could stop herself. It was as though keeping the secret about the baby was too much and she had to at least let something else out of the bag.

Nathan's eyebrows rose. 'Really? That dude in the next James Bond movie?'

She nodded.

'What's he like?'

'He's very... ambitious. A good actor. He'll do well. *Is* doing well, obviously, but he's on his way up.'

'And as a *person*?'

'Let's just say, his career is worth more to him than anything else.'

'Ah, say no more then.' He put his hand over his heart. 'And I won't say a word. Except that it's his loss.'

Lacie smiled and lowered her head shyly. 'Oh. Well, thanks.'

'Do you want me to boycott the next Bond flick in your honour?'

She laughed, and was tempted to casually slide a friendly arm around him in gratitude for his humour and loyalty, even though they hadn't known each other for long. 'No need, go enjoy it, it looks good.' She kept her arm firmly by her side.

She didn't know if she could watch any movies with Xavier in them anymore. But she would be curious regardless, from a professional perspective having been on so many movie sets, to see how his acting evolved.

'Exes are always a bit complicated, aren't they?'

'You're telling me.' She looked him in the eyes, they shone and sparkled from the reflection of the nearby fairy lights. 'Speaking from experience and not just observation, I assume.'

He inhaled deeply. 'Yep.'

And as his mouth remained firmly shut, she decided not to pursue any further lines of questioning.

'Tonight was really nice,' she simply said.

'It was indeed,' he replied. 'Really, really nice.' He patted the back of her hand with his, and they looked in each other's eyes again, Lacie's train of thought and speech frozen in time.

Laughter burst forth from inside the house, breaking their moment of connection, and his hand retreated. 'I better go inside and thank the hostess,' he said, standing. He tipped water from the watering can into what was left of the fire. 'I hope yours and everyone else's wishes do come true.'

'And yours?'

'Time will tell.'

CHAPTER SEVEN

After a busy weekend with various fun activities, Lacie awoke around 2am Monday morning, stomach grumbling and craving something cold like yoghurt or ice cream. She put on her slippers and walked quietly down the hallway, and with each footstep, a sound became clearer: sniffles, sobs, sighs. She approached the entrance to the kitchen and living area, and knew it was Ellie. Her crying sounded so fragile and innocent, reminding her of a little Ellie, around seven years of age.

Lacie gently tapped on the door frame as she made her way into the room. She peeked around, and Ellie was sitting on the couch, her face resting in her hands, dark brown hair falling to the sides of her shoulders that trembled with the vibration of her tears. 'Ellie?' She approached her sister and sat next to her.

'I'm sorry. I'm sorry.' Ellie sobbed and wiped at her eyes. 'I didn't want anyone to wake up.'

'It's okay, I was feeling a bit peckish. Looks like I came at the right time. What's up?' She placed a comforting hand on her sister's back.

'Nothing, don't worry. You get your snack and get back to sleep, I'll be fine.'

'You don't look fine. Talk to me, what's on your mind?' It made her heart ache to see her little sister like this.

'It's just...' Ellie attempted an explanation. 'Just...' Her sobs intensified, and Lacie hoped her mother wouldn't wake up, though her room was at the far end of the house upstairs.

'Oh, Ell... it's okay.' Lacie wrapped her into an embrace. She let her cry to get out whatever needed to be released, until the sobs became short, sharp whimpers.

Ellie tucked her hair behind her ears, her side fringe falling back over her eyes. 'I just feel so... down. I can't seem to get out of it.'

Lacie rubbed her back. 'Ever since Dad?'

She shrugged. 'Guess so. But I dunno, it feels like it's not only that.'

'Oh?'

'Life feels hard, that's all. I'm studying, writing poetry, watching my friend's band play their gigs, but it all just feels... flat.'

'Hmm. Have you spoken to a counsellor? Remember how Mum went for grief counselling?'

'Yeah, I went to her too back when it happened, but started feeling better, like I could get on with things. So I just... got on with things.'

'What about a doctor? Or a naturopath? Maybe they can check if you're deficient in anything or do some tests to see if you have any hormone imbalances?'

She shrugged again. 'Maybe. But I did see a doctor a while ago when Mum made me go, for the insomnia. She told me to stick to a regular routine and get sunshine each morning, not use my phone at night. She gave me melatonin, and a sleeping tablet to use occasionally when really necessary. I think I'll need one tonight to be able to get back to sleep.'

'Oh.' Lacie's shoulders slumped. 'I'm sorry you're having such a hard time. I wish I could stay longer to help a bit more.'

Ellie sniffled and it looked like she might begin crying again until she somehow straightened up and wiped her eyes, as though not willing to go through it all again.

'Don't say anything to Mum. I don't want her to worry.'

Lacie nibbled her bottom lip. She hated the thought of Ellie suffering again once she'd gone back to Chicago. 'But talk to her if you feel down again, okay? She's a mum, it's her job to be there for you and she won't mind at all.'

'Okay. I'll be all right,' she said. 'I just need to get through my studies and feel like I've got a new purpose. I was going to try to get a job in a library or something when I graduate, maybe that will be good for me.'

'Yes, for sure. Go for what you want and try to enjoy all aspects of life. You gave up your job in the shipping warehouse to start studying and find more meaning in life, so keep going. Keep learning, keep discovering. It'll all work out.' Lacie gestured to the kitchen. 'I feel like ice cream. Want some?' She smiled.

Ellie shrugged. 'Maybe. Okay then.'

Lacie quietly opened the freezer and got out two bowls and spoons, scooping the Vanilla Dream into them. She added a couple of teaspoons of Milo powder onto the top. 'Remember we used to mix it all up with Milo to make a chocolate and vanilla gooey mess?'

Ellie gave a faint hint of a smile and nodded.

'Wanna do it again?'

She took the bowl Lacie gave her and nodded again, her smile restrained but nonetheless there.

Together they stirred and mashed the ice cream until it melted slightly into a thick, smooth goo of yummy goodness.

Lacie spooned some into her mouth and sighed. 'Oh my God, I forgot how good this was.'

Ellie did the same, quickly having another scoop.

They sat there with nothing but the sound of the spoons clanging against the ceramic bowls, and their 'mmm's after each and every mouthful.

'Done. How good was that?' Lacie stood to take the bowls to the sink.

'Pretty damn good,' Ellie said, and Lacie grinned.

When she returned to the couch she said to Ellie, 'Hey, Penny and I are going for a pampering session tomorrow morning while Mum's hiking with her walking group. We're getting facials and stuff, wanna come? Do you have lectures?'

Ellie thought for a moment. 'I'm not too good in the mornings, especially if I need the sleeping tablet tonight. Maybe I could meet you after for lunch or coffee?'

'Sure, sounds perfect. Just get a good night's sleep and everything will feel better in the morning.'

Ellie opened her mouth but nothing came out.

'Ell?'

'Do you think... could we maybe go and visit Dad's grave?'

Lacie's heart fluttered with emotion. She knew it might be a good idea to see her dad's grave, having not been there since the funeral, but she wanted to leave it till the end of her holiday. Which was only three days away.

'If that's what you'd like to do, then yes, let's go. We'll take him some flowers, and... have a moment there.'

'I think I need to. I wish I could talk to him one more time.'

'Me too, sis, me too.' Lacie slid an arm around her sister and sniffed. 'Now, before *I* turn into a blubbering mess, let's get some sleep, hey?'

'Okay. Hopefully.'

When Lacie returned to her bed, it was her that had trouble

sleeping. Thinking, worrying, planning, trying to solve the world's problems and hers all in one night.

The alarm woke her, and she got up straight away, not wanting to miss her appointment with Penny at the day spa. It wasn't often she was the one being pampered. She got up and stretched, noticing more and more a feeling of tightness in her lower abdomen, as though it was stretching by the minute, which it probably was, if only minutely. Thin streams of sunlight peeked through the sides of her curtains, and she pulled them aside to reveal a glorious day. She smiled, glanced around, enjoying the view of the garden. Something near the pot plant caught her eye, and she did a double take.

She opened the patio door, stepped out, and picked up the jar. It had two bright red bottlebrushes poking out of it, and a lone leaf of foliage. Some kitchen twine was wrapped around it, also securing a small gift tag.

> *Lacie,*
> *Never stop believing in wishes.*

Her heart smiled. It wasn't signed but she knew it was from Nathan. She held it close to her and stood on her tiptoes, peering above the shrubs. Where was he?

The wrought-iron gate to her left, separating the garden from the adjacent guest cottage, creaked and Nathan walked through it, a broad hat shading his face, and hedge trimmers in his hand. He walked straight ahead until she sent him a sneaky wolf whistle, then covered her mouth as though to say 'oops'.

Was that inappropriate? Oh well, too late now. He stopped and looked her way, a big smile on his face.

She stepped off the patio onto the soft grass, still in her pyjamas but not caring one bit, feeling like if there was anyone she could be comfortable around at any time, it was him, for some reason.

He approached slowly. 'That's cute.' He eyed the jar.

'I wonder who it's from?' She fiddled with the twine. 'Must be someone who knows how much a simple flower or two in a jar means to me.' She stepped closer to him and lightly touched his arm. 'Thanks, Nathan. It's really special.' Her cheeks became warm under the morning sun.

'Just a spontaneous idea I had.'

'Those spontaneous ideas are often the best.'

Their smiles grew. 'So, what's on the schedule for today? Any flower picking?'

She shook her head. 'Nope, I am off to get pampered with my sister. Time to relax and get those endorphins flowing.' She didn't want to mention she'd also be visiting the cemetery. 'I could get used to being on holiday.'

'Enjoy! That reminds me, I must book in for a massage sometime, haven't had one for ages. My muscles don't know how to relax.'

She glanced briefly at the muscles on his forearms, tendons solid and strong pushing out from underneath the skin. She swallowed a lump in her throat. 'Massages are the best. You must need one with all the physical work you do. That firepit alone must weigh a tonne!'

'I'll make a booking as soon as I'm done here for the day. You've motivated me. Thanks, Lacie.'

'Anytime.' Massage was a service she loved providing to clients, helping them relax and feel wonderful. A vision flashed in her mind of giving *him* a massage. She scratched her head.

'Well, I better go get ready before Penny picks me up. It's a beautiful day, enjoy the sunshine.'

'I will. Living the dream, I am. I guess I'm kind of like a... *nature* beauty therapist.'

Lacie chuckled, then went back inside, twirling a strand of her hair, and placing the jar next to her bed, her cheeks feeling warmer than they had out in the sun.

CHAPTER EIGHT

They arrived at Soul Skin, a franchised salon that Penny said was expanding into more and more locations, offering bespoke treatments in a stylish and minimalistic setting, which the company proposed reduced stress and overstimulation in today's busy world. Lacie knew they would provide standardised treatments, which was fine, but she loved that in her own business she could customise her treatments in any way she liked, so the client got a unique experience each time. She was glad they hadn't booked in for a hot stone massage as she remembered that massage and heat wasn't recommended in the first trimester of pregnancy, but facials were okay.

They changed into robes and laid down on the treatment tables in the couples' room. Penny said she'd try not to talk too much, but couldn't promise anything. Lacie hoped she wouldn't fall asleep, so as to not miss any of the luxury. She had made Penny promise not to say anything about Lacie working in beauty, as she knew it could make the therapist more self-conscious because she sometimes felt that way herself when treating a fellow professional. She wanted to relax, chill out and feel good, and hoped the morning sickness medication would continue to work, as some strong smells had been making her a bit queasy.

'Your skin is already glowing,' the therapist said to Lacie. 'What products do you use?'

Lacie's glow was no doubt intensifying as heat filled her cheeks and the therapist ran the back of a finger up along her cheekbones to check for hydration levels and skin elasticity. Pregnancy hormones often made skin plumper and dewy. 'Um, I use a few different things. An American brand. That's where I live.'

'Oh, nice. Well, you'll make my job easy for me, but I'm sure you'll be even more radiant after your treatment.' She slid some cotton circles with make-up remover soaked on them over her eyes, then lathered a creamy cleanser onto her skin in rhythmic movements.

'All my radiance goes to my nose in winter,' said Penny. Her therapist commented that the treatment would boost circulation and warmth in her skin to counteract the effects of the cooler weather.

Lacie tried to relax, but kept anticipating what was coming next. A faint blueberry scent reminded her of one of the facial scrubs she used with her clients, and in her mind was transported back to her salon. She imagined a baby in a cradle, rocking it back and forth with one hand while trying to massage a client with the other. She held back a laugh at the ridiculous image. How would she manage running her business on her own with a baby? At least in the early stages before the child went to school. She'd met many in the film industry who had nannies, and she had clients who sent their kids to daycare, and she would probably have to do that at least part time. But if she was going to have a baby, she'd want to be there as much as possible. That's how she always thought it would be when the time came. Hands on, balancing the care with her partner. But there would be no partner or family to help her.

Chris's face popped into her mind, and his wife's tears. So many people struggled to have children. Was this a sign that she should give this baby up to someone who desperately wanted one? Guilt surfaced when she realised she wasn't desperate for a child, yet here she was, having what others yearned for.

'Try to relax your forehead as much as possible,' the therapist said as she painted on a cold, thick paste, 'to aid in circulation and absorption of the mask.' It was only then Lacie became aware she was furrowing her brow. She took a deeper breath and imagined the creases softening. The therapist's guidance and magic hands soon did the trick and her thoughts became foggier and scattered, and a quiet sense of calm relaxed her shoulders. While the mask took effect, she enjoyed a soothing neck and shoulder massage, followed by hand and arm massage, and by then Lacie wanted to stay in this very spot all day. Often clients would ask her if she had more time at the end to extend the treatment, and sometimes she'd give her regulars a bonus fifteen minutes for free if she could spare it, despite them insisting on paying. Being here now, reminded her of how blissful these treatments could be. Skin care was one thing, but stress relief and relaxation were even better. Not just airy-fairy luxuries, they were essential to many, and she loved that she could help people in this way.

At the end, the therapist lightly touched her arm. 'There we go, Lacie. Hope you enjoyed that.' She faintly heard something similar from Penny's therapist, and she nodded her thanks and yawned.

'How long do you reckon we can get away with laying here?' Penny said sleepily.

Lacie smiled. 'Five minutes max. After that they'll probably gently tap on the door to see if we're okay, or in other words, make way for the next client.'

Penny yawned and sighed. 'Are the holidays really almost over? Back to work for me on Wednesday, and back to Chicago for you on Thursday.'

'Shh, don't remind me. Let's forget about all of that for today, okay?'

'Okay.'

Plus, they still had the cemetery to contend with. They needed these five minutes of blissful peace.

———

Miracle Park was spotted with patches of delicious sunshine, many already taken up by people on picnic rugs or sitting on benches. In the shade they shivered, but in the sun they loosened their scarves. They found a sunny patch near the Wishing Fountain and sat, laying their takeaway lunch from Café Lagoon on a few napkins.

'I could get used to this,' Lacie said. 'Being the pamperee instead of the pamperer.'

Penny chuckled. 'I'd be happy getting five minutes to myself once a week!'

Lacie smiled. 'You should book yourself in for regular pampering, make yourself a priority. You deserve it. If I lived here, you know I'd do it for you.'

'I know, I wish! Yeah, I should schedule more me time. I just get so caught up with the kids and then the house and then school, and someone always wants me to help out with things.'

'That's because you always say yes. Try saying no sometimes, too. You're allowed.'

'Yes, okay. I mean *no!*'

'Haha, keep practising.'

Penny gave a resigned nod.

They tucked into their lunch and Lacie glanced around the park. With children back at school, there were only toddlers, parents and adults around, a couple in business suits scoffing sandwiches at a picnic table, one of them checking their watch. Lacie loved that she didn't have to rush anywhere right now, she could take her time and be in the moment, like Nathan said.

A mother pushing a pram stopped on the path and reached into it, picking up a tiny baby that only looked a few weeks old. Lacie's heart fluttered and she couldn't turn her gaze away. The mother held the baby close to her chest, patting it on the back and swaying side to side as the little one cried. An elderly couple walking past stopped to admire the baby and the mother smiled, though when they left her smile faded and she continued trying to soothe her infant.

Lacie imagined herself picking up a baby – *her* baby – and swaying side to side. The vision was so surreal she felt like shaking her head at how bizarre it was. But her bottom lip trembled and she blinked her eyes as they stung with unshed tears.

Penny looked in the direction Lacie's gaze was locked on. 'Do you recognise her?'

Lacie shook her head. She clamped her lips together but it was no use, emotion rose up within and a couple of tears dropped from her eyes.

Penny placed her hand on Lacie's forearm. 'Hey, what is it?'

'Nothing, it's okay,' she mumbled in response, wiping her eyes with the heel of her hand.

Penny tilted her head as she glanced back at the mother and infant. 'Aww. Cute, eh? Little humans like that are sure to put our ovaries on overdrive. I remember when mine were that young, but only barely. It goes so fast!' She glanced back at Lacie who nodded, then let out a sudden cry.

'Oh, Lace, it doesn't seem like nothing. Are you wondering when it'll be your time, is that it?' She rubbed her sister's back.

Lacie shook her head. She wiped her eyes again and straightened her back. 'It already is my time.'

Penny narrowed her eyes, beckoning for more information.

'I'm pregnant, sis. It's Xavier's.'

Penny's eyes went from narrowed to wide in a flash. 'Oh. Oh, wow. And you're sure?'

She nodded. 'Confirmed by ultrasound. I had a sneaky one before my hairdresser appointment.'

Penny's face softened and a big sisterly smile emerged, her eyes becoming glossy. 'Oh, my goodness, you're going to become a mum. I can't believe it!' She wrapped Lacie in an embrace.

'I haven't really decided what to do yet, I mean, it's early days and this wasn't in my plans, and Mr Hollywood wants nothing to do with fatherhood of course, so I'd be a single mum, and what about Chris and Melina? It's so unfair for them, and here I am with an accidental pregnancy and I feel so guilty and maybe I should give the baby to someone who can't have children, does that make me a bad person? Or am I bad if I have the baby when I wasn't ready or planning to?' Lacie felt a wave of dizziness despite being seated, and Penny handed her a drink.

'Hang on, one thought at a time.'

Lacie exhaled and took a sip. She glanced back at the baby, whose mother was placing them back in the pram, having settled the little one down.

'Does all look healthy? No medical concerns?'

'All good. I'm just taking some vitamins and some tablets for morning sickness.'

Penny glanced at her sister's belly as Lacie rubbed it.

'Why haven't you told me till now?'

'I didn't want anyone fussing over me or taking the focus off our precious family time. And I needed to think, to process... decide what to do.'

'But you're definitely having the baby?'

Lacie nodded. 'Oh yes, I mean, I couldn't face the alternative. Anyway, I just don't know if I'll be able to handle it all on my own, or if I should give the baby up. I have to go back to the States soon and it's not like you guys and Mum will be around. I've got friends who'd be thrilled, but I'm scared, I guess.'

Penny held Lacie's hand. 'You will be a fantastic mother. Don't have any doubts about that. And who's to say we couldn't come over sometime and help you in the early stages after the birth, or heck... would you even consider moving back here? You could start up a new salon down the track. I know it's not Hollywood and you've got your loyal clients, but when things change, sometimes you have to change things too.'

Lacie shook her head. 'It's all just too much.' She rubbed at her temple. 'My life is all set in Chicago. I love it there. But how is this going to work? Oh man, I don't feel ready for any of this.'

'Hun, no one is ever really ready for motherhood, no matter what they say. It hits you like a tonne of bricks even if you've planned everything to the nth degree, I won't lie. But you know what? We, us women, just somehow figure it out. We have to. When there's a little life relying on us, some unseen force kicks into gear and pushes us along. It'll all be okay. Focus on one step at a time, take care of yourself, and I'm sure the solutions will present themselves and soon you'll feel clearer on what to do about it all.'

Lacie nodded, a flicker of confidence alighting.

'No pressure, but I kinda like the idea of being an aunty.' She smiled and rubbed her hands together. 'Oh, and Jessie and Dane will have a new cousin! They will be so excited.'

'Please don't tell anyone yet, promise?'

'Sure, but Mum? You should talk to her about it.'

'Talk to me about what?'

Lacie flipped her gaze to the left where her mother approached, red-faced and glowing from her hike.

'Oh. Mum. Hi.' She tucked a strand of hair behind her ear.

Penny clamped her lips shut and gave a little wave.

'So? What have you girls been talking about?' She eyed each of them, as though they were kids all over again and one of them had found and eaten all the chocolate eggs before Easter (like Lacie had once done).

The tears Lacie had wiped away resurfaced and her resolve softened. She curved her hand to beckon her mother closer, and Martha sat next to them.

'Mum, it looks like you're going to be a grandma again.'

Martha gasped. 'Chris and Melina? Did they get good news, have you spoken to them?'

Lacie shook her head. 'Not them, Mum. Me.' Martha's face took on the same expression Penny's had before, and this only encouraged Lacie's emotions to have their moment. She sniffled. 'I just don't know what to do yet, but I am pregnant, and that's all I can process right now.'

'Oh, sweetheart,' she clasped both her daughter's hands, 'are you okay? Is everything okay? How can I help?'

Lacie nodded. 'Don't tell the others yet, I wanted to enjoy this holiday before reality kicks in, and I need to feel more certain about it all, and I don't want Chris and Melina to get upset.'

Martha nodded. 'Of course.'

Lacie's phone beeped. 'It's Ellie. She asked if we could get her a takeaway coffee and pick her up on the way to the cemetery.' She replied to the text in agreement.

Martha stood. 'I'll go get her some goodies, you girls wait here and then we'll head back to pick her up along with some flowers for your father's grave.' She gave a nod and Lacie noticed that her mother had rushed the last few words as though it still hurt to say *father* and *grave*, which of course it did. Martha, her hand on her heart, head tilted to the side and an emotional smile on her face, looked at Lacie before turning and walking across the road to Café Lagoon.

The cemetery wasn't far from South Haven, so it wasn't long after hopping into Martha's car, that the four of them hopped out again, stepping onto the pebbly parking area. A crisp breeze from the beach across the nearby highway tightened Lacie's chest... or was it from the impending emotions she was about to confront?

Ellie carried the bunch of flowers they'd gathered from the garden, and a few shells she'd picked up from the beach a while ago. 'Here, one for each of us to give.' She held out her hand of seashells and they each took one.

They walked along the track towards the back, where the more recent graves were. Lacie paused along the way, her eyes scanning the row of headstones. So many new ones had taken residence since her dad's funeral. Life was so fleeting.

She continued with her sisters and mother, Martha pointing out some cute birds flitting from branch to branch on the overhanging trees, and Penny switching her phone to silent when a message beeped. Ellie simply walked on, her gaze remaining straight ahead.

Even though she hadn't been here since it happened, Lacie instinctively knew which row to turn into, and there it sat, the fourth grave to the right, the fifth an empty one for Martha's eventual place next to her husband.

They stopped in front of it and Martha drew an audible breath.

Edward Jonathan Appleby – loving husband and father.

Lacie swallowed a lump in her throat. Her heart wobbled, and her legs weakened.

Ellie got straight to work, filling the removable vase tray with water from a nearby tap, and adding the flowers. She busied herself arranging them and adjusting them, as though she couldn't get them to sit just right.

Penny placed her shell down next to the flower tray. Lacie did the same, followed by Martha. Ellie held her shell close to her heart, twisting and turning it in her hand as though unwilling to let it go. Then she gave it a quick kiss and placed it down.

Martha held her hand to her heart and closed her eyes, drawing another deep breath, as though breathing in her husband's energy. Lacie tried to do the same, but just as fast as she'd breathe him in, her lungs would breathe him out again. She wished she could give him one last hug.

'Miss you, Dad,' Ellie said quietly. Martha rubbed her youngest daughter's back, and slid her other hand into Lacie's grasp. Lacie squeezed it and gave a solemn smile. Tears threatened, but she clamped her lips tight. It was Ellie's tears that burst forth first, and she knelt down at the foot of the grave, her palms placed on the cold granite.

'Oh, my darling,' Martha said, bending but not quite willing to kneel, probably on account of her bad knees. Lacie knelt down next to her sister instead. It wouldn't be long before she would probably find it difficult too, to get back up at least.

'We all miss you, Dad,' said Penny. 'The kids are doing well. You'd be proud of them. And we're keeping your Christmas in July tradition going no matter what.'

'You betcha,' added Martha.

Lacie helped Ellie to stand and wrapped her in an embrace, much like the one from the middle of the night. She waited until her sister's tears reduced to sniffles, then eyed her mum, silently asking if she should reveal her news. Perhaps it would give her a boost. Martha gave a little nod.

'Ell, I have some news to share with you, and maybe I should share it with Dad too, while we're here.'

Ellie raised her gaze to meet her sister's, wiping her eyes with the corner of the sleeve on her grey woollen hoodie.

'Life is so unexpected, isn't it?' Lacie said. 'So precious.' She glanced down at the headstone again, the glossy plaque glinting in the afternoon sunlight. She looked back at Ellie. She was about to say the words when she remembered she hadn't shown the others her ultrasound photos or video. Desperate to see them again herself, Lacie got out her phone from her back pocket and opened the link the clinic had sent.

She had a quick look at the flickering white heartbeat then turned the phone screen towards Ellie.

'What's that?' she asked.

'Oh my, is that what I think it is?' Martha added. Penny's mouth gaped open, knowing all too well what it was.

Lacie grasped Ellie's hand and placed it gently on her lower belly. 'That's what's happening inside.' She smiled.

'You're pregnant?' Ellie asked, a slight smile stealing some of the sadness away.

Lacie nodded. 'Bit of a surprise. I'm still getting used to it. Don't tell anyone else yet.'

'Does that mean you'll stay here till the baby's born?' Ellie asked eagerly.

Lacie's heart sunk. 'Afraid not. I'm still going back, but I'm sure we'll work something out when the time comes. I haven't really figured anything out yet. I wasn't even sure whether to keep it or give it to someone who–'

'Oh, you must keep it.' Ellie gripped her hand. 'Don't let this baby grow up without you.' Her eyes were strong and purposeful, as though endowing Lacie with an important mission.

'Surprise, Dad!' Lacie turned to face the grave again. 'I haven't exactly done things in the traditional way, but hey, that's life sometimes, eh?' She shrugged.

'As long as you're healthy and happy, my dear,' Martha said, as though relaying a response from her father.

'If it's a boy, can you name him after Dad?' Ellie asked.

Lacie's eyebrows rose. 'Um, I haven't even got to thinking about names. But that's a nice idea. And what if it's a girl?'

'Martha, of course!' said her mum, and they all laughed. 'No, just kidding. You name the little one whatever feels right to you.'

Lacie slid her arm around her mother's back as multiple thoughts clouded her head and her heart swelled. She slid the other arm around Ellie, and Penny stood on the other side. Four women, arm in arm, in front of the grave of the man who'd been there for them all through thick and thin. Leaving a family legacy in his wake, and many happy memories.

One life may have ended, but a new one was just beginning.

CHAPTER NINE

Nathan squinted up at the cloudy sky as a few tiny rain droplets tickled his skin. *C'mon, make up your mind.* It had been doing that all day, a tiny sprinkling of rain here and there, then nothing. At least it meant he could finish his work day without getting wet, but it would be great to get some rain too.

He continued digging out the hole in the soil with his hand shovel, then scooped away some extra with his gloved hands to get the right shape and depth. He only used tools when needed, and much preferred getting stuck in with his own hands... there was something satisfying about tending to the garden in a natural way, and feeling the earth beneath his fingertips. It helped him feel connected. He couldn't connect to his family's roots to gain a sense of belonging, but he could connect with Mother Nature's.

The front gate clanged, and he turned to see Penny's daughter, Jessie, skipping into the yard in her school uniform. Penny waved beyond the fence as she got out of her car with Dane. He waved to both, and Jessie smiled and stopped under the willow tree in the front corner of the property, the leaves draped over the side fence. He'd hardly seen anyone else all day, with school back the kids weren't frolicking in the gardens until late afternoon, and Lacie hadn't had her morning visit to her bedroom patio. Martha had brought him out a muffin at 10am, but had scurried back inside quickly. He assumed they were simply making the most of family time with Lacie's impending departure in less than two days. Yes, he was counting. Although their interactions had only been going on a short time, each was increasingly pleasurable in an indefinable way. Somehow, she brought out the chatterbox in him, whereas usually, he'd be the observer, giving an occasional remark when appropriate.

Jessie dumped her schoolbag on the ground and eagerly rummaged through it, extracting a brown paper bag and tipping the contents onto the grass.

He narrowed his gaze in curiosity. 'Are you taking over my job, Miss Jessie?' he asked in a playful tone.

'No! I'm a kid, not a gardener.' She giggled. 'I made these at school today, come and look.'

He took off his gloves and accepted her invitation, and walked towards her. He was never one to get in the way of a child who looked like they were on an exciting mission, unless they showed interest, remembering what it had been like for him as a kid, getting into the zone where the outside world no longer mattered and everything revolved around the fun he was creating with his imagination.

She held up one of the smooth, coloured pebbles, 'Jessie' written on it. 'My teacher helped us paint pebbles, and I made pebble names for the whole family. I'm going to make them into a family tree right here!' She pointed to the patch of grass at the base of the willow tree.

'What an awesome idea.' Nathan crouched and picked up

the pebble with her brother's name on it. Then his gaze caught a movement to his right, where Penny was peeking through the gate as though to check on Jessie. Nathan gave a thumbs up to say *all good* and she waved and disappeared towards the front of the house. 'You've done a great job with the lettering. Neater than my handwriting, that's for sure.'

'We used paint pens. Then to protect them from rain, my teacher grazed them.'

Nathan frowned. 'Grazed?' Then his face softened. 'Ah, you mean *glazed.*'

She nodded, seemingly unperturbed by the mispronunciation, and too busy arranging the pebbles.

'I just need some sticks for the branches, and something for the trunk.' Her gaze darted around. She picked up a twig, then got up to search further.

'Here, I'll help,' he said, checking his watch on standing to make sure he kept track of time and stayed a bit longer to account for his hourly pay.

He found some loose bark from another tree and pulled a bit off. 'Will this make a good tree trunk?' he asked.

'Yes!' she exclaimed, taking it and placing it down under the willow tree.

They gathered a few extra twigs for the branches, and Jessie placed them around the top and sides of the bark, before adding her mother's and father's pebbles next to one of the twigs. She added her and Dane's pebbles underneath.

'My teacher said I had too many pebbles, until I told her what I was making and then she let me have them all.' She looked at Nathan with a satisfied smile.

'I hope there were some left for the other students to paint.' He winked.

'Yes, there was a whole box of them.' She picked up two that simply had the letter A on each. 'I didn't have much room for Anastasia's name so I just put A, and then I didn't want her to feel left out so I gave Allana one with A too.'

Nathan wracked his brain until he remembered Martha's son Chris had two stepdaughters.

Jessie arranged, then unarranged the pebbles, her brow furrowing. 'I can't remember where they go.'

Nathan knelt in front of the tree. 'How about we start at the top? With your grandma and grandpa.'

Jessie nodded and placed the pebbles with Martha and Edward at the top of the makeshift tree. Jessie giggled. 'Martha and Edward,' she said in a posh voice. 'My teacher said I should use their proper names. But Grandpa, I mean Edward, isn't alive anymore. But she said I should still give him a pebble.'

Nathan's heart sank. Death was such a difficult yet inevitable thing for children to have to understand and accept. 'Of course,' he replied. 'Even those who aren't around always live on in your heart. And your memories.'

'Is your grandpa alive?' she asked him.

Nathan sat back on his heels. 'No. I don't think so. Well, I don't really have a grandpa.'

'Oh.' Jessie frowned. 'What about a dad?'

Nathan exhaled. Kids conversations could get tricky, and he didn't want to burden the girl with the complexities of his upbringing. 'Not anymore, unfortunately. But hey, you are lucky to have yours. Steve, I see.'

'Yes.' She laughed. 'Steve!' she said in a masculine voice.

He helped her correctly place the remaining family members' pebbles, his eyes lingering on Lacie's and the empty space next to hers. Ellie's was also on its own. He scanned the complete family tree and shook his head in awe. Nathan's family tree, if he made one, would only have one pebble. He could add his mum of course, but he barely remembered her. He wondered what she was like before she got into trouble and her life went downhill. There was no one to tell him funny anecdotes, or stories of times gone by. Moist sprinkles on his forearms brought him back to the present moment, and he glanced up.

'Is it raining?' Jessie asked. 'Will the pebbles get washed away?'

'No, it's just sprinkling. They should be fine here under this tree, but sometimes bugs and little creatures like lizards like to crawl on things like twigs and rocks, so keep an eye on it regularly in case you have to tidy it up a bit.'

She nodded.

'Would you like me to take a photo of it so you always remember the correct arrangement just in case?'

'Yes please!'

Nathan snapped a photo, showed Jessie, then texted it to Martha. 'Well, Miss Jessie, I better finish up my work for the day before it gets dark and cold.'

'Okay.' She jumped up onto her feet in one swift movement. Oh, to have the limber joints of a seven-year-old. 'What are you planting?'

He walked over to the three holes in the soil he had prepared, put his gloves back on, and picked up one of the small olive trees. 'Well,' he said, in a documentary-worthy voice, 'here I have an olive tree, or, *olea europaea*, to be exact.' He pointed to the roots. 'These need to burrow deep into the soil to get nutrients, so the tree can grow.' He placed the tree into the first hole and filled the gaps with soil, patting it down until it was secure.

'Wow, that was quick,' she said.

'Yep. I did most of the work beforehand, and the tree had

first grown in a pot, so it's already started, and now it'll get a bit bigger.' He realised he had forgotten to continue in his documentary voice. He cleared his throat. 'And now... for the next one.'

He did the same, this time encouraging Jessie to hold the trunk of the small tree as he compacted the soil around the roots.

'What is the middle one?' she asked.

'That, young lass, is a fig tree. Or, *ficus carica*.'

Jessie giggled at his David Attenborough impersonation and the strange tree name.

He planted the tree with Jessie's help, and she asked, 'Are you going to put more trees in between them?'

'No, you see... trees need room to grow, and for their roots to lengthen underground. However,' he held up his pointer finger, and continued in his accent, 'in the next few days, I will plant some marigolds, also known as *tagetes*, underneath the trees, because they *deter* unwelcome bugs and insects, and can prevent the fruit on the trees from being *spoiled*.' He made sure to emphasise certain words to give his impersonation more credibility, even though he didn't know if Jessie knew who the legend was. 'Plus, they add a bright *burst* of orange colours to the garden.'

Jessie's eyes widened. 'Orange is my second favourite colour!'

'It is? And what is your first?'

'Red! Like roses. Roses have thorns to stop the bugs getting to the top.'

Nathan smiled and took off his hat. He placed it on her head. 'I now declare you, Miss Jessie,' he resumed his impersonation, 'the second-best gardener at...' he held his arms out to the sides as though on a stage, 'South Haven!'

The girl exploded into laughter and bowed as he clapped.

More clapping sounded, and both Nathan and Jessie turned around to see Penny, Martha, and Lacie watching them with delighted grins from the side door. Warmth crept onto Nathan's cheeks, and he wished he had his hat on to shade his face. Lacie caught his eye and although she grinned too, it soon faded into a smile that looked more... bittersweet.

CHAPTER TEN

After a productive day assembling and painting the new beehives for South Haven and unclogging the gutters after a night of rain, Nathan tidied his hair in the bathroom and patted on some cologne, in readiness for the trivia night that would begin in twenty minutes. He managed to find decent footwear that didn't have mud or paint stains on them, slid his phone into his pocket, grabbed his keys and wallet, and got into the Ute. He hoped he would be able to answer some questions that weren't only about nature. He also hoped he wouldn't have to answer any more about his family background or past.

Nathan entered the bustling school hall. Bright pink lipstick caught his attention first. He approached the table. 'Hi, Lacie.' He did his best to avert his gaze to the other members of the family too, as they took their seats at the table. 'Martha, long time no see. Hi, everyone,' he added, making eye contact with each.

'Our nature guru is here,' Martha said. 'Let's hope Penny and her colleagues have chosen some questions my tired brain can handle.'

'You can handle a lot more than you give yourself credit for, Mum,' said Lacie. She patted her hand.

'Nathan, this is Gloria.' Martha gestured to the older lady at the head of the table to his right. Her pixie-like white-grey hair framed her face, and she offered a kind smile.

'Thanks for having me. Since Leonard passed, bless his soul, I don't get out much. But thought this a perfect opportunity to make some new friends and contribute to this wonderful school.'

Nathan grasped her hand gently in greeting. 'Sorry for your loss.'

She waved his condolences away. 'Oh, thank you, but it was four years ago now. Still, life must go on.'

'Indeed it must.' Nathan nodded.

Once again, he had brought an offering... this time, corn chips and salsa, to add to the smorgasbord of cheeses, dips, crackers, fruits, and sweets lining up along the centre of their rectangular table. 'Some good brain food here,' he said, licking his lips as he hadn't had time for a proper dinner. 'We should win for sure.' He winked at Martha, who put her hands in the prayer position. Over Martha's shoulder he waved at the Delaneys; Hannah's parents. Mrs Delaney had tried to set him up with Hannah a few times, in a trying-not-to-be-obvious but still-obvious way. She was now most likely relieved Hannah had found herself a good man in Luca who knew with all his heart he loved her. Nathan had only once felt that way about someone, until Tess took that gift away from him. Back then he didn't know if he could feel, or even trust himself to feel, anything like that again.

Penny, dressed in a smart skirt suit approached the table and leaned in. 'Hope you Haven Heroes all behave yourselves.' She smiled.

'That's the name we thought we'd use for our team, if that's okay with you, Nathan? Since most of us are connected to South Haven.'

'Of course. Love it.' He smiled.

'And we'll have to invite Gloria over for afternoon tea one day, won't we, Gloria?'

The woman nodded eagerly. 'I used to make afternoon tea every day without fail for Leonard when he retired. I miss those days.'

Martha offered her an understanding but sombre smile.

'Oh.' Penny glanced at Nathan before turning back to the stage. 'Your prize is all sorted. Thanks for that!'

'What prize? We haven't even started yet,' said Lacie.

'Nathan generously donated a garden tidy-up as a raffle prize,' Penny said.

'Oh, how nice.' Lacie smiled. 'Someone is in for a treat.' She took a sip of water or whatever was in her glass bottle.

'Ah, it's nothing. Glad to be able to give something back to the school that supports my work and values outdoor nature play for kids.'

Penny gave his back a quick pat then returned to the front of the hall, waving in greeting at a few other people taking their seats.

Penny tapped at the microphone. 'Attention, everyone.' She tapped again and the chatter gradually died down. 'Thank you, all, and welcome! Glad to have you here on this night of nights. And I'm glad to have a night off from mum duties! Lucky my husband is taking care of the kids tonight, because I can't be sure he didn't sneak a *peek* at some of the questions.' A few chuckles sounded. 'But rest assured, all questions have been chosen with the utmost care and security, and none of the contributing staff are allowed to participate tonight.'

Nathan piled some finger food on his paper plate, hoping he didn't appear too desperate, but his stomach was grumbling. He munched away while Penny explained the rules, and that there'd be a prize for each round, plus a grand prize hamper for the winning table with donated items from local businesses to share between them, and a set menu dinner for eight at Home, Luca Antonescu's restaurant.

'If we win, you'll have to video call me into your dinner, promise?' Lacie said.

'Of course,' Martha replied. 'We'll have to see if Steve can take your seat, if we can organise it for one of his nights off work and get a babysitter for Dane and Jessie.'

'Hey, we haven't won, yet, Mum,' Chris remarked.

'Just thinking ahead, no harm in that.'

Nathan felt like he'd already overdone his quota of family events, and he didn't want anyone to feel obligated to include him, or get in the way of family discussions, but for some reason they didn't seem bothered by his presence. He wasn't used to being part of something bigger than his small circle, which was so small it couldn't even really be classed as a circle.

'Okay, everyone,' Penny said in what must have been her teacher voice, as it was more direct and authoritarian than before. 'Time for the first round of questions. Each round has a topic, plus a random question at the end, so if a particular topic is not your thing, you'll still have a chance to earn bonus points from a general knowledge question.' She cleared her throat. 'As one of my colleagues – who I won't name – said, "let's get the boring questions out of the way first", so our first topic is... history!'

A few people laughed, and one man called out, 'Hey, history is the most fascinating area of study that ever existed, I'll have you know.' He waggled his finger up and down towards Penny, who raised her hands in the air as if it had nothing to do with her. The man chuckled and took a sip of wine. 'Bring it on, Penny! We've got this round, haven't we, team?' They all nodded and leaned in close together to collude.

Penny read out each question with perfect annunciation, so much so that Nathan thought she could probably do a good David Attenborough voice of her own. Martha immediately got the first three questions before anyone else on their table, until the fourth question about the Amazon rainforest when Nathan responded, though a few others chimed in with conflicting answers. Martha was the scribe, jotting down each answer on the scoresheet, and at the end of the round, papers were collected and tallied up, and, not surprisingly, the history buff's table won.

Nathan often simply observed... people, animals, and general goings-on of life. It was fascinating to him, the differences, similarities, behaviours, and diversity that existed, and he sometimes wondered if he should be a philosopher instead of a gardener.

'Hey, Ellie, you're studying philosophy, aren't you?'

The young woman's eyes lit up from their often dark gaze, and she nodded. 'Why do you ask?'

He shrugged. 'Couldn't remember and wanted to double check. I find it interesting too.'

'I'd be happy to recommend some books to you if you like.'

'Sure.' He smiled, and so did Ellie, and he was glad that he'd seemed to brighten her mood a little. She was always quiet and lost in thought and, a bit like him, only spoke at length when it was a subject she was passionate about.

'Will they have a philosophy or books topic, I wonder?' Lacie asked.

Martha shook her head. 'Penny said they have entertainment questions, so I guess anything related would go in that.'

'Philosophy's not entertainment though, Mum,' said Ellie. 'It's an art and science all rolled into one.'

'But it's not really science,' said Matt, Nathan's gaze flitting from one Appleby to another. 'Otherwise the theories would be proven, and most aren't. They are simply observations and perceptions.'

'Exactly,' said Ellie. 'In my opinion if someone has observed something then it's true. Even in some way. Even if it's not true for everyone.'

Matt shrugged.

Nathan was even more fascinated by their interactions, having grown up without siblings.

'Now it's time for... entertainment!' Penny exclaimed. 'Be careful, folks, we have an ex-Hollywood make-up artist somewhere in the room.'

She pretended to peer around through the crowd as though she didn't know where Lacie was, while Lacie and her flushed cheeks hid behind her water bottle, and a few excited gasps emerged from the crowd.

Nathan grinned. She was like a pink, glowing bubble of joy. Her eyes sparkled with the light reflecting from the silver lid of her bottle, and she caught his gaze and whispered, 'Wait till the nature section comes around, then it'll be your turn in the spotlight.' She gave him a friendly elbow nudge.

'You worked in Hollywood, dear?' Gloria asked.

Lacie nodded. 'But not anymore.'

'Okay, question one: what is the name of the third Harry Potter film, or book?' Penny asked.

'Ooh!' someone yelled out from a nearby table, then was shushed by a teammate.

'*Chamber of Secrets?*' Matt suggested in a whisper.

'No, man, it was *Prisoner of Azkaban*,' Chris responded.

'Ahh, of course.' Matt rested back against his seat and Martha wrote it down.

'Know anyone famous?' Gloria asked Lacie, seemingly uninterested in the questions.

Lacie smiled. 'Umm, a few. No close friends though, more like passing acquaintances. When you're on set everyone's close-knit, until the end and then it's on to the next film and the next temporary family.'

'Nothing like real family, is there?' Gloria clasped Lacie's hand gently.

Lacie glanced around the table, her eyes glistening even more than before. 'No. There really isn't.' She spoke so softly Nathan strained to hear.

'Next question! One for the locals. Which instrument does musician Grace Forrester play?'

'Piano!' someone accidentally called out, followed by 'Oops!' and everyone laughed. Martha wrote it down, shaking her head at the obvious lack of discretion.

'Is she a local?' Lacie asked.

'Her mother is. Dr Greene,' Martha said.

'Oh! I didn't know. I'll have to look her up later.'

Martha leaned in. 'She first played a while back at one of the local charity concerts, when Sylvia first introduced Grace as her daughter. She was adopted, came back to meet her birth mother. Such a beautiful story.'

'Oh wow. That must have been...' Lacie's eyes took on a distant look.

Nathan waited but she didn't continue.

'Anyway, ten bucks says Mum gets the next question right.' Lacie placed her elbows eagerly on the table.

And she did, followed by the next, until Lacie, Matt, and Sophia became the clear team leaders during the round. Their table tied first place with one on the opposite corner of the hall, and Lacie straightened up and waved with a smile at the woman who owned the bookstore, Nathan wasn't sure of her name.

The technology round was blitzed by Chris, with extra help from Ellie, and the table won a wireless charging dock and portable speaker, which everyone agreed Chris should take home.

'And now for science and nature,' Penny said.

Everyone looked hopefully at Nathan, and Chris and Matt clapped their hands on the table in rhythm, saying 'Haven Heroes, Haven Heroes, Haven Heroes!' making the chips bounce in their bowl.

Nathan laughed. 'I'll do my best, guys, but I'm sure you'll probably know many of the answers too.'

'Which flower can survive by getting nutrients from the air instead of soil?' Penny asked.

'Orchid!' Lacie said with enthusiasm, just as Nathan opened his mouth to say the same. He clapped in her direction.

'Next... what is the largest fish in the world?'

'Whale?' Sophia said.

'Shark!' Lacie said.

'Close. It's actually a whale shark,' Nathan explained.

'Is that like a crossbreed?' Ellie enquired.

Nathan shook his head. 'It's one hundred per cent shark.'

'Cool.'

Martha wrote it down and whispered, 'Thank God you're here, Nath.'

'Okay, now which bird can fly backwards?' Penny continued.

'Hummingbird,' Nathan said without a second thought and Martha didn't even look up to check for any other suggestions. He held back an honoured smile.

There were a few science questions about the human

body, medical advancements, and the planets, and then Penny asked, 'Which flower is most commonly known as the flower of love?'

'Any flower that Matt gives me!' Sophia said, patting her boyfriend's arm.

'Rose.' Lacie said it at the same time as Nathan, and they exchanged smiles.

'Too easy,' Chris said.

'Oh yeah, then why didn't you say it?' Ellie asked.

'Wanted to give these two flower gurus their moment.' He winked.

'Thanks, bro. I feel so smart now.' Lacie laughed.

'May I add,' Martha said, 'I think we might get bonus points if we indicate which *colour* of rose. Which is of course *red*.' She wrote it down in confidence.

'Good idea, Mum,' Lacie said. 'Red roses for sure. Though I personally find the Love and Peace rose the most beautiful.'

'Ah, the one with the yellow and pink petals.' Nathan knew it well, such a delicate yet definite scent.

'Indeed.' Lacie smiled and held his gaze for a moment. 'Not many guys know such details.'

The table fell silent for one brief moment before Penny continued, and the round ended, Haven Heroes winning a collection of organic seedlings.

'Perfect!' Martha exclaimed. 'Let's hand them around and, of course, I'm just going to give mine to Nathan to choose which ones to plant at home.'

They took a brief break to nibble, drink and chat, and as he and Lacie were discussing the best types of flowers to plant together versus display together in a bouquet, Gloria was watching them intently.

'Ah, so nice.' She focused in on Lacie. 'He looks at you the same way my Leonard used to look at me, dear.'

Lacie's eyes widened and her cheeks flushed the same pink as a Love and Peace rose, while Nathan's became warm.

'How long have you two been together?' Gloria asked, eyeing both of them.

Nathan gulped.

'Oh, goodness,' Lacie said, hand on her heart, 'that's so sweet but we're not a couple, I'm afraid.'

Nathan scratched his head, wishing Penny would start reading out the last round of questions. Why wouldn't any words come out of his mouth? He hadn't been presumed to be part of a couple with anyone for a long time. Was he really looking at her in a *certain* way? He was just interested in what she was saying. That was all. Wasn't it?

'Oh, my mistake. Apologies,' Gloria said, then subtly winked in his direction.

What?

Nathan simply offered a polite smile. 'Corn chips, anyone?' He picked up the bowl that only had a few broken fragments left and held them up.

'Attention, everyone!'

Oh, thank God.

'Now, there's no prize for the last round of random questions, but the scores will go towards the final tally to determine who wins. So, it's anyone's game!'

The crowd clapped, cheered, and Chris and Matt did the whole 'Haven Heroes!' table clapping thing again, and this time Nathan joined in.

The round had some tough questions nobody knew for sure, and some that they did, so it really was anyone's game.

When the results had been tallied, Penny spoke, 'Before we announce our winning team, I'm going to draw the winner of our raffle, and they'll get a professional garden tidy-up and mini makeover from Nathan Sharp Gardening.' His team mates clapped. 'And of course, if you don't have a garden, you may either benefit from a balcony garden design, or you may wish to pass on the prize to a loved one.'

Penny dove her hand into the raffle box and took her time rummaging around, eventually plucking out a ticket.

'It is blue, number thirty-eight. Mrs Gloria Stenman!'

Nathan's gaze shot to his right where Gloria sat and laughed. 'Cool!'

The woman's hands flew to her gaping mouth. 'Oh my stars!' She grasped Nathan's hand and mouthed 'thank you'. Gloria stood, but Nathan held out a hand to say 'wait'. He went up to Penny and took the voucher, then took it back and presented it to Gloria, along with a light kiss on the back of her hand. She fanned her face and said thank you another five times. 'I think my Leonard is pulling some strings up there,' she said.

'And now, it is time…' Penny held the scoresheets in her hands and straightened them into a neat, upright pile on the surface of the lectern. She grinned. 'As I said before, we've created the night with the utmost professionalism and objectivity.' She glanced around at each of the tables. 'And I'm thrilled to announce the winners are… Haven Heroes!'

Nathan let out a 'woohoo!' and everyone clapped and cheered. Nathan held up a hand and Lacie high-fived it, and somehow it morphed into a celebratory hug. They all clapped the table again and sang 'Haven Heroes!' one last time, then Martha went up to the stage and accepted the large basket courtesy of her daughter.

'Rigged!' History Man called out, then laughed. Penny held up her hands as if to say, 'Hey, I can't help it if my family is the best!'

'Okay, let's share these prizes around, who wants the candle from April's Glow?' Martha held up a coastal blue and white themed candle, then other prizes, and somehow managed to figure out who would take home what without too many disagreements. Nathan declined the offer of a prize and said the night was a fun gift in itself, but she slipped the coffee vouchers into his hand regardless.

Another half hour passed as people mingled and chatted, took selfies, and staff cleaned up. Nathan had been introduced to several new people he'd probably forget the names of, but a couple had asked for his business card.

'I think we probably scraped through thanks to blitzing the nature round,' Lacie said.

'Maybe, but that tech round was pretty good too, and who knows, the random round may have been the clincher. It was a team effort anyway.'

'Yep. I can't believe I remembered that flower question, it's been years since I did my basic floristry course.'

'When you're passionate about something the information is retained more easily.'

'So true.' She yawned.

'Tired?' Martha asked as she approached them both.

'Me? No, not at all.' She covered another yawn. 'I'll have hours and hours to sleep on the plane tomorrow. So glad I've got a window seat I can rest my pillow against.'

'We're going to head home now, ready?'

Lacie shifted her stance to the other foot and back again.

'Lace?'

'What else does Tarrin's Bay have to offer? I'm not ready to go home yet!' She glanced around as though some form of entertainment might suddenly pop up.

'Nothing except the pub or Café Lagoon, my darling, that's pretty much it. And you won't be drinking, so...'

Nathan noticed Lacie give her mother a light tap on the

arm. Ah, so she probably did hear about the jet lag hangover situation.

Nathan didn't feel ready to go home yet either. He'd forgotten how enjoyable it was to hang out and interact with a group of great people.

'Actually, I was planning on grabbing a hot beverage at the café, you're both welcome to come along if you like.'

'Not me, bedtime calls,' replied Martha. 'But thanks, Nathan. Lacie?'

A small smile grew on her pink lips. 'I would love a hot chocolate right about now, actually.'

'Great. Happy to drive you and drop you back home then.'

'See you in the morning, I guess, Mum. Everything's ready and I don't have to leave till eleven thirty, so there shouldn't be any rush to get to the airport.'

Martha gave her daughter a hug. 'Oh, let's not even think about that until the time comes, shall we?'

Lacie nodded, clamping her lips together.

Though they probably only had the next hour to connect, Nathan smiled. He was glad to have some more time with this delightful human, before life would inevitably go back to exactly how it was before she'd arrived.

CHAPTER ELEVEN

The warmth of the heating welcomed them into Café Lagoon, and Lacie eyed the cakes in the window. She hadn't eaten much at the trivia night, pacing herself so she wouldn't get nausea from food overload, but the cakes on display looked too good to resist.

'That hummingbird cake looks amazing.'

'It does. Let's get two slices,' Nathan said. He looked at Jonah, whose smile was ever-present. 'And a hot chocolate was it, Lacie? My shout.' He smiled and held out his coffee vouchers.

'Yes, thanks.'

'And I'll have a chai latte, thanks, mate.'

'Perfect for a chilly night like tonight.' Jonah glanced out at the street, where a firm breeze was cutting through the air. 'Now, we are closing, in...' he looked at his watch, 'twenty-five minutes, but you're still welcome to sit in until then, unless you wanted takeaways?'

Lacie raised her eyebrows at Nathan. 'I know it's freezing,' she said, 'but I'd love one more beach stroll before my departure.

Is that crazy? Plus, the full moon on the ocean is so beautiful, I want to snap a pic.'

'Not crazy at all. I've often camped in winter. Being out in nature is my passion, after all.' He winked.

'Takeaways coming right up,' Jonah said, then got to work.

Soon after, they were parked in Nathan's Ute beside the beach. 'Want to have these in the car first, or do you want the full outdoor nature experience?' he asked her.

'Hmm, I don't want to get sand in my cake, but...'

'I've got an idea. I've got a small pop-up tent I sometimes use when fishing late at night.'

'Oh, that's okay. No need to go to any trouble.'

'No trouble. It only takes about ten seconds to set up. It just unfolds, like a kids' play tent.'

'Why not? One last little adventure before I...' She wondered how many times she'd said 'before I go' today.

'I'm not sure it'd be classed as an adventure, but it might be a... fun moment.' He smiled and got out of the car, and she followed, tightening her scarf, popping on her beanie, then carrying the cake bag and tray of hot drinks.

'So,' he said, grabbing the tent from the back of the car, 'apart from the Love and Peace rose, do you have a favourite flower?'

'My answer to that question has always changed over the years! Depends at the time. But one I always turn to no matter what is the tulip. I love the smooth simplicity of it. Their curved petals and bright tones. Perfection.'

He nodded. 'Did you know tulips can also be eaten? Mainly the petals and the bulb, as long as they're not sprayed with chemicals. They're from the onion family.'

'Really?'

'Only if one was desperate of course.'

'Yeah, I wouldn't want to waste their beauty.' Lacie

imagined munching on her favourite flower. 'Tulips, edible. Who'd have thought?'

'I know. Amazing earth we live on, eh?'

She gazed across the expanse of ocean, the shimmer of moonlight caressing the ripples on the surface. Lacie drew in a deep breath and tried to memorise the salty aroma, the cool and soothing sensation – an all-encompassing freshness in the air as though it was part of her, absorbing not only through her lungs but her skin. She popped the cake and drinks into the tray of the Ute for a moment and got out her phone. She took a few photos of the full moon commanding the sea.

'Not as good as the real thing,' she said as she appraised her photography, 'but nice to have some extra memories to take back with me.'

'After tonight, you can say you've been camping on the beach too.' He smiled. 'At least the tent part.'

'Let's go. I'm so looking forward to this cake.' She picked up the items and they walked down the narrow sandy pathway. Luckily, she was wearing boots so sand wouldn't get in her shoes, and only with a mid-rise heel so she wasn't too wobbly. She didn't feel like taking them off and freezing her toes.

Nathan wore tan suede boots and dark jeans. He'd covered his checked shirt with a thick jacket, and looked every bit the rugged Australian outdoors type.

'I'm curious to see how we're both going to fit in that tiny tent.' She giggled.

'You'd be surprised.' He found a good spot at the base of a sand dune and he pulled the tent out of its circular zip-up bag. In a flash, he had popped it out and it formed a triangular shape.

'Ladies first.' He gestured, then held the bag and drinks as she climbed inside, giggling again.

'Reminds me of our childhood cubby houses. We used to make them out of tablecloths and blankets, draping them all around the dining table and chairs, so much fun. But we had five of us to squeeze in.'

'What was it like, growing up with so many siblings?' he asked as he climbed in after her and sat the food in front of them, and took a sip of his drink.

'Fun. Annoying. Crazy. Loud. All those things.' She sipped her drink and let its warmth calm her soul. She observed him as he watched the ocean through the gap in the tent. 'I hope that didn't sound ungrateful. What was it like for you? Did you get to make many friends in the places you grew up?'

Nathan sighed. 'A few. But then I'd get moved again. Or, as I got older, I'd make friends with the wrong types. I got used to making my own fun.'

Lacie couldn't imagine growing up on her own and without a loving family. She thought of her baby, and if she gave it up for adoption, would the parents adopt more or would her baby be an only child? She felt a pang of sadness, and of longing... although it still hadn't sunk in, the thought of adoption still flashed through her mind sometimes... giving hope to a desperate couple, giving her baby a stable home... and the story of Dr Greene's child coming back years later as an adult with a happy reunion, made her wonder if that would be for the best. But she longed for her baby to have a life like she'd had. Lots of kids running around together, even if they were cousins or friends' children. If she gave up her child, would she always wonder what their life was like, to the point it would become an ongoing obsession, or a regret?

She shook her thoughts away. There'd be time for them on the plane. She remembered Nathan and Jessie the other day and laughed. 'I can see that. You sure had fun with the second-best gardener the other day.'

He chuckled, and a sudden breeze whipped at the flaps of

the tent. 'Oh, that. Yeah, she's a good kid. Lots of energy. Smart cookie too.'

'She sure is. Oh, I'm going to miss them all.'

'I bet.'

She dug her wooden fork into the cake and devoured a chunk, savouring the comforting texture and the mix of flavours from the tangy pineapple to the creamy sweetness of the icing. Cold air tickled her cheeks as it rushed in through the narrow gap at the front of the tent.

'Your family is pretty awesome,' he continued. 'I'm a lucky man to get to work for them and be treated so well.'

'Oh, Mum loves you. And she enjoys the company, with all of us except Ellie living our lives elsewhere, she can get a bit lonely sometimes.'

'Must be hard for her after your dad. And all of you.'

'Yeah. It is.' Lacie sipped more hot chocolate, her hands snug and warm around the cup. 'You remind me a bit of him actually. Not in a dad way, in a man way. He was always so grateful, so empathetic and understanding of other's feelings and points of view. Mum said he was a rare breed.'

'Oh, well thank you, I'm honoured. I know what it's like to be misunderstood, not listened to, not accepted... I guess I figured I should do my best to give that to others since I know what a gift it can be.'

'You definitely are a rare breed,' Lacie said. She thought of Xavier, who would often be on his phone when she was trying to talk to him, or would just say 'get over it' when she'd had a bad day.

For a few moments there was nothing but silence between them, apart from the whistling wind and gushing ocean waves. Lacie felt fully awake, alive, and... something else.

She glanced at Nathan just as he glanced at her, then quickly looked away, suddenly self-conscious for some reason. A butterfly flitted about in her belly, and she knew it was too early to feel the baby move.

'Nice cake,' said Nathan, finishing off the last of his slice.

'Yeah, delicious,' Lacie said, putting the last piece in her mouth despite the fact it was a bit of a mouthful. She covered her mouth with her spare hand as she chewed, desperate to swallow it and hoping she hadn't overloaded her stomach to the point of nausea. She drew in a deep breath, the air in the tent a bit heavy.

'Want to go for that beach walk?' Nathan asked. 'It's stuffy in here now.'

'Sure. But...' She got onto her knees and peered through the gap in the tent, the wind instantly hitting her face. 'I think out there it's the other end of the spectrum.'

'A bit fresh, huh. I'm game if you are.' He shrugged.

She looked at him and smiled. 'Don't they say cold exposure is good for the immune system?'

'Sure is. Want to go for a dip too?' He cocked his head toward the ocean and she laughed.

'I'm not that keen for an immune boost, I'll just take some vitamin *sea* from a bottle instead.'

She popped their empty cups into the cake bag and scrambled through the opening and he followed, pushing the metal pegs further into the sand with his foot, and tossing a few pieces of driftwood into the tent. 'Don't want it flying away,' he said.

Lacie rubbed her arms and jogged lightly on the spot as a large wave crashed onto the shore, sending with it a rush of cold air. 'On second thoughts...' *Maybe the cold wasn't good for the baby?*

'Let's make it a quick walk, shall we?' He crooked his elbow and she hooked her arm through, and they walked in quick, stiff steps up to a sand dune and back again, laughing at how silly they must look, and why they would choose a cold winter's night to have a beach picnic. But it was her final night, and she was no stranger to the cold, so she let herself enjoy the moment and breathed in the salty air with gratitude. 'I'll miss the smell of this place.'

'It's funny, isn't it, how places smell different to each other?'

'It is.'

'What does Chicago smell like?'

'A bit of everything. Car fumes when you step outside, a bit of salt from the lake, sewage sometimes,' she crinkled her nose, 'but I love the fresh grass in the park after the rain, and my favourite – popcorn. There's a great popcorn shop near my salon.'

'Some things to look forward to then.'

She nodded. She was looking forward to getting back. It was her home, after all. But her home was also here, and in her heart, always would be.

Lacie stood still in front of the tent and Nathan's eyes sparkled as the full moon shone onto his face. 'I'll miss you too,' she said.

'My smell, or me?' He laughed.

She giggled, shaking her head. She leaned close to him and breathed in; a hint of something spicy yet sweet catching her awareness. 'Both,' she whispered. She glanced up into his eyes, and suddenly the air wasn't cold anymore. Whatever she was feeling overtook all other sensations. Until the loud crash of another wave stole her focus.

'Let's get this tent back to the car before it blows away,' he said, scratching his temple and averting his gaze.

'Sure.' Lacie's heart sunk a little, not sure exactly what she was feeling but knowing she didn't want this night to end.

She tried to help him fold up the tent while holding the

rubbish from their feast, but wasn't much help as the wind kept flipping the material around.

'These things are tricky sometimes,' he said, trying to twist and fold it. 'Supposed to be easy and instant, but not on a night like tonight!' He grunted as he tried to force it back into a folded position, but it popped straight back up again like a jack-in-the-box, one corner hitting him in the face. 'Oh, man!' He rubbed at his cheek, and Lacie tried to bite back a laugh but it escaped.

'Here, let me try and help again.' She held one side while he pushed and twisted the other, their laughter making it hard to hold it steady.

'How about we drag it back to the car, it might be easier there with a bit of a wind break?'

'Good idea!'

She held one side and he held the other, and, laughing as the wind flapped the tent about, they walked quickly back up the pathway to the car park, and she tossed the rubbish in a nearby bin.

Nathan stood by the Ute and with one mighty twist, managed to hold the tent steady in its closed position, and she helped attach the clasp.

'Victory!' he exclaimed, and she clapped.

'That was definitely a fun night to remember!' She rubbed her hands together as she got into the passenger seat, Nathan chuckling and putting the car's heating on right away.

'Forgotten anything?' he asked, twisting to face her and checking the back seat. 'We did leave in a hurry.' As his gaze returned to the front it rested on hers, and his pure smile and slightly red nose endeared her.

She was still panting from the mad dash back to the car, and his breath tickled her cheek as his face seemed closer than it was a moment ago. Unable to look away, unable to move away, their eyes locked like a laser onto each other in mutual knowing.

Heart beating double time, in an instant their lips were pressed together. A warm rush flooded her entire body, drenching her in a longing she didn't know she had. His hand grasped hers and he threaded his fingers between her own, his other hand meeting her cheek with the gentlest of caresses. The cold from a moment ago long forgotten, as his kiss transported her somewhere else completely.

When they broke away for a breath, only centimetres separating their lips, he spoke.

'Lacie...' They both panted. 'I wish you were staying. Even one more day.'

She held his hand more tightly. 'I wish that now, too.'

He leaned his forehead against hers with a sigh, and she licked her lips, wanting to savour the moment.

'It'll be a special, secret memory,' she whispered, touching his cheek with the palm of her hand.

'I guess it'll have to be,' he whispered back.

Reluctantly, she pulled away, and exhaled loudly. 'Wasn't expecting that.'

'Me neither. Sorry.'

'Don't be.'

She searched his eyes, trying to make sense of what was happening and wondering how they could possibly go on with their own lives after a kiss like that. Her lips wanted more, her body wanted more, her *heart* wanted more.

But his eyes looked as confused as she felt.

'If things were...' he said, his gaze finally leaving hers as he glanced out the window.

'Different. I know,' she completed his sentence.

If I still lived here...

If you lived in the States...

If I wasn't pregnant with someone else's baby...

If, if, if.

Lacie realised her life would never be the same. If she ever got around to dating again as a single mother, she wouldn't be able to go out on a whim anywhere with anyone. It would be her and the child, and the mystery man would have to be up for that. She'd probably have to be home and in bed by 10pm to be able to wake in the middle of the night to tend to her little one.

Nathan caught her gaze again. 'If you were staying, I'd probably ask you out on a proper, even better, and temperature-controlled date,' he said with a soft smile.

'Probably?'

'Okay, *definitely*.' His smile widened. 'I like being with you. Talking to you.'

'Me too.'

He held her hand again. 'Let's keep talking then. Distance doesn't have to get in the way of a good convo at the very least.'

'I'd like that. We may not be able to date, but we can try to be...'

'Friends?'

'Friends.'

Her words conflicted with her emotions, but she had to push them down, way down. It was a simple holiday kiss in the heat of the moment, nothing more. It couldn't be. For more than one reason.

'Deal,' he said, getting out his phone. 'Can I friend you on Facebook?'

'Sure,' she said, opening the app on her phone. 'I don't post much except on my business page, but I use messenger a lot, so let's chat on there.'

'Anytime you want a trivia challenge, let me know. I'll send you some questions and see if you can answer them.'

'I look forward to it.'

They friended each other and Lacie put her phone in her

bag. 'So, I never got to find out. What's *your* favourite flower? Is it another edible one like tulips?'

Nathan shook his head. 'Actually, my favourite flower is a weed.'

Lacie's eyebrows drew together and she chuckled. 'A weed?'

'Lantana. The flowers are cute and I like how it can thrive wherever it is, no matter what. A bit like me.'

'Ha. Cool,' Lacie said. 'I know the one, it has those tiny pink and yellow petals.'

He nodded. 'I'm weird, huh?'

His favourite flower was a weed.

A rare breed indeed.

CHAPTER TWELVE

D espite grey clouds looming above, rain had not yet fallen, and Lacie hoped it'd stay that way until she was safely on the plane and in the air. She stepped out of South Haven's grand entrance, and had no idea when she'd be stepping back in. If she was able to come to the next family reunion, she'd have a young baby to bring along. Unless she could somehow get her family to visit the States instead, to reunite and of course meet their new family member. But one plane ticket was a lot cheaper than several. And she couldn't think that far ahead yet.

Penny wheeled out Lacie's suitcase and Ellie carried the overnight bag, Martha fiddling with the scarf around her neck as though she couldn't get it in the right position. 'You sure you don't want one of us to come with you, help you with your bags, see you off?'

Lacie shook her head. 'No need, Mum, I'll be checking in the suitcase pretty much right away anyway, and the carry-on bag isn't too heavy, and I'm not...' she glanced around to make sure no one else had suddenly appeared, '*that* pregnant yet.'

'Still, make sure you take things easy when you get back

okay?' Martha rubbed Lacie's arm. 'And give yourself some time to catch up on sleep and get over the jet lag.'

'I will, I've got a few days off before I start seeing clients again.' She glanced at her watch. The airport shuttle should be here any minute. Her mother had insisted on paying for it, to save her having to handle her luggage on the train, though she'd managed perfectly well when she'd arrived, but after seeing that little heartbeat on the screen... maybe she should take things easier from now on.

She was glad she'd already said her goodbyes to the other members of her family earlier, and Penny had arrived with the kids extra early for aunty cuddles before they got dropped off at school. It was hard to hold back the tears, knowing they'd have grown even more by the next time she saw them, but she'd make sure to have lots of extra video calls with them. 'Don't forget, Mum, don't tell anyone else about you know what until I've... until I say, and wait till after the twelve-week mark anyway. Especially with Chris and Melina, I don't want them getting upset.'

'My lips are sealed.' She drew a line with her fingers across her mouth. 'But do keep us posted.'

'Of course.'

The sound of a car gradually became louder, followed by the sight of a shiny black sedan. 'I thought it was going to be a van or a bus,' Lacie said.

'No, I wanted you to have a comfortable car all to yourself.'

'Thanks, Mum.' She smiled, then sighed. 'Well, this is it.' She held out her arms to her mother as the car turned into the driveway, and Martha gripped her tightly.

'It's been wonderful having you here again. Oh, I'm going to miss you!'

'I know. Me too. But I'll call as soon as I get home, and I'll update you regularly, don't worry.' She imprinted the sensation of her mother's hug into her memory, knowing too well how quickly life could change. She wanted to be able to draw on the memory whenever she needed it, and she had a feeling she might need it a lot in the coming months.

The driver got out of the car with a smile on his face. 'Lacie, I presume?'

She nodded.

'Let me get your luggage into the boot.' He took the suitcase then the bag from Penny and Ellie, leaving their arms free for goodbye hugs. 'I'll give you all a moment.' He got back into the car.

She hugged Penny, whose eyes had already become glossy, and her sister sniffled into her shoulder. 'Hey, no tears. If I start, I won't stop,' Lacie said, clamping her lips together tightly. Penny pulled back and wiped her eyes with her sleeve. 'Have a safe flight, and let us know when you land.'

Lacie nodded then turned to Ellie, but her youngest sister's eyes were clear and strong, as though she'd been practising holding it together after her big night of emotion at the start of the holiday. 'Send me a silly selfie when you get back. Something fun I can look forward to,' she said.

'I promise.' When Lacie pulled back from their hug, she saw over Ellie's shoulder that Nathan was peeking through the half-opened gate next to the garden entrance. She gave him a smile, at least she hoped it appeared as one. A bittersweet feeling twisted inside.

He held up his hand in a firm wave; not a 'see you tomorrow' wave, but an 'I may not see you for a long time' wave. She returned it with a knowing wave of her own. Martha waved too, then ushered for him to come over but he pointed his thumb over his shoulder. 'I better get back to what I was doing. Just wanted to wish you a safe flight, Lacie.'

'Thanks, Nath.' She gave a nod. 'Can't wait to see what you do next with the place.'

And can't wait to see you again... whenever, *if*, that was going to happen.

'I'll take photos,' he replied, then offered a final wave and a smile before disappearing behind the gate and the hedging. Lacie swallowed a gulp, and tried to imprint the image of his goodbye into her memory also. Not to mention last night's kiss. What a whirlwind two weeks she'd had.

She managed another quick hug for all three of them, then got into the car before she got too emotional, double checking she had her passport and travel documents in her handbag. She plastered her best smile on her face as the car slowly moved, waving with enthusiasm at her family as they waved back, and Ellie pulled funny faces that made her laugh. It was good to see her sister smiling again after how down she'd been at first. The visit to their dad's grave must have helped with her healing.

When they were out of sight, she leaned her head back on the headrest and exhaled.

'Going on holiday?' the driver asked.

'No,' she replied. 'Just had one. I'm going home.' Her voice broke on the word home and she cleared her throat. She didn't know if that was because she also missed Chicago and couldn't wait to get back, or because her home was also here in Tarrin's Bay and she didn't know which home was more *home* to her anymore.

CHAPTER THIRTEEN

Despite the onslaught of noise in downtown Chicago when she got out of the Uber – cars, horns, people chattering as they walked by – when Lacie set foot in her apartment, everything was eerily quiet. No 'dinner's ready!' from her mum, or game shows on the TV, or birds outside the window in the morning, or the sound of Nathan using the leaf-blower or lawnmower. Just muffled noises from outside, and the whoosh of the window blinds when she opened them to let in some much overdue light.

She took her luggage to the bedroom and plonked herself on the bed.

Where would a baby sleep? She found herself thinking.

Her apartment was spacious enough and could fit a baby's cot near her bed or in the living room, but with only one bedroom the apartment wouldn't be suitable in the long term. A growing child would need their own room and space... she'd need a new home if she were to keep the baby.

Lacie hopped off the bed before overthinking engulfed her mind and fatigue claimed her body. She'd wait until it was dark before trying to sleep, she needed to get back into her normal circadian rhythm as soon as possible to be okay to return to work in a few days.

After unpacking, she remembered she had to take a silly selfie for Ellie. She got out her cosmetics bag and applied a bright red lip liner but extended the line beyond the margins of her lips, then filled it in with lipstick to create a big pout. She did the same with eyeliner, extending it beyond her usual limits and drawing an accentuated flick upwards at each corner. Her eyebrows went back in time to the 1980s, and the blush on her cheeks gave her natural pregnancy glow a run for its money.

She gave her best pout and took a selfie, laughing as she edited it with a filter to make her look extra fake and overdone, and sent it to Ellie. After pizza for dinner, and, satisfied it was getting dark enough outside, she got into her summer nightgown and hopped into bed, barely aware of her head touching the pillow.

Strange, to be leaving for work at the same time her family in Australia would be asleep or getting ready for bed. Lacie did one last check of her bag, making sure she had everything and that jet lag hadn't affected her memory, before locking up and leaving her apartment after a weekend of pretty much sleeping constantly.

Sunshine lit her way across the bridge over the Chicago River, and Lacie smiled as she walked. It was one of her favourite parts of the day, taking in the views of the skyscrapers surrounding her like a large embrace, and sunlight glinting on the water below. The walk to work always gave her time to think, to dream, and enjoy the beginning of a new day with unlimited possibilities. And the exercise had always helped keep her healthy. She may need to use another form of transport in a few months when she got big and heavy, but for now, she wanted to make the most of it.

Lacie grabbed her morning coffee from La Bella as she rounded the corner near her salon, and hoped it was okay to continue drinking coffee during pregnancy. She made a mental note to google that later, but for now, it would help her remain focused for the day, or a few hours at least.

Before entering The Galleria shopping mall, she paused for a moment, admiring the welcoming gold frame of the double glass door entrance, and the burgundy wooden trim that gave the building an elegance that flowed through to her salon. She walked in to the building and reached her ground floor premises.

'I'm back, baby!' Lacie mused to the empty reception area, after she'd unlocked the door. Her part-time assistant wouldn't arrive until 10am. She flicked on the lights, set the relaxing music up for the day, and filled the diffuser with lemon oil. She then checked everything was in place for her impending client in the beauty room, and got the nail polish samples ready. Which colour would Mrs Maria Elvarez choose today?

At five minutes to nine, the automatic bell sounded its gentle ding as her client stepped through the door.

'Hello! Anyone home?' Maria called out, as though she was simply dropping in unexpectedly to a neighbour's house for a cup of tea. Lacie smiled, glad her first client after her holiday was one of her favourites. She felt a bit guilty having favourites, but couldn't help it.

'Come on in!' Lacie opened the door to the beauty room and gestured for her smiling client to enter. 'It's nice to see you again, Maria. You're looking extra rosy today.'

'I started drinking turmeric lattes,' she replied, patting her cheeks. 'For my health. Gives me a bit of a flush.'

'Good on you. I haven't tried them myself.'

'Supposed to be good for the heart and the liver, apparently. Not to mention my joints.' She wriggled her arthritic fingers, which she – no matter what – made sure were perfectly manicured, and today was her regular appointment.

'Let's give those joints a bit of pampering today, shall we?'

'Can't wait,' she said, 'your hand and foot massages are the best. I'm sure I've been going this long without pain medication because of your expert care.'

'Oh,' Lacie waved her hand, 'I do my best.' She gave Maria an extra pillow behind her head for comfort, then held out the colour samples.

'A few new ones arrived before I went to Australia. If they pique your interest?'

Maria popped her glasses on the bridge of her nose and peered at the rainbow of samples, focusing on the new range of fresh, summery colours. 'Hmm, maybe one of each?' She laughed. 'I do have ten fingers and toes after all.'

Lacie didn't know if she was being serious or not, as some clients did like having different coloured fingernails, but most of her older clients opted for a more traditional and classier look.

'I'm kidding. I'll look like a fool. No offence to anyone who wears multiple colours but I don't think it'd suit me.'

Lacie smiled. 'Whatever makes you feel your best, I'm here to follow your wishes.' She thought back to painting rainbow nails with Jessie and her heart ached. Barely home and she already missed her family.

'In that case, I wish for...' Maria's hand roamed over the samples as though one might jump out at her and say 'pick me!'. 'Morning Glow,' she said with a nod, pointing to the light, bright orangey-pink. 'It'll give me a boost.'

'Nice choice, it's perfect for your skin tone.'

Lacie prepared the polish equipment and then sat on the low stool near Maria's feet. 'Feet first, let's get that blood flowing back to the heart, then hands, and while it dries, I'll do your head, neck, and shoulder massage.'

Maria smiled in anticipation and wriggled her toes.

Lacie started with a foot cleanse and scrub, followed by a gentle but rhythmic massage that flowed in time with the relaxation music.

When she had finished applying the layers of nail polish, she rose from the stool and a wave of weakness made her legs wobble, and a large lump in her throat caused her to gulp. She leaned on the massage table nearby.

'Whoa. Got up too quickly, I think.' She took a breath and raised the stool higher, manoeuvring it to beside Maria to work on her hands.

'How far along are you, my dear?' Maria asked with a curious arch of her left eyebrow.

'I'm sorry?'

She gestured to Lacie's belly with a soft smile. 'I remember my closest friend, Sandra's pregnancy back in the day. Some smells set off the nausea, yes? And sudden movements can make you dizzy.'

Lacie's face became warm and she was sure it must resemble Morning Glow. 'Oh.' She lowered her head a moment. 'Well, considering all is confidential within these walls, you're right. I'm about a couple of months, early days. But...'

'It was unexpected?'

Lacie nodded.

'Consider it an unexpected blessing. You know, if it wasn't for an unexpected pregnancy, I wouldn't have had my beloved Carlos.'

Lacie furrowed her brow. 'He was unexpected? I thought you mentioned a while back that you and your husband waited a long time for him.'

'Oh, we did indeed, my dear. We adopted him. From a

young mother who wasn't ready to give him the life he deserved.'

'Wow, I never knew that. Thank you for sharing that with me. How lucky you were to find him.'

'Indeed. We are beyond grateful every day for the blessing. And now of course he's in his thirties and his wife has our first grandchild on the way. I can't wait!'

'I'm so happy you got to have your dream, Maria.' Lacie lightly massaged her client's hands; hands that had held and cared for a much-wanted child for many years. Having a baby hadn't even been on her mind at all. And suddenly, she was immersed in the reality, the uncertainty, the fear, the guilt... that she didn't know if she could be the best mother for this child... that other parents would surely be more worthy of such a gift.

She managed to get through the rest of the manicure without feeling nauseous, and got up slowly from the stool to grab a sip of water before beginning the neck massage. She avoided talking during it so Maria could properly relax and get the most out of her treatment. Some clients liked talking the whole way through, others liked silence, and others liked a balance between conversation and relaxation, so she was always sure to make sure she wasn't overstepping the mark with anyone.

'That concludes your treatment, Maria, I hope you enjoyed it,' Lacie whispered to the woman who may or may not have been asleep in the armchair.

'Oh my goodness, not even midday and I'm ready for a nap.' Maria yawned and stretched her arms above her head, then admired her new nails. 'Love this new colour, I'm going to do some shopping now and show them off!'

'Have a wonderful time, and it was so nice to chat with you today,' Lacie replied as she left the room with Maria, and Lacie's recently arrived assistant, Madeleine, took her payment and booked her next appointment.

'Likewise,' Maria replied, sidling up to her as though she was about to say something else, but on glancing at Madeleine she bit her lip and simply said, 'it was lovely chatting with you too. You take care, okay?' She arched her left eyebrow again.

Lacie nodded.

'Jet lagged?' Madeleine asked, getting up from her chair. 'Welcome home!' She embraced Lacie with her slim arms.

'Thanks, hun, and yes a bit, but I'm okay.'

'Good to have you back, how was the reunion?'

'Fabulous,' she replied. 'God, I miss them all so much, but then I'm always glad to get back here too, it's like I've got two homes.'

'I was like that when I moved here from France, like being caught in limbo, but now I'm much more settled,' she said with her slight French accent.

'I still can't believe you chose Chicago over Paris.'

'With true love comes change and sacrifices,' the young woman said, smoothing her straight black hair with her palm. 'It was hard at first, but I'm so happy here with Lachlan. His work at the museum is his passion, and my job, well, I can do that anywhere, so...'

'How are the studies coming along?'

Madeleine was studying part time to become a beauty therapist and make-up artist while working for Lacie on reception the other half of the time.

'Great. Won't be long and I'll be fully qualified.'

Lacie did some calculations in her head and wondered if perhaps Madeleine could be of help to her if she did keep the baby. She could take over some of her clients until she was able to return to work, though many would only want Lacie's expertise, and then she'd need a babysitter or nanny as well. Her heart rate rose as she began to feel overwhelmed again and as she prepared the beauty room for her next client, she found herself thinking about her conversation with Maria, and with Chris back home about his struggles with Melina and their fertility issues. She had no time to think further as her next client arrived, and as the day kept her busy, she barely thought about it again until later.

When saying goodbye to her last client of the day – a woman who'd suffered scarring from burns and had been given a collagen and vitamin C infusion facial – she noticed a nicely wrapped package on the reception desk and a note from Madeleine:

Maria brought this back for you xx

Lacie smiled at her client's thoughtfulness. With a yawn, she popped the gift in her bag, deciding to open it later when she got home and could focus better.

With a craving for mac and cheese, she picked up some takeout at a restaurant on the way home and devoured it when she arrived at her apartment. Sleep came soon after she'd showered and next morning she woke to texts from Penny and her mother.

PENNY:

Miss you already! Please keep me posted on everything xo

MUM:

How is it being back at work? Hope you're not too jet lagged!

Lacie checked the time difference and texted Penny:

Miss you too! Ok xx

Then she called her mum; she'd probably still be awake.

'It seems my pregnant body clock is happy to sleep at any time of day or night,' she said when Martha Appleby answered.

'Oh good, so no trouble sleeping normal night-time hours on Chicago time?'

'Nope, out like a light after dinner last night.'

'Fabulous. Any nausea?'

'Comes and goes, depends on certain smells, getting up too fast, temperature changes and things like that. The nail polish at the salon was a bit of an issue.'

'Oh dear. Perhaps a mask?'

'Yes, I think I will, even though I use natural-based formulas, they still have a strong scent.'

Martha was silent a moment, then said, 'I was thinking, for next year's reunion, it might be, ah, difficult for you. I'm wondering if we can somehow manage a family trip to the US and come to you?'

'Mum, it'd cost a fortune for everyone's airfares, it's much easier for one person – aka *me* – to travel and visit everyone.'

'Yes, but with a baby, it's a big ordeal.'

Now Lacie was the silent one.

'Lace?'

She sighed. 'Mum, let's think about all this another time, yeah? I haven't even...'

'Haven't even what?'

'Decided. I mean, I'm still wrapping my head around the whole thing, and...'

'Okay, I'll try not to get ahead of myself. I just like to plan in advance and be prepared, and thought I could allow enough time to save up.'

Lacie got up from the bed and stretched. Her stomach felt funny and a dry retch erupted.

'Oh dear. You okay, sweetheart?'

'Yep, yep. I'm good.' She gulped and took a deep breath, then grabbed a banana from the fruit bowl. 'Just need to get something in my belly.'

'Maybe keep some crackers beside the bed. Anyway, the other thing I wanted to let you know was that Chris and Melina had a good talk apparently, and he's agreed to take things further and investigate other options like IVF. They've booked an appointment with a fertility specialist in about three months, and are going to take things easy in the meantime and enjoy a week away together next school holidays when I can mind the girls.'

'Oh, that's good, although three months must feel like a long wait.'

'I think it'll be good to give them a break and reduce some stress and pressure, then they can be prepared and ready for the next step. Plus, they need to save some money too as it's quite costly.'

'I'm happy to dip into my savings if they need a bit of a contribution.'

'Oh no, not at all, you're going to need it. And Chris has a couple of nice properties listed now so with any luck he might be able to negotiate a good deal or two and get some extra commission.'

Lacie's head was spinning. So much time, money and stress, all to try for a baby, with no guarantees. And here she was with the opposite experience: it didn't take time, it hadn't cost money, and there wasn't any stress involved except on finding out and needing to comprehend how her life was going to change.

'Mum?' She sat back on the bed. 'I've been thinking. I spoke to a client yesterday who adopted a son thirty years ago. Without that gift, she wouldn't have been able to become a mother.' She waited for an 'uh-huh' but was met with silence. 'I think I'm going to talk to Chris.'

'Sweetheart, that's not necessary.'

'I know, but they're struggling, and here I am not even knowing if I can – if I *want* – to do this. I feel guilty.' Her bottom lip trembled. 'I don't deserve this as much as them.'

'Oh, love. Of course you do. It wouldn't have happened to you otherwise.'

A sharp intake of breath surprised her. She wasn't usually this emotional, but her hormones were obviously taking over. 'I just...' A sob escaped and she sniffed. 'I just wasn't expecting this, that's all.'

'Oh, my girl, I know, I know. But sometimes things happen for a reason. You might not think you're ready, but somehow, we just become ready when it happens.'

Lacie took a deep breath and straightened her back. Conflicting emotions fought within her heart. 'I feel like I should talk to him. Let him know the situation, and give him the opportunity at least to discuss it with Melina. I could just be Aunty Lacie, while they get to be parents to a new baby together. It would save them going down the IVF road and spending bucket loads of money, possibly without success. I should do it now, before...'

Before I get too attached.

Martha exhaled slowly on the other end of the line. 'Well, if you feel it's the right thing to do.'

'I do. Even if he's not open to the idea, at least I made the offer and won't have any regrets.'

'You're a special sister,' Martha said. 'And daughter.'

'I have a good role model.' Lacie's lip trembled again. 'Thanks, Mum.'

'Love you.'

'You too.' She ended the call and held a hand to her heart for a moment, before clicking on Chris's name in her contacts.

She sent him a text:

> Hey bro, would love to chat to you about
> something. Give me a call when it suits xx

She left her phone on the bedside table and walked into the open-plan kitchen, popped on the kettle, and put two slices of toast in the toaster. What was with all the carbs? It's all she felt like eating. Pizza, mac and cheese, toast... She was about to cut open an avocado but it wasn't ripe, so opted for sliced tomato, and fried an egg so she'd at least get some protein although she didn't much feel like it.

Her stomach more settled, she got dressed into slim black pants that were now a little tight and a watermelon-coloured tunic that flared at the waist, and put her standard make-up on. Comfy ballet flats and she was ready for the walk to work. She filled her water bottle and placed it into her bag along with her phone, then noticed the present she'd forgotten to open last night. She eyed the wall clock; plenty of time as her first client wasn't due till 10.30am. She sat at the kitchen table and eased open the floral wrapping paper.

Her heart fluttered at the sight of the beautiful neutral-coloured, fabric-covered journal with gold embossed lettering that read, *For my baby*.

'Oh.' Her hand flew to her mouth.

Inside the book was a handwritten note:

I saw this and thought of you. I know you will make a wonderful mother.
Love, Maria.

Her hand shook as she closed the front cover and shut her eyes for a second.

Tears built up and a few drops fell out and ran down her

cheeks. An unexpected sound disoriented her for a moment, and she took a few seconds to realise it was her phone ringing. She picked it up. Chris's name was on the caller ID. Her finger hovered over the green button. She'd have to head to work soon, but it'd be the middle of the night if she called him back later.

'Chris, hi!' She hoped she didn't sound unnaturally excited.

'Morning, Lace. Just got out of the shower and ready for bed. How's things?'

'Good, listen, um...' She gulped down a lump of uncertainty. 'The thing is, I'm... well...' She stood and paced around.

'Off to work? No worries if you're strapped for time, we can catch up another time. But there was something you wanted to chat about?'

'Yes. I mean, yes, I have to get to work, but...' The gold lettering of the journal sparkled under her gaze. 'I wanted to run something by you.'

'Go ahead.'

'Mum told me you've booked an appointment with a fertility specialist?'

'Yep, it's all happening. I got cold feet, but we had a good talk and we're on the same page now. I get it. Time is limited and it's now or never.'

Now or never. For her too.

'That's great. Well, I was wondering if...'

She paused at the table and ran her hand over the comforting fabric of the journal, and it left tingles on her skin.

I know you will make a wonderful mother.

'If... I can contribute in any way?' The right words wouldn't form. 'Financially, I mean.' Oh God, she couldn't do it.

'Oh, sis, please, there's no need.'

'I know, but if it helps take some of the pressure off, even a small amount, it might... help?' *Or I can give you a baby I prepared earlier?*

She shook her head at her lack of resolve. She thought she'd been certain. But now it was time to speak the words, something held her back. A simple journal, was that all it took to back down? It was simply a thoughtful gift from a lovely lady, no need to read further into it or treat it like some kind of sign from the universal powers that be. She could even pass it on to Melina. But...

'Thank you, I really appreciate it. But we'll figure it out, don't worry.'

'If you're sure.'

'I'm sure. We'll see how we go with the first round and go from there.'

'Okay.' She nibbled on her lip.

'Did you want to chat about anything else?'

She tapped her foot on the floor. 'Um, no I think that was it.'

'Rightio, have a great day at work then, and I do appreciate the offer, I really do.'

'My pleasure. Here to help if I can.'

'Take care, sis.'

'You too. Say hi to Melina and the girls.'

'Will do.' He ended the call, and Lacie sunk into the chair.

> I chickened out.

She texted her mum, who was probably *still* awake on account of all the things she'd have on her mind after their discussion, then sent her a photo of the journal and note.

> My client found out and gave me this.

She opened the first page; the scent reminding her of childhood storybooks and special moments with her mum and dad.

A keepsake for your precious child.
Record your thoughts, hopes, and wishes for your bundle of joy
during your special pregnancy.

The next page had space to write basic details like name, year, and due date, followed by a journal prompt asking her to write an introductory letter to the baby. The other pages were a combination of more letters to write throughout the pregnancy and on their first five birthdays, and short prompts about how you were feeling at each stage, any food cravings, ultrasound photos, bump photos, name ideas, and things you wanted to teach your child and activities you were looking forward to doing together.

The significance of the road ahead took her breath away.

Oh how lovely. Maybe it's a sign?

Lacie released a tearful chuckle.

I just couldn't do it.

Trust your heart, my love. This is your baby and we're here to support you. Why not wait till the 12-week mark (which is only a month away), check all is healthy, then either share the news with everyone else or talk to Chris again if you decide you want to.

Lacie's muscles softened and she exhaled slowly. Her mum knew how to make sense of things, like her father used to.

Okay, I've got this. A few more weeks and I'll make my final decision, she thought.

Thanks Mum, sounds like a plan.

A few minutes later she had booked some medical appointments and was finally ready to head to work. When she arrived, she used the work phone to send a message to Maria:

> What a beautiful, thoughtful gift. Thank you so much, Maria.

Her client replied with orangey-pink heart emojis that resembled her current nail polish, and Lacie smiled. She made herself a peppermint tea and took a few moments for herself in the beauty room while waiting for her client, and strangely, in that moment, an image of Nathan flashed in her mind and she wondered what he was doing right now.

CHAPTER FOURTEEN

Nathan had made the mistake of having an afternoon nap after work, and now at just past midnight, he couldn't sleep. He sat on the couch with a peppermint tea, deciding to watch a documentary to pass some time and help him relax. He couldn't decide whether to watch David Attenborough or Nigella Lawson. Well, Nigella wasn't exactly a doco but it *was* enticing viewing, and it might inspire him in the kitchen, among other things.

While flipping through the options, he paused and checked his phone, wondering whether it was appropriate to contact Lacie yet. It'd only been a few days and he wanted to give her time to settle back home, but he was keen to connect with her again. She hadn't contacted him either, maybe she was too busy settling back in, or maybe she wasn't as keen.

He selected a random Nigella episode and sipped his tea, getting up to grab a biscuit a few minutes into it. As she prepared her slow roasted garlic and lemon chicken, he licked his lips and wished he had her meal in front of him, even though he'd eaten a not very Nigella-ish basic steak and mashed potato for dinner not too long ago. He thought back to the Christmas in

July dinner at the Applebys' and smiled. For someone without any family, he was certainly starting to feel like he belonged somewhere.

He eyed his phone. *Ah, why not.*

He opened messenger and typed:

> Hey there, hope you arrived home safely. I was up late watching Nigella's cooking show and it reminded me of your family dinner and all the delicious food.

He checked the time in Chicago... morning, so she was probably busy working.

> Hi, nice to hear from you! Jet lagged but good. Oh, she's great, you a big fan? ;)

Nathan smiled and pressed pause. Not much would interrupt his Nigella viewing but Lacie won out.

> Yeah, she's probably my second favourite celebrity. Not that I'm much into 'celebrities', but she's got a special charm.

Like you, he thought.

> And your first favourite celebrity?

> David Attenborough :)

> Of course! You're just like a younger version of him. Maybe you'll follow in his footsteps one day.

> No one could ever replace him, but I do have some ideas for educational videos about nature.

> Awesome, send them to me when ready! Gotta
> go, my day of work awaits! x

He smiled at the little x and his mind rushed back to their kiss. Such a shame she was now on the other side of the world. But as they'd agreed, better to be long-distance friends than nothing. The kiss would have to remain a memory, and he'd have to stop thinking about it.

He pressed play and resumed salivating over Nigella instead – well, her *food* – and decided to try out her chicken dish sometime soon. Maybe he could make extra and take some over to Martha as a thank you for her recent hospitality and, of course, for his ongoing employment.

He placed his phone on the coffee table and noticed a text message he'd ignored earlier, and his moment of bliss dissolved.

> Hey. Saw these and thought of you. I
> remember you always liked them. Hope you're
> having a nice evening.

With the text was a picture of some tiny flowers – lantana. Tess was the only other person he'd mentioned his favourite flower, or weed, to apart from Lacie. She hadn't responded to his last text saying he was busy and it wasn't the right time for a catch-up until now. He simply pressed on the message and selected the thumbs up, hoping his ex would get the message. He had many good memories with her, and she shared his love of the outdoors, but sadly, the bad memories of her deceit overtook them and he didn't want to dig up the past. Digging up gardens and creating new ones was much more fun. He turned his phone to silent, placed his feet on the coffee table, and leaned back on the couch, taking in a deep breath and pushing out all thoughts of Tess with his exhalation. When he breathed back in, he pictured Lacie. Her pink-highlighted hair, the vibrant colours in her choice of clothing, the way she carried those flowers in the basket like it was a precious child, and... oh no, there it was again... her lips on his.

———

> So, I know your favourite celebrity and your favourite flower (I mean, weed). Next up... what's your favourite animal?

Lacie texted Nathan as she sat on a hard chair in the waiting room of the pathology centre early the next morning, trying to take her mind, and stomach, off the rising nausea, as she was having a fasting blood test.

Little dots moved up and down on the screen while butterflies flitted in her belly as she tried to guess what his reply would be. Dog? Too standard a response, and he didn't appear to have one, at least, he hadn't mentioned it. Maybe a cat. No, probably birds.

'Next up,' the woman in a clinical uniform said as she opened the door and the previous patient walked out.

Lacie popped her phone back in her bag and got up quickly. Too quickly. She wobbled and grasped the door frame.

'You okay?'

'Yep, just need to eat.' She sat on the chair inside the small room.

'Ah, pregnant I see,' the woman said as she read the request form. 'I'll be as quick as I can.'

In a few moments her blood was drawn and she immediately grabbed a muffin from her bag and took a bite. She sat back in the waiting room for a few minutes to steady herself and raise her blood sugar, before walking to work. Her phone pinged as she stepped out into the morning sunshine.

Oh!

She couldn't believe she'd forgotten about Nathan.

She slowed her pace to check the message that had come in during her blood test:

> Hard to choose, I love them all. But I'd have to say ladybirds. Or ladybugs, but I don't like that term, they are indeed like little birds.

And just now, he'd added:

> Been fascinated with them since I was a kid, I loved how they'd crawl on my arm, and just when you try to place them somewhere else, they'd fly off. So small but powerful. They do eat some plants of course, but they're so unique and beautiful.

Lacie stopped along the path and smiled.

> OMG I love them too! But my fave would have to be cats. Boring, I know.

> Not at all, cats are special creatures too. Do you have one?

> Used to. Lightning passed away earlier this year. Haven't been ready to get another one yet.

And she might not be for a while.

> Sorry to hear. I don't have one, or any other pet apart from the birds that frequent my garden, but I might commit to having a long-term pet at some stage.

> They become like family. So, your fave flower is actually a weed and your fave animal is actually an insect. Let me guess, your fave food is probably not really a food?? :)

She chuckled as she continued walking, conscious not to be late for work.

> Haha! Actually, you're right. I love a lot of different foods, but when I think about it, gravy is actually my favourite.

A laugh burst from Lacie's mouth and a man walking past her flinched as though she scared him. She slowed to type a reply:

> Gravy? Well, you're right, it is delicious, but yeah is it a food or not? Might have to ask Google!

> It might be liquid but it tastes good so I'll just call it a food. :)

Lacie pondered her favourite foods.

> Am I also boring if my favourite food is chocolate? I sound like every other woman on the planet.

> I'm sure not everyone likes chocolate, and how can chocolate be boring, it's delicious!

> Just not if it's paired with gravy.

She chuckled. Nathan replied with a vomiting emoji and she laughed again. He sent another message:

This is fun. I'm going to have to think up some more questions over the coming weeks. And each question you ask me, you have to answer too, deal?

Deal.

Lacie put her phone in her bag and got out her keys, unlocking the door to her salon and looking forward to the day ahead, and what his next question might be.

CHAPTER FIFTEEN

The next couple of weeks were a flurry of daily messages, fun questions and answers, and sharing of photos: Nathan's gardening progress, his own garden, pictorial responses to the questions; and from Lacie: photos of her salon, her apartment and its tiny fake garden on the windowsill, and her deceased cat Lightning (bless his furry soul). It had helped distract her from everything that was happening, while awaiting the important twelve-week mark.

She popped her second iron tablet of the day as she finished her dinner, having shown to be slightly deficient in her blood results, and after checking her appearance in the gilded mirror above the side table, opened her phone's camera and cleared her throat, then pressed 'video'.

'Hi, everyone,' she said with a wave and a smile. 'I wish I could be there tonight for your prize dinner, but sadly I'll be fast asleep by then, so this'll have to do, and I expect a video in return, thank you very much!' She turned the camera to the dining table. 'As you can see, I've just finished my gourmet dinner for one of crispy chicken wings with beetroot salad, and unfortunately no dessert. I hope you get to have more than I did.' She turned the phone towards the windows and pulled back the curtains. 'It's a beautiful warm night here in Chicago, as you can see there are lots of lights everywhere, hence my blackout curtains. But it's such a pretty sight, like thousands of colourful stars.' She moved the phone from left to right to take in the view, then turned it back on herself, conscious that Nathan would probably be attending the dinner too. 'Steve, I hope you enjoy this free meal courtesy of yours truly since I couldn't be there, and Mum, enjoy a night off from cooking.' She smiled and looked up at the ceiling, wondering what else to say. 'Miss you guys already. I'm sure you're all taking advantage of the new fire pit, and I bet the supermarket is running low on marshmallows.' She grinned. 'Anyway, have a great night, video me when your meals arrive so I can have a squiz and pretend I'm there with you.' She yawned. 'I think it's time for me to wind down, so I'll leave it there, and also long videos take too long to load so better wind things up. Okay, see you, guys, have fun, bye!' She waved and ended the recording, then sent it to her mum, who responded a few minutes later:

> Ohh, we miss you too. That's great, thanks, my dear, I'll show everyone at dinner tonight and when you wake you'll have a video from us to look forward to. Have a good sleep, Mum xx

Lacie smiled. Thank goodness for technology, it made being away from family much easier. Before getting in the shower, she scrolled through her saved videos and clicked on one of her dad. He was opening his presents at the last family reunion she'd attended when he was alive.

'Yes! I've been wanting a new crossword book, thanks, guys. This'll keep my brain going well into my nineties.' He smiled and put it to the side then opened another present. 'Best Dad Ever socks, well I am going to put these on right now.' He took off his slippers and slid the bright stripy socks onto his feet, pulling them up as high as they would go, almost to his knees, and laughter filled the living room. He stood and surveyed his gift, lifting his feet one at a time. 'Nice, eh?'

Little did Lacie know then that he wouldn't live into his nineties, or even his eighties, and not long after, he would be buried in those very socks along with his favourite suit which he wore on special occasions and had always said made him feel like a million bucks. Martha had wanted him to wear the things that made him feel his best when he was alive, novelty socks included.

Lacie wiped the corners of her eyes. 'Oh, why did I go and click on that?' She cursed her nostalgia. 'Oh, Dad,' she whispered. 'Life is changing so much, and I don't know what to do.' She wondered what message he might write and leave on her pillow if he were able to...

Trust your heart, love.

Or: *Wait until morning when your mind is clear to make important decisions.*

Or perhaps: *Trust your mother's wisdom now, Lace. She's here for you.*

Yes. She was lucky to have her mum, and her family. Some people, like Nathan, didn't have anyone. Her dad may be gone but she had years of memories to be grateful for. Her mum had wise words to say too, and like she said, wait for the twelve-week scan then decide. Next week, she'd get to see the baby on the screen, knowing it would be more than a flickering white blob by now, and hoped all would be healthy. And then, she'd have to trust her own wisdom and make her decision – have this baby for her brother and sister-in-law to raise, if they wanted it, or keep the baby and learn how to become a single working mother, without family support nearby. Plenty of women did it, and many without the luxuries she had in life. But seeing Melina so disheartened at the reunion broke her heart. She was such a great mother to her girls, and it was clear she wanted to have a second chance at motherhood with Chris, instead of with her ex who hadn't been the most supportive husband. What if it never happened for them? Melina was older, and maybe her window had now closed. Maria Elvarez had said she'd waited a long time for her adopted son, and she had no idea how adoption, egg donation, or even surrogacy even worked in Australia, if it came to that. How long would they have to wait to grow their family? Maybe there was a reason why this was happening to her and them at the same time, so she could step up and offer this gift.

The pros and cons of each choice swung in her mind while she showered, and until she succumbed to sleep.

When she woke, she had a brief sense of clarity and a clear mind, until it all came back again. This time next week, she'd make her decision.

She stretched and nibbled on a few crackers she'd left beside her bed, and eagerly grabbed her phone, clicking the WhatsApp icon and then the video her mother had sent during the night.

'It's a big howdy and hello from the Haven Heroes!' Matt's face and voice burst through the screen and Lacie grinned. 'We're all dressed to our best and ready for a night of food, fun, and family.' He swung the phone along the table until it settled on Gloria, the lady who'd been added to their table the night of the trivia event. 'And the lovely Gloria, who is now practically family. She insisted we give her share of the prize to another member of the Appleby clan, so we insisted in return that she join us. Besides, Penny said she was looking forward to an evening of... what did she call it, Steve? Oh yes, peace and quiet, after the kids go to bed.' He turned the camera to Steve who nodded and shrugged. 'So, Lace.' The view returned to Matt's close-up face. 'We all enjoyed your video and quick tour of the Chicago lights. We all miss you too. I'll pass you around the group.'

There was a swish of blurriness as the phone was moved around the table, first up she saw Sophia's heart-shaped face. 'Bonjour, Lacie!' She pressed her hands to her lips and blew a kiss, then passed the phone to Chris who gave a wave and a hello, her heart tugging at the subtle weariness on his face. Ellie in comparison looked wide awake, the night owl that she was, and she wore dark eyeliner on both top and bottom eyelids. She pulled a funny face for Lacie, pushing her cheeks and lips together, then chuckling. Martha gave an exuberant wave and blew a kiss also, saying how much she wished she were here with them, and hoping that she was 'taking good care of herself', and thankfully not saying 'hope the pregnancy is going well'.

Poor Gloria, immersed in the loud and silly Appleby family fun, she looked slightly overwhelmed and lost but happy to be there nonetheless. She gave a single wave, a bit like the royal wave, and then Nathan came into view and her stomach somersaulted. He had slightly more stubble than the last time she saw him, as though he was growing it out a little over winter. He was wearing a navy shirt, the top button undone and the collar gently cradling his collarbones. 'Sorry you can't be here to join us,' he said. 'Loved seeing a bit of Chicago, you'll have to send more tour videos for this small-town guy.' He smiled. 'Hope you have an amazing weekend.' He waved and handed the phone back to Matt.

'Ooh, perfect timing, our meals are here!' Matt turned the

camera to face the table and Lacie watched as plates were placed in front of each person. Whatever they were having looked delicious and beautiful. 'And we'd like to thank Luca, here, who made tonight possible with his generous donation in honour of the local school. Thanks, Luca.' The face of Home restaurant's owner, Luca, came into view, as he received a round of applause, his dark hair and eyes commanding the screen as he waved hello to her and held a hand to his chest at the accolades. He had been in the same high school year as Chris, until he'd moved away, only to return twenty years later. He'd been Nathan's roommate temporarily at one stage, Nathan had mentioned during one of their chats, when she'd asked him more about his home life. She wondered if he ever got lonely, but by the looks of things, her mum had welcomed him into the family like a lost puppy.

'Well, I think that concludes the show, folks, I mean, Lacie.' Matt winked at her. 'Dinner awaits! Take care, Lace. We love you, and we'll talk again soon. Bye!' He moved the phone around and everyone waved and choroused, 'Bye!' The video cut out just after it landed on Nathan, and she giggled at the entertainment her brother had provided. She may not be there, but she was still part of their lives. Living far away wasn't so bad. She could see and talk to them any time she wanted, really. It was only hugs and sharing meals and experiences that she missed out on.

Lacie yawned and stretched again, easing herself out of bed. She could have a lazy breakfast, take it slow, and let the day unfold however it wanted to. Then tonight, she'd be enjoying a much-needed night out with her friend Rosie. They were going to watch her client and friend Lulu perform on stage at a local club. Lacie often did Lulu's make-up for her shows, but tonight she'd be part of the audience at Lulu's first gig at a new upper-class venue for up-and-coming stars. Rosie didn't yet know Lacie was pregnant, and would no doubt find out when she ordered a mocktail instead of her usual cocktail, but hopefully she could avoid having a long, deep conversation about it and just enjoy the night. That was the plan anyway.

CHAPTER SIXTEEN

Nathan watered his plants on Monday morning with extra enthusiasm. Rain wasn't forecast for another week, so he thought he'd give the plants some love in the meantime.

He'd enjoyed his weekend; dinner with the Applebys, seeing Lacie on video, and then a rainforest walk on Sunday to soothe his soul.

His mood was also boosted knowing that when he messaged Lacie at this time of day she was more likely to respond, with it being the later part of the day overseas. When he heard the ping from Messenger, he smiled and glanced at his phone. He'd told her how much he'd enjoyed dinner with her family, and seeing her face on the video, and said maybe they should do a video call sometime.

No time like the present, she'd replied.

Nathan's heart beat a little faster. When the screen showed her call coming in, he turned off the hose and answered.

'Hey, stranger,' he said, holding the phone in front of his face. Her smiling face appeared, and with her hair splayed out to the sides it looked like she was nestled against the back of a couch.

'Hello yourself. I see it's a bright, sunny morning in the land of Tarrin's Bay.'

'Indeed. Another early start for me.'

'Off to the house?'

'Not today. I'm working on Gloria's garden makeover, the prize she won at the trivia night.'

'Oh yes, I'm sure she'll love that. She looked to be enjoying herself at the meal.'

'She sure did. It gave me a chance to speak to her about what she wanted done too, so I could get prepared. I'll do what I can today, then get anything else I may need and go back sometime this week to finish things off.'

'You'll have to send before and after photos. If she doesn't mind, of course.'

'Sure, I'll ask.' He waved away an insect then walked onto his back porch. 'How was your weekend?'

'Great. Watched a friend sing at a club, caught up with another friend, and had a nice lunch out by the river today. It's beautiful here this time of year. Oh, I took some photos, I'll send some through after the call.'

'Awesome. Sounds like you lead a busy and fun life over there. My weekends are usually much less social: pottering around the house and garden, a hike up in the hills, and going with the flow.' He smiled.

'That sounds awesome too. I also like my downtime, though living in a small apartment I don't potter around much, so I usually prefer to get out and about.'

'I can imagine.'

'So, what's today's question?' she asked, and he loved the way her eyes narrowed slightly with curiosity.

'I hadn't thought of one, but now that I'm on the spot...' He tapped his temple. 'Oh yes, I haven't asked what's your favourite movie?'

'We haven't discussed that yet? I can't believe it. Anyway, that is a hard one, there are so many I love and so many I've worked on in the make-up department – some of which weren't that great to be honest,' she said with a lower voice, as though her employers might hear. 'I could say *Titanic*, or *Mary Poppins*, but you know what, I actually love those gorgeous little films that take you to a different place and help you escape for a while, nothing too dramatic or violent, nothing too sappy either. One that stands out is *The Guernsey Literary and Potato Peel Pie Society*.'

'Hang on, the Potato Literary what?'

She chuckled and spoke slowly. '*The Guernsey Literary and Potato Peel Pie Society*.'

'Ah, I'll have to google that one. But it does sound... unique.'

'It is. Based on a book. I love watching books become movies. If they do it justice.'

'The only other book to movie I can think of is Harry Potter.'

'Well, that's great too of course, defined my younger sister's teenage years. Anyway, maybe check it out if you want to try something different. You might like the scenery in it.'

'Will do. And as for my movie, hmmm, most of my favourites are documentaries, but I'll try to cast them aside in order to think of a fictional one...' He ran through the options in his head, though he didn't watch many films. 'This is hard. Oh, I do love *The Shawshank Redemption*. The victory at the end, so rewarding. But if I think of another one that trumps it, I'll let you know!'

He could enjoy watching films if he had someone to chill on the couch with. Movies were best watched with company. Probably why he hadn't seen many since he was with Tess. He sat on the wooden armchair on his porch for a moment, and something caught his eye in the young potted olive tree next to it.

'Lacie, check this out.' He angled the phone to face the trunk of the tree. 'Can you see it?'

There was silence, and then, 'Oh, a ladybird! How nice. Your favourite too.'

Nathan shook his head in awe. He hadn't seen one for a while, it was winter but they often liked to camp out on tree bark and between rocks. He held his finger near the ladybird and it crawled onto his skin. When he tilted his hand, it flew off, and he returned to face the phone screen. 'Just like you; here briefly in all her glory, then off she flies!'

Lacie chuckled. 'Well, I hope the ladybird comes back for you.'

He hoped another lady would come back too. But by the looks of things, she wouldn't be back for another year, and even then it would only be for two weeks. Anyway, he couldn't change the way things were. A least he was having fun chatting to her regularly, and that's all it would ever – could ever – be.

When Nathan arrived at Gloria's small duplex, she had a cup of tea and scones waiting for him. 'The least I could do, after your generosity in helping me with my garden.'

'Gloria, you shouldn't have,' he said, taking a seat at the outdoor wrought-iron table for two. 'Although, I'm glad you did.' He smiled, and Gloria seemed excited to have a visitor. 'I make them with a dash of lemonade, the scones. My secret trick.' She waited for him to take a bite and he nodded his approval.

'Delicious,' he said. 'How long have you lived here?'

'About eight years. We – Leonard and I – downsized in the

hope of having an easier retirement. After four years, though, he got sick. And another four years have gone by and things are exactly the same as when he passed. A little garden makeover will be just the thing to freshen things up and bring a little joy.'

Nathan was glad she had won the prize; it was clearly meant for her.

They finished up the scones and Nathan helped her take the plates into the kitchen.

'Now, I know you have other gardening jobs during the week so I don't want to keep you. Whatever you can manage today is fine.'

'I'm happy to come back again to finish anything up, or acquire anything else you may like. I was thinking a birdbath even, though they can be costly. But the free plants and pebbles included in the prize will go a long way to bringing some colour and joy to the garden.' Thankfully, he was able to secure some donations from the plant nursery he spent so much time at. Anything else Gloria wanted would be at her expense, but he'd do what he could with what was provided.

'I was thinking perhaps a cute row of pansies along the border of the bed here,' he said, pointing it out as they walked around the tiny grassed area which had a few small trees and shrubs, but not much colour. 'Pebbles too, along the border. And then in this corner here, perhaps some cornflowers. If I plant them now, you'll have nice blooms in spring.'

Gloria's face lit up. 'Oh, that sounds wonderful. Leonard was more of a green thumb than me, though he couldn't do much in his later years.'

'Do you have someone who cuts the grass?'

She nodded. 'A young chap from up the road, gives him some pocket money.'

'I used to do that here and there when I was a young chap too.' He smiled.

'And now look how far you've come.'

Nathan waved away her compliment. 'Ah, I just do what I enjoy, nothing to it.'

'Martha tells me what a gift you've been in helping her with the gardens of South Haven, especially after her husband died. And she enjoys your company.'

'The Applebys are great. They're more a family than I've ever had.'

'Oh?' She raised her eyebrows. 'You're not close with yours?'

'None left, as far as I know. Dad disappeared when I was a baby, Mum died and she was estranged from her parents, so I was in foster care by the time I was four years old.'

'Oh my goodness.' Gloria held a hand to her heart. 'Well, you should be even more proud of yourself for how you've taken hardship and created a positive life out of it, making a contribution to society.'

'Thanks, Gloria.' Nathan's cheeks warmed. He'd never had anyone say he should be proud of himself, never had anyone say *they* were proud of him. He'd just done what he needed to create a life for himself.

'And there's no... special person in your life?' She eyed him with a curious tilt of her head.

'There was, but it wasn't to be. And...' He thought of Lacie. 'There's no one with any promise at this stage, unfortunately.'

'Oh well, I'm sure that person will come along. But don't you wait around for it to happen, go out there and make it happen. Meet new people, take some risks. Don't overthink things. Goodness, it took so long for Leonard to get the guts to ask me out, I thought I would die an old spinster by the time he did!' She smiled, then her face turned solemn. 'And to think we could have had a couple more years together if he'd been confident enough to ask me sooner. Back then, it wasn't proper for a young woman to pursue a man. Some did of course, but it wasn't how I was brought up. So I waited.'

'I'm glad you finally got together. And I'll definitely try to be more... gutsy. Thanks, Gloria.'

'Anytime.' She wandered to the side of the garden that had an old, splintery bench. 'Nathan, if I may ask, could you also help me set up some kind of memorial for Leonard? I mean, not as part of the free makeover, but a special thing for down the track, when I've saved up some money to purchase a few things, like a new bench?'

'Of course,' Nathan replied. 'And we could even do a plaque at the end of the garden, next to the seat if you like, with perhaps a small tree planted in his honour?'

Her eyes lit up. 'Yes, and I could add some of those stones, you know, with the words on them, like love and peace?'

'Great idea.'

'Oh and why not, add a birdbath. I can sit on the seat and remember him, talk to him, and watch the birds.'

'Sounds like a beautiful way to keep his memory alive. I'll get onto it after today and get back to you with a plan and a quote.'

'Wonderful. Now, what colour will the cornflowers be?' She rubbed her hands together.

As he explained more about what he planned to do, took some 'before' photos, then got busy weeding, trimming the grass and shrubs, and adding some fresh soil and fertiliser before planting some seedlings and arranging the pebbles, he wondered if it was wasted energy getting close to Lacie. She was delightful to chat to, and they had a strong connection, but how could he be gutsy with her when there was no way it could become serious with her living overseas? He didn't want to mess her around either. Or was he overthinking things? As he worked, he had an idea. She loved flowers, tulips, to be precise. Maybe it was time to move on from just chatting and show her how special he thought she was. So it might not be able to go anywhere, but life was short and he may as well let loose and make some memories. Even if that's all they'd be.

CHAPTER SEVENTEEN

Lacie arrived at the salon early on Friday, wanting to catch up on admin and organise some work for Madeleine to do, knowing she'd have to leave early for her ultrasound appointment. At 9am on the dot, the door opened with its gentle ding, but her first client wasn't due till 9.30am.

A person she didn't recognise walked in with a bunch of colourful tulips.

'Delivery for Lacie Appleby?'

'That's me. Wow, thank you.' She stepped out from behind the desk and accepted the blooms with a smile.

When the delivery person left, she opened the attached envelope and read the card:

Thanks for brightening up many of my days, hope these brighten yours. Nathan.

Her heart fluttered and she couldn't hold back the huge smile erupting onto her face. *What a nice surprise!*

She was glad Madeleine wasn't here yet so she didn't have

to explain who they were from... a charming Aussie guy she kissed once who she couldn't stop thinking about and whom there was no chance of having an actual relationship with.

She arranged them into a vase and placed them on the table next to one of the chairs in the waiting area, then she took a photo and sent it to Nathan.

> Wow, thank you so much! You remembered my favourite flower and my business name. Thank you, they've certainly brightened my day. I wonder if there are any florists that will make up a bunch of lantana weeds so I can return the favour!

She was then hit with a sudden feeling of guilt, that she should probably tell him she was pregnant. Not that there was anything real between them and it wasn't technically his business, it was just a nice long-distance friendship with a hint of attraction. But she should say something perhaps, at least after today's scan, just so he knew.

She was about to text, *hey – let's have a proper chat sometime over the weekend*, when the screen came to life with an incoming video call. She checked the time before answering, and pressed accept.

'Hi!' she exclaimed on seeing his face, which held a warm, orangey glow, like he was in a dimly lit room. 'Another surprise.'

'Good morning, I thought I'd stay up a bit and see if the flowers arrived safely.'

'They certainly did.' She angled the phone towards the flowers displayed beautifully on one of the side tables.

'Nice. Just what I hoped they'd send. What's your favourite colour tulip?'

'Hmm, I do like the pink ones, but that other slightly watermelon colour is pretty too.'

He nodded. 'Salon looks nice. You sent me some photos

before, but it looks even better on video. I hope I'm not interrupting your work? I figured if I was, your phone would be on silent or packed away.'

'All good. I have about twenty minutes before I start. Here, let me show you around.' She panned the phone around the reception area of the salon, then opened the door to the beauty room; rich and opulent with burgundy walls and gold accents in the decor. 'And this is where the magic happens.'

'Amazing, so stylish. And,' he yawned, 'that massage bed looks especially good about now.'

'Past midnight there?'

'Yep. But the good thing about starting work early and finishing early is I sometimes have a little nap afterwards.'

'Naps are the best.' She was thinking she might have to start scheduling some into her work day as her pregnancy progressed. 'It was nice to see your face again. I guess I should let you get some sleep.'

'Nice to see yours too. We should do this more often. Video calls, I mean.'

'Sure. I mean, texting is great, but I do miss our garden chats, so video is the next best thing.'

His eyes seemed more awake for a moment. 'I do too. When your mum and sister's not around, I only have the plants to talk to.' He grinned.

'And do you talk to them?'

'Am I crazy if I do?'

'Hey, no judgement from me. Almost-florist, remember. I think I used to talk to the flowers, things like, "oh, you're going to look so great alongside these lilies, aren't you?"' She giggled.

'I feel much better then. Nah, mostly I just hum and sing to myself, not that I *can* sing, just whatever random music pops into my head.'

'When you hum or sing to yourself that means you're enjoying what you're doing.'

He smiled, then hummed a tune.

Lacie's lips widened into a smile, knowing what he meant. 'I enjoy talking to you too,' she said softly. Their eyes locked for a moment and she wished she could reach out her hand and touch him, just a little caress of his face. She shook the thought away as the sound of the door opening brought her back to the present. 'Gotta go, my client is here early.'

'Okey dokey, goodnight. I mean morning.' He gave a wave.

'Night, sleepyhead.' She smiled and ended the call.

She checked all was ready in the room then welcomed her client, while she tried to stop herself grinning from ear to ear like a teenager who'd just been asked out.

After three back-to-back appointments and a quick bite for lunch, Lacie left Madeleine to do her work, and set off for her appointment. She'd pop back in afterwards to pick up the tulips to take home, and lock up when Madeleine finished her shift.

Butterflies fluttered around her stomach, knowing how important this scan was. What if it was all a big mistake and there wasn't really a baby after all? What if there was something wrong? She didn't know what to expect. By twelve weeks the foetus would be fully formed, though small, and from then on it was all upwards and outwards. She'd already seen the heartbeat, and she hoped it was still flickering away in there. The nausea had settled somewhat, though still recurred if she was overtired or hadn't eaten often enough, so she was learning what to do and what not to do. She wasn't really showing yet either, just looked slightly bloated, but she could feel a roundness in her lower belly when she cupped her hands around it. Soon enough, it would start to become obvious.

She opened the door to the women's health clinic and took a deep breath. A couple of other women were waiting; one who didn't look pregnant and another who clearly was. After a ten-minute wait, Lacie was called in. She lay down on the table and lowered the waistband of her skirt. Cold gel tickled her belly, and as the transducer was moved over her skin by the sonographer, she closed her eyes and took a deep breath.

'Here we go,' the sonographer said. 'Baby's heart is beating and as you can see, he or she is doing a little exercise!'

Lacie's eyes snapped open and she gasped. 'Oh my God.' The baby looked much more like a baby, still small but with a largish head, a rounded body, and skinny little arms and legs which were kicking and moving about. 'Last time it was a little blob!'

The sonographer chuckled. 'They grow rapidly. I'll do a few measurements now and let you know what I find as we go along.'

Lacie's unblinking eyes were mesmerised. She couldn't feel any movements yet, it was too early, but the baby was definitely active and having a great old time in there. Maybe it was the caffeine in her occasional coffees? Or maybe it was normal. Either way, relief flooded her veins at the fact that everything looked okay.

'Heart rate is one hundred and fifty-five, which is normal,' the sonographer said. 'And the size of the baby is normal for twelve weeks too.'

'That's great to hear,' Lacie said.

'I'll just have a closer look at the fluid at the back of the neck, that will give us an indication if there could be any chromosomal problems, but your blood test will also check for any issues.'

Lacie was filled with an indescribable sensation: a warmth, a cosiness, a sense of awe at the mystery of life. She was once this small, and now she was a grown adult. If all went well, one day this baby would be a fully-fledged adult too. It was so surreal to imagine.

'Fluid thickness looks normal too.' She pointed out the little band of white behind the neck. Just then, the baby's head moved, it lifted its chin up and down as though swallowing.

'Oh!' Lacie laughed. 'This is amazing.'

'First baby, I guess?'

She nodded. The sonographer did several other measurements and checks, then told her the report would be available for her doctor tomorrow but all looked good, and after she had her blood test, those results would take seven to ten days and she'd be able to find out if there was any increased risk for genetic defects.

'Did you want to find out the gender through the blood test?' the pathology collector asked when she checked Lacie's form.

She had thought about this over the past few days, and had made her decision. 'No. I'm going to wait until they're born.' She gave a confident nod.

Soon enough, she was on her way back to the salon, a lightness in her step, as though she was encased in a bubble, buoying her along the sidewalk. It was a strange feeling to be carrying this tiny human around inside her, and no one even knew. When she arrived back at YOU Beauty, Madeleine was finishing up. She wanted to talk to her about opening up a few small spaces in her schedule throughout the days for breaks, so she could get off her feet and keep hydrated and fed. She could earn extra money if she wanted to by doing some make-up work again for the Chicago theatre scene on evenings and weekends, but she had a decent amount of savings and didn't want to push herself, not now.

Madeleine stepped out from behind the desk. 'Perfect timing, I've squeezed in a few clients for next week as best as I could, a few others had to wait for the following week. Did you want to open up any new appointment spots? I made a waiting list for cancellations too.'

'Thanks, Maddy, that's okay, but starting the following week I actually want to create some space in my schedule for a couple of extra breaks each day.'

'Sure. Show me where.'

Lacie joined her behind the desk and eyed the computer screen. She pointed out where she could stretch out some of the gaps between clients, and also added a block of time on Wednesday mornings so she didn't have to start until 11am. That way she could attend regular medical appointments and have an extra sleep-in or slower start to the day if needed to help her energy mid-week. This was what she loved about being her own boss, she could work around her own needs and not be overworked and underpaid somewhere else.

'Is everything okay?' Madeleine asked. 'With you?'

'Yep. All good.' She smiled and walked over to the flowers, picking them up and wrapping them back in the paper they'd arrived in. 'Just going to take these home, don't want them to be wasted sitting in here all weekend. Here, one for you.' She handed Madeleine a single pink tulip.

'Thanks! I noticed these when I arrived. *Belles fleurs*. Where did you get them from?'

'They were a gift, delivered this morning.'

'Oh?' She eyed Lacie curiously. They were employer and employee but had also become friends, though Lacie tried to keep things as professional as possible between them.

Lacie's face become warm. 'Um, a friend back in Australia.'

'It's not your birthday, is it? Oh God, I didn't forget, did I?' She held a hand to her forehead.

'No, no, mine's in April. This was a "just because" kind of gift.'

'Oh.' She gave a sigh of relief.

Lacie placed the flowers on the desk momentarily, took the vase to the sink in the bathroom and tipped the water out, then put it back in the storage room. When she came out and picked up the flowers again, the image of her baby flashed into her mind, and her eyes stung with warmth. Before she could process what she was feeling, her bottom lip trembled, and she brought her hand to her heart.

'What is wrong? Are you okay?'

This only made Lacie's emotions increase in intensity. A sharp intake of breath surprised her and a few tears slid down her cheeks.

Madeleine put her hands on Lacie's shoulders, eyeing her with concern. 'Lacie?'

'The flowers were from my mother's gardener. I kissed him while I was in Australia, but now nothing can happen between us because we live in different countries. And I'm twelve weeks pregnant. Just had my ultrasound. And I don't know whether to keep the baby or give it to my brother and his wife who can't have children.' She sobbed a little and Madeleine gently embraced her.

'Oh my, I had no idea you had so much going on,' Madeleine said.

'Sorry, I shouldn't let my personal issues come into the workplace,' Lacie said, drying her eyes with the collar of her shirt.

'Don't be silly, we are human, yes? It is natural for life to merge with business. And pregnant, oh my goodness!' She held Lacie at arm's length and looked at her belly. 'Is the gardener the father? Oops, sorry, you don't have to answer that!' She covered her mouth.

Lacie smiled and sniffed. 'It's okay, what is said in here stays in here, right?'

'Right.'

'No, he's not, it's my ex. But we're not back together and we won't ever be. So I'm on my own, unless I decide to give the baby up for adoption to someone more ready and deserving than me.'

'Oh, that's very generous and brave of you, but don't give up so quickly. You would make a wonderful mother. And I'm here, I'll be qualified at the end of the year. I can hold the fort or work part-time until you can return. Whatever you need.'

'Thanks, Maddy. I haven't had time to process it all. I'll be doing a lot of thinking this weekend, that's for sure.'

Madeleine looked at Lacie with wide eyes and a smile. 'Ooh, a little *bebe*! I wonder if it's a boy or girl.'

'I'm going to leave that as a surprise for later. I've had enough of surprises for now!'

'Let me know if there's anything you need. I better get going. Thanks for letting me know. Your secret's safe with me.' Madeleine winked and grabbed her handbag.

Lacie said goodbye and took a deep breath, leaning on the desk with her hand. Tired and relieved about the scan and getting things off her chest. But she also had some remaining tension and uncertainty. She needed to get home, have a lie down, an early dinner, and give her body some much needed downtime.

She started walking back but decided to hail a cab instead. When she got home, she put the tulips in a vase on the dining table, and flopped on the couch. She awoke after a brief nap and a strange sensation had her walking over to the pile of papers and books on the table, and she picked up one in particular.

CHAPTER EIGHTEEN

Dear Baby,

I don't know exactly what I'm going to write. But here goes...

Right now, you are about the size of a plum. I can still hardly believe I have a living, growing human inside my belly. When I first saw your heart beating, I had never seen anything like it. Nature really is amazing.

I wonder what it is like for you in there, surrounded by darkness and warmth. I hope you are comfortable. I was a baby once too, of course, and began just as you are, but I don't remember it, I don't think any of us do.

No one can tell that I'm pregnant yet. I know that soon you will start growing even more quickly, and so will my belly! I will have to buy some new clothes; they are already feeling tight.

I am excited about the journey ahead, but I have to admit, I am also a little scared. This is a first for me. I don't know what to expect, or how I will change, and it all feels surreal.

I feel like eating a lot of carbs lately. I guess that's sort of a craving... they say you can crave certain foods in pregnancy. I wonder what your favourite food will end up being. Mine is usually chocolate, but a healthier favourite would have to be strawberries, or watermelon.

L acie lifted the pen off the page for a moment, tapping it against her chin. Her mind was trying to swerve around the deeper issues and distract her with food. Would she really show the baby this letter in the future? It was in the journal – in ink – so she couldn't rub it out at least. Time would tell. For now, it felt good to let some thoughts and feelings out into the open, in writing, so she could process things her own way. The pen seemed to buzz against her skin and she put it back onto the page...

Anyway, I'm blabbering. Sometimes I do that when I'm nervous, or in a new situation. This is definitely new to me. I wonder if you will love a good chat when you're older, or if you'll be more of a quiet observer in life. It's interesting how different people are, even those in the same family. My two sisters are completely different from each other. But each of us have our own unique strengths and gifts, and you will too. It's exciting to ponder what they might be. You are about to become a new person in the world, with your own personality, hopes, and dreams. I want you to know that you can achieve anything you set your mind to in life. You are always stronger than you think, and more capable than you know. I can't wait to...

Lacie sat up straight, a jolt of energy coursing through her. Something was building; something unknown but energising. Her heart beat faster and her breathing quickened, and it was as though she was writing the words to herself too. Resolve strengthened her grip on the pen and her eyes blinked back tears.

I can't wait to discover who you are. I can't wait to be your mum.

The pen fell from her grasp as her hand trembled.

That was it. Decision made.

Time seemed to stand still in that moment, as though the universe had been waiting for her to decide and was equally stunned.

Chris and Melina popped into her mind, and her heart ached at them having to struggle to achieve what she was experiencing. But maybe what she was experiencing was *hers* to experience, and her right to enjoy. At least she'd considered the idea of helping out her brother, but she wasn't even sure if they would agree to such a thing, and even if they did, she wasn't sure how she would handle being an aunt instead of the baby's mother. Maybe she would regret her choice down the track. And how would the child feel if the truth was disclosed to them later on? While she empathised with her brother and his situation, she realised the most important consideration right now was her child. And for some reason, this child, or the universe, or a higher power, had chosen her to bring this soul to earth. It was time to step up and handle the responsibility given to her, and... allow herself to feel deserving of this gift. Sure, her brother and Melina would probably feel a little envious, and she didn't want them to feel cheated. But the baby was the most important individual to consider. Yes, she'd be a single mum, whereas her brother and his wife would provide double the love to a child, but plenty of children had happy single parent families. She'd never let fears stop her from achieving her goals in life, so why start now? A baby hadn't been on her list of goals, but now it would be right at the top. Life was changing, and she had to change with it.

Lacie closed the journal and grabbed her phone.

> Hi Mum. Baby looks healthy so far. The 20-week scan will be most important, so until then, I'll still keep it on a need-to-know basis. But I've decided. I'm keeping it. xx

She thought she might cry on putting it in writing, but surprisingly she chuckled, then laughed heartily, at the strange but exciting sensation that she – independent and ambitious Lacie Appleby – was to become a mother.

> Oh! Lacie that's such a lovely message to wake up to. I'm so glad to hear this :)

> I thought I'd spend all weekend deliberating, but on writing in that journal, something happened, something clicked inside, and I knew.

> Sometimes it's good not to rush into decisions, I'm glad you gave yourself some time.

> Thanks for the suggestion.

> Do you want me to tell Matt and Chris, since Ellie and Penny already know?

Lacie released a nervous breath.

> Yes. I don't want to keep it from them. But no one else at this stage.

> You got it. And don't worry, I'm sure he and Melina will be happy for you. Xx

After the clarity of her decision and knowing that her mum

would handle telling her brothers, Lacie was suddenly hit with exhaustion. She hadn't realised how much the indecision and waiting for the scan had worn her out. She switched off her phone and placed it in the charger, got into her pyjamas, and flopped on the couch, ready for an evening of escapism with a good movie. Next thing she knew, she was watching the credits roll and had missed half the film. She laughed, and scrambled her way to bed to continue sleeping, and intended on spending most of the weekend doing the same. She had a lot of things to plan and organise, but it could wait until Monday.

CHAPTER NINETEEN

Nathan's finger hovered over the phone, wondering whether to add anything to the text message he'd sent Lacie several hours ago. It'd be bedtime over there, and she usually replied to him as soon as she finished work, but lately her replies had been delayed and... brief.

> Hey. I noticed you've been a bit quiet lately, hope all is well. And I hope my flower delivery a couple of weeks ago wasn't crossing a line or anything.

He put the phone down and went to the kitchen to make a cup of tea. He needed to get out of the house, maybe catch up with a mate, or even better, do a good workout at the gym, something to get his mind off the ridiculousness that was his feelings for an unavailable woman.

His phone beeped and he rushed back to the coffee table where he'd left it. So much for that idea.

> Hey, sorry for my delayed reply, I just got home after being out with a friend! I've been super busy and tired, but yes, all is well. Hope you are too. As for the flowers, no line crossed. They honestly made my day. You really are such a sweet guy. I've also

Nathan smiled in relief, then said, 'Also what?' The typing bubbles appeared, then disappeared, then reappeared, as though she was thinking of what to say.

> Sorry, accidentally pressed send before I'd finished! I've also been doing a lot of thinking about my life, reprioritising, setting goals, that sort of thing. I'm in a bit of a 'transition' stage I guess, pondering my life's direction.

Nathan nodded to himself. She had probably just needed some space for herself lately. He got that. The bubbles continued as though she hadn't yet finished.

> But I'm glad you texted. The past couple of weeks have flown by, and I've missed our daily Q&As! And, maybe we should have a chat sometime?

Nathan sat on the couch and grinned. He thought he'd scared her off with the flowers, but maybe not. Now, he just had to think up another interesting question. What else did he want to know about the lovely Lacie Appleby?

Lacie put down the phone and exhaled slowly. It was late and she needed to get ready for bed. A shower could wait until morning. She stripped off her loose slinky evening dress that showed only the slightest baby bump, and got into loose cotton pyjama pants and a spaghetti strap singlet. She started removing her make-up. Her phone pinged but she continued her bedtime routine, making sure her face was reasonably cleansed. Moisturiser giving her face a dewy sheen, she turned off the bathroom light and sat on the side of her bed, the dim lamp giving a warm glow to the bedroom.

She rubbed hand cream on and thought of what she had been going to type when she'd accidentally pressed the send button...

> I've also been meaning to tell you something, up for a chat?

With her proposed sentence cut off after the first two words, she'd then hesitated for some reason, deciding to be broader in her update of what was going on in her life. It was all true, she was going through a transition and pondering her future, but she didn't know how, when, or if she should tell him about her pregnancy. She hadn't even announced it to her wider circle of friends yet, so why did she feel compelled to tell Nathan? He was just a friend, despite their one-off kiss, because that's all they could be. He didn't really need to know at this stage, did he? It was her business, and like she'd told her mother, now that the immediate family knew, and some of her regular clients, she'd wait until twenty weeks to share the news more widely. Then it would no doubt feel even more real, she'd have an obvious baby bump, she'd be more organised with her plans for the rest of the pregnancy and the postpartum period, and she'd have had more time to process this life change and be confident in what it meant for her future.

So she'd changed her plans and simply suggested a chat sometime. She smiled as she remembered the chats they'd shared so far, and she always looked forward to hearing from him. He was a fresh, welcome end to her days, and she'd never really been able to chat with anyone else so easily and effortlessly before.

Her hands no longer greasy from the cream, she pressed her phone and opened his message.

> How about now? If it's too late no worries, I'll catch you another time.

If only she'd read his reply before getting ready for bed, she may have done a quick video call when she still looked decent.

She started typing *let's aim for tomorrow* when his profile photo appeared on screen as an incoming video call.

Lacie's heart raced and she froze. If he was just a friend then why did she want to look her best for him? He'd probably seen her typing bubbles, so she couldn't pretend she'd fallen asleep. She pressed accept. At least the lighting was dim.

'Hi!' She offered a goofy smile. 'If I'd known I'd have the pleasure of your company tonight, I would have dressed for the occasion.' She chuckled.

'I can hardly see you, oh, are you in your PJs?' He peered closer at the screen and she nodded, making sure to keep the phone above waist height, not that much was obvious at this stage. 'No need to look fancy, I never look fancy.' Now he chuckled.

'Oh, I don't know about that, you looked pretty spiffy at the trivia night.'

'That was a while ago. You remember? I did make an extra effort; I don't go out to events that often.'

'Yeah, you looked nice. Not that you don't the other times, just that...'

Nathan smiled. 'My occupation requires more... practical attire.'

'Yes.' She nodded with a slight smile, noticing he was wearing a plain grey T-shirt with a rip in one shoulder.

'What's on the agenda this weekend?' he asked.

Visiting the baby shop for the first time to get an idea of what I'll need so I can budget and research my shortlist of essential items.

'Bit of shopping, some housework, replying to messages, life admin, that sort of stuff, I guess.'

'Ah, never ends does it, there's always something to keep on top of.'

'Indeed. And you?'

'Visit to the gym... gotta lift my game a bit so I can be fitter for when the beach season begins in mid-spring. I'll be putting on my lifeguard hat for the next school holidays.'

Lacie's eyebrows rose. She didn't think with his practical occupation that he'd need to do much else. 'How much fitter can you get? You seem pretty strong and fit to me already.'

'One can always improve. Gardening, small landscaping and construction jobs are one thing, but being able to have endurance and aerobic fitness are another. I'll start swimming again soon too in preparation.'

'Do you ever rest?'

'Only if I have a good documentary in front of me.'

'Like Nigella Lawson?'

'Haha.' He laughed. 'I wouldn't say her shows are documentaries, but yeah I can definitely rest while watching her, or David.' He smiled. 'Who's your favourite celebrity? You never told me before.'

It used to be Xavier Black.

'You know, I don't think I have one,' she stated after a brief moment of thought. 'After meeting so many in my line of work, actors at least, I feel like I can't think of celebrities as celebrities anymore, I just see them as people who have a public occupation. So I can't really determine a favourite unless I've met them and know more about them personally.'

'Fair enough. Makes sense,' he replied. 'Let me think of another question then for our Q&A...' He made a show of thinking by rubbing his jaw between his fingers, tapping his temple in an exaggerated way, and saying 'hmmm' loudly.

Lacie giggled like she was ten years old. Talking to him was so easy. So natural. So enjoyable. She never wanted their conversations to end. And at this point, she definitely didn't want to disrupt the flow of their interactions by sharing her serious personal matters.

'I know!' he declared. 'What's the most embarrassing thing that's happened to you?'

'Apart from throwing up in a plant pot in front of you?'

Nathan laughed. 'I'd forgotten about that.'

'Hmm, I think my most embarrassing moment would be telling you my most embarrassing moment.' Her face was getting warmer already. 'Okay, here goes. When I was a teenager, and went to my first party – at least, one without parental supervision and pass the parcel – I had arrived with a friend and gone into the house. A small crowd gathered on the patio, including a guy I had a crush on. I was a bit too eager and went to walk out the door to greet them, but didn't notice that the glass sliding door was closed, and I walked straight into it.' She shook her head at the memory. 'Bumped my nose and forehead and had a headache the rest of the night, not to mention people laughing at me every time they saw me, and telling me to "watch out!" for invisible obstacles.'

'Nice one, Lace.'

'Thanks, Nath.' She eyed him curiously through the screen. 'What's yours?'

'Me? I don't have one. I don't really get embarrassed.'

'Oh, c'mon, that's a cop out!' She shook her head. 'A question for a question, remember?'

'Well, I did fall out of a tree once, when I was a kid. In front of a couple of bullies. They laughed, but I wasn't embarrassed for long as they saw I was able to climb back up quickly and easily like Tarzan. They wanted to outdo me, but couldn't. One of them almost fell out of the tree too.'

'Ha! So, they didn't bully you anymore?'

'Nah, and after a while I started hanging out with them, more as an attention-seeking thing, I think, and to protect myself, I guess.'

'I can't imagine you being a bully.'

'I wasn't. Just did stupid things like *borrowing* other kids' bikes and taking them for a race, but I always returned the ones I took.'

'Naughty Nathan I'm going to call you now.' She giggled.

'Guess I was a little naughty back in the day, but I've become nicer with age.' He winked.

She smiled and tilted her head. 'I can see that. But I better tell my mum to keep any stray bikes locked up just in case.'

Nathan tipped his head back with a laugh. 'Fair enough.'

When their laughter had subsided, there was a moment of silence between them, and their eyes held each other's gaze through the screen.

'You look really nice, by the way. Pyjamas and all,' he said.

She lowered her gaze a second. 'Oh, geez, thanks.' She smiled, noticing the way the sunlight lit up one side of his face. 'I expect you to show me your pyjamas next video call, so that we're even.'

'Can't do that,' he said.

'Why not?'

'Don't wear any.'

Lacie's mouth opened slightly then she cleared her throat. 'Oh. In that case...'

Don't let that stop you.

'Unless it's super cold, but then I just turn on the heater and put an extra blanket on.'

A vision of him in bed under the blankets flashed into her mind and she willed it to disappear. And then a question popped into her mind as if to replace it with something equally enticing, and before she could stop herself, she blurted, 'Next question; I bet you're someone who's been skinny dipping, am I right?'

As he scratched his head and diverted his gaze for a moment, Lacie winced, knowing she'd have to answer the same question. 'Okay, let's answer it at the same time so we can get it over with,' she said.

'Aha! That means you have,' he said. 'Okay then, one, two, three, go!'

'I did it once in a lake when camping, purely as a substitute for a shower,' he said quickly, at the same time as she said, 'I did in a pool on holiday after I was dared to by a friend, but it was dark!'

They both laughed and Lacie fanned her hot cheeks with her hand, no longer feeling sleepy.

'Phew, glad that one's out of the way,' she said.

The same look as before graced his face, and with a softer voice, he said, 'If you were here right now, I'd...'

She locked eyes with his gaze. 'You'd what?' Her voice was barely audible.

He looked away and ran a hand over his head. 'Nothing, it's okay.'

'You'd what, Nathan?' Her breath paused halfway to her lungs, awaiting his answer.

He looked into her eyes again. 'I'd do what we did in the car at the beach, the night before you left.'

She swallowed her breath quickly so she could take another. No words came out in response.

'I miss you,' he whispered.

She glanced away then returned his gaze. 'I miss you too.'

Certain his heart was beating faster than ever like hers, the tension rising within like a boiling pot, she released a breath. 'Life, huh?' she mused. 'Crazy how things work out.'

'Yep.' He nodded.

'I should, ah...' How to tell him?

'Should what?'

Tell you that I want you to kiss me again like you did in the car that night. I wish I could teleport there right now, and any time I wish, so we can do it again and again. Have midnight snacks on the beach in the cold of night, and walk among the gardens talking about our favourite plants and flowers, discussing our very different childhoods, and hear your David Attenborough impersonation, and, and, and, I want ... you. Also, I'm pregnant. Crazy, huh?

'I should... invite you over for dinner! A virtual dinner, that is.' Maybe that would be the next best thing.

His eyebrows rose. 'Dinner?'

'Yeah, why not? Since we can't hang out in person. We only chat at random times, so why not...'

'Make a date?'

She nodded.

A smile formed on his lips, and he nodded too. 'A date it is then. Next weekend?'

'Okay. Oh! But my dinner will be your breakfast.'

Nathan chuckled. 'That's perfectly fine. Maybe I can get Nigella to help me whip up a breakfast feast.'

'I'm looking forward to seeing what you come up with! And no pyjamas allowed.' She winked.

'Definitely not. I'll wear my best outfit.'

'Me too.'

'Say, my Saturday morning, your Friday evening: 7pm?'

'It's a date.' She smiled, waving him goodbye. Things had shifted between them now. She knew she had feelings for him and he had feelings for her, but they both knew it was futile. Maybe with a more formal conversation over dinner/breakfast, they would be able to enjoy the limited experience the distance allowed, at least in some way, but also she could tell him what was going on with her, before they got too close.

CHAPTER TWENTY

Spring couldn't come around fast enough. Nathan had practically leapt out of bed the following Wednesday morning. After a few days of rain, the skies were now clear, sunny, and the air was warm. Flowers were beginning to bloom, the hard work from the months prior now ready to be rewarded. He smiled, wishing he could pick flowers for Lacie, but instead, he'd take photos and send them to her as a virtual gift.

He snapped a photo of some bright blue cornflowers he'd planted back in July when Lacie left, like those he'd planted in Gloria's garden – which reminded him, he had to check how her garden was going and when she'd be ready for him to create the memorial for her husband. He sent her a quick message and she replied telling him early October would be good, and added the text she'd like engraved on the memorial plaque. He took a screenshot and would order the plaque next week. The birdbath and bench seat would be next on the list, but they were easy to buy quickly once she had the funds.

He whistled as he surveyed the growing garden, proud of his handiwork.

'Yoo-hoo,' Martha called and waved from the living-room window on the second floor.

'Hi, Martha,' he called out. 'You should come outside, the weather is sublime today.'

'Oh I sure will at lunchtime, a salad on the back deck sounds good to me. Feel free to join me around midday.'

He smiled. 'Thanks.'

'For now, I'm rearranging the books on the new shelves. I started to do them alphabetically and by genre, but I saw this fancy thing online with books arranged by colour, so I'm going to try it!'

'Sounds fun, you'll have to take a photo when it's done.'

'I will, but I'll bring you up to see them too. My Edward – bless his soul – would probably have a fit, though, if he knew they weren't in logical categories or alphabetical order.'

He smiled again, a sense of ease and belonging washing through him. He didn't know what he'd do when the garden of South Haven was as complete as it could be. He would still be able to do maintenance of course, but that wouldn't be a full-time job. He'd have to secure another long-term project or several minor jobs. But he'd miss the Appleby family and hoped he'd still be able to connect with them regularly.

He waved as she disappeared from view and continued his assessment of the progress of the garden. Martha wanted a gazebo with a centre table and chairs installed out the back between now and Christmas, so they could have fancy high teas in the warmer months. That would be his next project, but for now, something he was looking forward to gave him a boost of energy in anticipation...

He walked around to the back of the house, on his way to the shed to collect the beekeeping materials and protective suit. He paused when he noticed Ellie sitting on the step of the verandah. He approached, mindfully, the young woman with her head low and elbows resting on her knees.

'Ellie, you're up early. I don't usually see you till the afternoon, except on your uni days of course.'

Her head shot up quickly. 'Oh hi, didn't hear you coming. I couldn't sleep so I came out here.'

'Sorry to disturb you, just on my way to do the first honey harvest of the season... see how much we've got.'

'Oh nice, Mum will love that. She always enjoys her honey on toast in the evenings. My dad used to love it too.' She lowered her head slightly again.

He had never met Mr Appleby, but had heard a lot about him... knew more about him than his own father who seemed like a mythical creature he wasn't sure existed.

'Must be hard without him,' he said, not sure of what else to say.

She nodded. 'He used to like sitting here, on this step. Plenty of other seating options around the house but he'd sit here, or on the ground, said it was his thinking spot.'

'I can understand that. And there's something about being outdoors that helps you think better.' He watched as she placed her palm on the concrete step next to her, as though it was still warm from where he'd sat. 'I guess you feel close to him again, sitting there?'

She glanced up and shaded her eyes from the sun with her hand. 'I guess I do.'

Nathan came closer and sat on the grass nearby. 'What was he like? I mean, I know a little, but what was he like, from your perspective?' He hoped his questioning would be comforting rather than upsetting.

Thankfully, Ellie's eyes brightened and she looked into the distance as though seeing the past. 'Oh, where do I start. He had so much energy, even though he was getting older. That's why it was such a shock when he… when the heart attack happened. He seemed so healthy. Always keeping busy and active, working around the garden like you, helping us kids out with whatever we needed, suggesting fun day trips and adventures. He just had a certain wonder about the world around him.'

'Sounds like he lived a full life.'

She gave a nod and tightened her ponytail. 'The only time he'd keep still was when he was sitting here, thinking, or sitting on an armchair reading a book at the end of the day. I used to think he knew everything there was to know about the world and life, so I'd ask him the deepest, craziest questions. He said I kept his brain active and healthy with all the difficult questions I asked!'

'I bet he taught you a lot,' Nathan mused. He had only his life experience to teach him, along with random things from school, but he'd never absorbed much in the classroom, had been too inattentive indoors at a desk, preferring to look out the window or be mischievous with his classmates.

'So much. And mostly, encouraged me to love learning, so I've kinda never stopped.' She managed a smile, then her chest rose high with a deep breath. 'Out of all my family, it was like he was the one who always *got* me the most.' She rubbed at the back of her neck. 'I didn't only lose my father, I lost my best friend.'

Nathan's heart plummeted, and a memory from long ago resurfaced in his mind. He stood and went over to Ellie, sat on the step next to her. 'I'm sorry. For you and your family.'

'Thank you,' she replied, wiping a tear from her cheek. He sensed she was trying to hold the rest of them back. 'Is your dad around?' she asked.

He shook his head even though her gaze was fixed straight ahead. 'Nah, never met him. I grew up in foster care.'

'Oh wow, sorry to hear that.' She glanced at him.

'I guess in one way I did lose a father, but I never knew him so it's not the same as what you're going through. I did lose a friend once, though.' He leaned forward on his bent knees, the memory of it heavy in his chest and weighing him down all of a sudden. 'I know how grief can really consume you and make it hard to feel like you'll ever be normal again.'

'Oh my God, that's exactly what I feel. Like I wish I could go back to how I felt when he was around. It's like it's changed who I am and I don't know how to get "me" back again.'

'Yeah.' Nathan nodded in understanding. He'd had more time than Ellie to find himself again after Cooper died two decades ago. To regroup and reset and focus on moving forward. It had been a shock for his sixteen-year-old self, let alone the fact that the boy had taken his own life. Cooper had been the only real friend he'd had growing up, having moved around to different homes so often. Since then, he hadn't really gotten too close to any other mate, or anyone for that matter, until Tess. And that had ended badly too, though not tragically. He was scared to get close to Lacie too but somehow the distance between them gave him a buffer of safety, a way to feel the connection without risking too much.

'I'm sorry about your friend,' Ellie said softly.

'Thanks.' He patted her hand and stood back up.

She gave a weak smile. 'Thanks, Nathan.' She stood too, as though she'd had enough of her thinking time. 'I know I have a great family and I'm lucky, but I just feel lost without him.'

'You'll get through it; I know you will.' Nathan turned in the direction of the shed then turned back again. 'You know, we are similar to bees in some ways.'

'Oh yeah,' she replied. 'How?'

'They need each other. And they need their queen... they are lost without their leader, their guide in life.' He placed his hands into his pockets. 'They can't do their job, or thrive, on their own. Neither can we.' Though he'd done a good job of that for quite a while. 'And they need a good home. If you move a beehive to a new location in the yard, they'll often get confused and try to find their way back to their old spot.'

'Huh. Interesting,' Ellie said. 'So what do the bees do if they lose their queen?'

'They create a new one from her eggs.'

'Cool. So they just start afresh and move on, find a new leader?'

'Pretty much.' He smiled. 'Us humans are more complex though, we can never replace those we've lost, but we can draw strength and guidance from other people in our life.'

'Guess I need to try to do that.'

'Have you spoken to your mum, or siblings about how you're feeling?'

'A little, here and there. But they feel the grief too, so I don't like to burden them.'

'That's understandable.' He wondered whether he should ask Lacie about her father. Maybe she was struggling too. Maybe the times she'd been quiet was also when she was trying to process her grief.

'You should start a counselling service.' Ellie said. 'I've felt better talking to you than any of the professionals I've seen.'

Nathan's cheeks warmed. 'Ah, I don't know about that. I don't have any training, just life experience, I guess. And nature is a great teacher, and friend, in a way. We can learn a lot from it. I've got a great book at home called *The Wisdom of Nature*, maybe I've learned more from that than I've realised!'

'Sounds interesting. And it does help being outside in nature. I'll have to try that more often now the weather's warming up. I'm such an indoor gal, though.'

'Maybe this spot on the steps is all you need.' He pointed to where they had sat.

'If it was good enough for my dad, it's good enough for me. Thanks, Nathan.' She turned and walked inside the back of the house.

Nathan stood still for a few moments, absorbing their conversation, and with a satisfied sigh at Ellie's new-found ease, he made his way to the shed to begin his honey harvest adventure. He may not be able to send any to Lacie, but he would definitely be showing her some photos, and probably making some cheesy remark about how she was just as sweet. He smiled and got on with his work, looking forward to their upcoming virtual date.

CHAPTER TWENTY-ONE

Lacie laughed on opening Nathan's message on Wednesday morning. A photo – a selfie – of him getting dressed into his bee suit, one arm hanging out to press the phone camera button.

> You look like an astronaut.

She texted, after heading downstairs in the elevator of her apartment building.

She swiped through the other photos he'd sent; blue cornflowers in the garden, trees starting to grow leaves and flowers, and Jessie's pebble family tree which she'd added some fairy statues around. He'd also sent photos of the wooden frames from the beehives, full of honeycomb. Another showed the frame after he'd scraped the honeycomb off, allowing the honey to drain from it into a tub. And the 'after' photo he'd called it; the richly coloured honey in glass jars, ready for consumption.

> Tastes delicious. But not as sweet as you ;)

She grinned. He was so cheesy, in the cutest, most endearing way. She sent back a selfie of her face looking all flattered and shy in response to his text, and then one of the front of the building that housed her business premises, and then had another idea. She went into her salon, and found exactly what she was looking for. She held the nail polish in her palm and took a photo of it, followed by the underside of it which showed the name of the rich golden-brown colour: Sweet as Honey.

> I'll have to change my nails.

She replied, then popped the small bottle into her bag to take home so she could update her nails later, knowing she wouldn't have much time at work.

> I look forward to seeing them. Have a sweet day at work.

> Thanks. Sweet dreams.

She added a heart emoji and then switched her phone to silent and put it away, got the room and ambience just right in preparation for her first client, with coconut and vanilla scented candles, and warm, dim lighting. When she heard the ding of the door, she also heard sniffles and sharp, short intakes of breath. Instead of entering the waiting room with a broad smile and welcoming gesture, she entered with a curious tilt of her head.

'Chloe, are you okay?'

Her client dabbed at the corners of her eyes with a tissue.

'Come in, lovely, let's have a chat.' She draped an arm around Chloe and guided the sobbing young woman into the beauty room. 'Can I get you a tea?'

Chloe nodded. 'Thanks.'

Lacie poured a cup of the ready-made superberry tea from the teapot sitting on its warmer, and handed her the small ceramic teacup as she sat on the chair.

'Sorry, it's just one of those days, and it's not even midday.' She offered a weak smile.

'Oh, no need to apologise. Do you want to talk about it?' Lacie sat on her wheelie stool and rolled up next to Chloe.

'It's nothing new, just the usual. Still coming to terms with the way I am now, I guess. It swamps me out of the blue sometimes.'

Lacie nodded her understanding. 'It's all part of the grieving process, and the healing process.'

'I know I should be grateful, I mean, I'm *alive* for crying out loud. But I didn't realise what an effect the physical changes would have on me. I feel guilty for feeling this way, when others who've had cancer aren't as lucky as me.'

'Your feelings are valid. You've been through a big scare, and the pain of surgery. And now you're coming to terms with your new appearance, not to mention loss of employment. It's normal, and perfectly acceptable to feel whatever you're feeling.' Lacie eyed the scarring over her client's cheek and the side of her nose, slightly disfigured with a caved-in appearance from skin cancer and the surgery to remove it. The scarring was also along her collarbone area, visible beneath her neckline of her dress. At their first appointment a month ago, Chloe had showed her photos of what she'd looked like before, when she had worked as a model, and the significant difference in her appearance meant she was no longer recruited for modelling work. Sad, considering what they could do with digital editing these days. But it was much more economical for photographers to have less to edit in the first place.

'Thanks, Lacie, it's just hard some days, you know? I miss

my life before all this. Things are so different now.' Chloe wiped her tears again and sipped more of her tea. 'If there's one thing I've learned though, it's to make the most of your life when it's good. Be grateful for what you've got. You never know when things might change. And as you taught me last time, I also need to make the most of what I have now, work with what I've got and focus on the positives.'

'Yes. But remember that you are always entitled to have bad days. Just don't let them get in the way of your life and what is possible now and in the future. The bad days are going to happen sometimes, but a bad day doesn't mean the whole week is bad, and a few bad weeks doesn't mean you've got a bad life. They are just part of the light and dark of our lives as a whole. Focus on the light. On the light within *you*. That's what matters.'

Chloe nodded. 'I never thought my beauty therapist would become my emotional therapist!'

'Happy to help in any way I can. I can't, and no one can, change what's happened to you, but you can change what you do and how you think, moving forward. Any progress with your idea for your Empowered clothing line?'

Chloe's eyes brightened. At her last appointment she had mentioned her idea to turn her experience into a positive, with an inspiring range of clothing for cancer survivors, those with scars and disabilities, and anyone wanting to embrace their unique beauty. She'd have a professional photoshoot, modelling the clothing herself, no digital editing required. 'Yes, I've made a list of all the quotes, words, and designs I want incorporated onto the T-shirts, so the next step is to find a service that can do high-quality printing. And I'll be using organic cotton only.'

'Nice. Well, I'll be your first customer. That is, if you're going to have...' she placed her hand on her small but rounded belly, 'maternity T-shirts?'

Chloe's eyes widened. 'Oh! I didn't even know you were pregnant! How far along?'

'Almost fifteen weeks.'

'Congratulations! In that case, I'll be sure to add a maternity option to the T-shirts. Perhaps the "Blooming Beautiful" quote would be suitable.'

'Lovely. What are some of the others?'

'There's also Brave and Beautiful, Perfectly Imperfect, Sassy Survivor, I Never Gave Up, and We're All the Same Inside.'

'I'm excited for you! Happy to promote your business to my clients as well. I know a lot who would love these.'

'Wow, so you're my beautician, my therapist, and my marketing assistant. I'm so glad I found your salon. I hope you'll be here forever. Although you'll obviously need some time off work when the baby's born. Boy or girl? Or is it too soon to tell?'

'You can find out early these days from a blood test, but I'm going to keep it as a surprise.' She smiled. She often wondered, sure it was a girl on some days and then convinced it was a boy on others. It didn't matter, she was still trying to get used to the fact she was growing a baby, let alone whether it was a boy or girl. 'Are you still up for your facial and vitamin C treatment?'

'Of course, though I know you might have to cut it a little short after our talk so that you don't fall behind.' She stood and handed the empty teacup to Lacie. 'I think it's going to help me, coming here regularly. It's nice to show my skin some love after all it's been through.'

'It's nice to show *yourself* some love after all *you've* been through.' Lacie smiled. 'I'll leave the room and let you get into a gown, and be back shortly.'

Lacie left the room and took a breath. She had so much to be thankful for. A family, though far away, who were always there for her. A place to live in a city she loved. A job, her own business, to earn money – one that satisfied her in even more important ways. A unique, enriching friendship with a charming man. And a new life growing within her.

The leaves on the tree in the small park near her apartment complex were a rusty orange colour, heralding the transition into autumn, or fall, as they called it in the States. Her second favourite season, spring being first with all its blooms and sunshine. It was nice to have Nathan's photo updates, he kept sending flower photos, knowing her love for them. And she would send him nature photos when she came across anything that he'd find interesting. She'd even sent him one of a stray twig on the ground, and a weed bursting through a crack in the pavement, to which he'd sent a laughing emoji.

When she stepped inside her apartment and kicked off her shoes, her phone pinged with a message. She smiled, wondering if Nathan was expecting her sweet as honey fingernail photo.

Her mouth formed an O shape when she saw it was from Melina. Chris had taken a few days to respond after her mother had revealed Lacie's news to the family, and she hadn't expected Melina to message her as they didn't often chat except when in person, or through Chris.

Hi Lacie, sorry it's been a long time between messages. Chris told me your news, and I know he messaged our congratulations, but I wanted to send a congrats myself, even though it's been a couple of weeks. I guess it's taken me a while to process, and to be honest, I was a bit jealous at first. But I really am very happy for you, and I know you'll make a fantastic mother. Let me know if I can offer any words of wisdom when it comes to motherhood, though I know Penny will probably help you with all that. But I'm here too, though it's been a long time since mine were babies. Chris also mentioned the gift you offered, and I want to thank you. Although we are okay at present, I do appreciate the gesture. Fingers crossed we get some answers, and more importantly, solutions when we see the specialist, and who knows, maybe IVF will work for us sooner rather than later. Stay well and all the best for this new stage of your life.

Lacie sat on the couch and sighed. She wondered how Melina would have responded if she'd offered a different gift, but her decision was made now, and Melina and Chris would probably want to give it their best shot for a biological child first anyway.

Hi Mel, thanks for your message and congrats, much appreciated. Miss you and the girls! Will definitely need your motherhood expertise, you are a pro. And I have a good feeling you'll get to experience it again too. Lots of love, Lacie.

She sighed again, in relief or tiredness she wasn't sure, and after making herself a cup of peppermint tea, she sat at the table where the journal was, and opened it to a new page...

Dear Baby,

I can't wait for you to meet our family. They live in another country, Australia, so it's not as easy to see them regularly, but we'll figure it out. And we'll do lots of video calls. Your grandma Martha is so looking forward to meeting you. Everyone is, especially your cousins Jessie and Dane, and Anastasia and Allana. I grew up with two sisters and two brothers, these will be your aunties and uncles. I'm sad you won't get to meet your grandpa Edward though, he went to Heaven a couple of years ago. That's a place some people believe in, where we go when we're no longer alive on Earth. I like to think he is looking down on us and guiding us through life.

I will be here to guide you through life too, from childhood to beyond. I will be learning as I go, but we both will. Life is an exciting adventure and there are so many great things to experience.

I can't wait to introduce you to ice cream, and Easter eggs, and slippery slides, and jumping castles, and picture books, and baby animals, and show you the stars in the sky. It's like you're a shining star that's come down to earth to be with me, magical and miraculous. I still can't believe it.

I'm so glad I was given this journal by a special client of mine, Maria. It's helping me connect with you and process what I'm going through. I hope that by me writing these words, you will somehow sense them, and feel connected to me too. This will be our special time together, through this journal, until we meet in real life. I'm sure when I see you it'll be like I've known you all my life.

Love, Mum xo

Lacie held a hand to her belly and breathed. It wouldn't be long before the baby would start kicking, and she couldn't wait to discover what that felt like. Her elastic waisted, wide-leg pants felt tight, and she decided she would go shopping at the weekend for some proper maternity clothes. And in a few weeks' time, after her morphology scan that would assess her baby's organs and growth and ascertain that everything was indeed okay, she would tell Nathan. She had to. She could bite the bullet and tell him now, but they were having such a nice time connecting virtually and she didn't want to spoil it, or change the dynamics. This would be her last chance to experience something like this – a simple but meaningful connection with a man, that although couldn't go anywhere, was giving her (and she presumed, him) such joy and fun. If he was local and they were dating, she would have told him already, and it would be becoming obvious, but he wasn't and they weren't, and she wasn't sure what to do in this unfamiliar situation. He might not want to continue their unique connection if he knew, and like Xavier had left her to it, he might do the same. She wasn't ready for that yet. Maybe it was the fear of motherhood, of whether she could do this on her own, but once the cat was out of the bag, she'd have to face impending motherhood head on.

Until then, it was okay to enjoy a little harmless flirting and friendship with the opposite sex, wasn't it? It would be her last chance for quite a while, I mean, who would want to date a woman with a newborn? And her interludes with Nathan would probably fizzle out at some point anyway, pregnancy or no pregnancy. Just like nature, it would run its course. She might as well enjoy his virtual company until he lost interest or met someone else. And that was something else she'd have to get used to, the day when his lovely messages and photos would be saved for someone else who *could* actually be a real part of his life.

CHAPTER TWENTY-TWO

W hen a thin strip of light shining through the blinds woke Lacie ten minutes before her alarm on Friday morning, she took the extra time to lay in bed and reply to some messages, one from Penny asking for a baby bump progress photo (*later, sis, there's not that much to see yet and I'm not yet out of bed*), one from Ellie with a picture of two books asking which one she should read next (*the romantic comedy, don't overwhelm yourself anymore with anything too serious*), and her friend Rosie who wanted to know if Lacie was free for a girls' night out on the weekend (*how about a girls' day out? I need to buy maternity clothes!*).

She was about to get up and have a stretch when another message came in, and she instantly smiled in anticipation, knowing her virtual date with Nathan was tonight.

> Morning! Just off to bed but looking forward to our breakfast/dinner. So, when I sent you the honey photos, I failed to send something else because I was too nervous, lol. So here it is, my first video on my new YouTube channel. Bee Kind... haha. P.S. Your mum gave me permission to film on the property, FYI xo

Lacie clicked on the link and pressed pause as soon as it started playing, so she could get herself some breakfast first and watch it while she ate to save time. When she sat at the table with her scrambled eggs and toast, she eagerly pressed play.

Nathan's gorgeous smiling face appeared. 'Hey, folks, welcome to my channel, Nature with Nathan,' he said. 'I'm looking forward to bringing you some tips and techniques on working with nature, and today I'm showing you how to do a honey harvest from a backyard beehive.'

Lacie grinned and rubbed her hands together in anticipation. She had no intention of learning beekeeping but every intention of subscribing to his channel and watching every video from start to finish. She watched as he scraped the honeycomb from the frames and slotted the frames into a large tub for the honey to ooze into, after which he let the honey drain like liquid gold through an inbuilt tap and into a jar. He had even added a cute video at the end of him eating honey on toast and saying, 'Mmm, delicious.' A memory jolted in her mind; it was just like her father used to say when he'd eat his honey on toast.

She clicked subscribe and replied to Nathan.

> Brilliant! Can't wait for your next video... what will the topic be? Hope you get lots of views. Have fun xx (oh and see you soon).

He replied immediately. So much for him going to sleep.

Phew! Now I can sleep knowing my only
viewer and only subscriber (thanks btw) is
happy with my content. Next topic I'm
thinking… the top 5 best plants for coastal
gardens.

Lacie replied *sounds perfect* and wondered if she should start a channel for make-up tutorials, but thought the market was probably saturated. And when would she have the time? She drank the rest of her orange juice along with her daily vitamins, put her plates in the dishwasher, then got ready for work.

'Have fun, Lulu!' Lacie said goodbye to her last client of the day after doing her make-up for her singing gig tonight, then packed up her things to head home. When she stepped through the door, she inhaled the warm, comforting scent of chicken casserole simmering away in the slow cooker, which she'd set up before leaving for work.

I wish he could be here to enjoy this with me, she thought, her stomach grumbling.

How long could they go on having dates via video instead of the real thing? And there could be no post-date kiss either. It was like they were stuck in romance limbo, hovering on the edge of satisfaction but never quite getting there.

Just enjoy it while it lasts, Lacie, she told herself.

Another hour and it'd be ready, and she could set the table and pretend it was a real date. She changed out of her work clothes and into her slinky dress which, being a shimmery black, was dark enough to hide her small baby bump unless she was visible from the side. She draped a long golden thread scarf around her neck which hung low on each side to her hips, sitting softly over her belly when she sat. A quartz pendant and an extra swipe of honey-coloured lipstick, not to mention her sweet as honey nails she'd done last night, completed the look. She took a selfie in front of the bathroom mirror, and as she giggled, a side-on view with her holding the base of her abdomen, for Penny's eyes only.

She texted her sister along with the pic:

15 weeks

OMG! It's starting to really grow. And where are you off to? You look fab.

A special dinner. Talk later, gotta go xx

Giggling with excitement, she set the table and lit two candles, and dimmed the overhead lights. She ladled the steaming casserole into a bowl, filled her glass with sparkling mineral water, and placed her phone in a stand in front of her so she could video chat and eat at the same time.

She waited till right on 7pm and was about to call Nathan, when he beat her to it.

'Good morning! I mean evening,' he said, and she laughed as he appeared on the screen.

'Are you wearing a tie?' She peered closer.

He nodded. 'Indeed I am. I wasn't sure I even owned one, but it's amazing what you find when you rummage around for a while. Haven't worn this since... I can't remember, but I thought what better occasion to wear it than our date!'

'I hardly recognised you, and a fancy shirt too, let me guess, it's the only formal shirt you own?'

'Correct. It's good to have such things in case of emergencies, like this.'

She laughed. 'You better hope no one knocks at your door.

A spring morning in Tarrin's Bay and the local gardener and lifeguard is dressed to the nines.'

He stood and showed off the fact he hadn't completed the outfit and was only wearing casual shorts on his bottom half. 'Sorry I couldn't find anything else, but at least my top half is dressed up.'

Lacie shook her head with a giggle. 'You are so entertaining,' she said.

'Enough about me, you look amazing and... sparkly! Go on, stand up and show me the whole look. Let me guess, pyjamas on the bottom half?'

She giggled and said, 'No,' while her heart rate rose a notch and she hesitated. 'Oh man, I only just sat down after a long day!' She fanned her face for effect.

'C'mon, I showed you my fancy pants, I'm sure you look much posher than me.'

Reluctantly, she stood, making sure to position her long flowing scarf in front of her body, gave a quick 'ta-da!' then sat back down again. 'I am in bare feet though,' she confessed.

He didn't seem to notice anything out of the ordinary, as he simply gave an appreciative wolf whistle. Had she been further along it may have been a different story, but she would tell him anyway before she got to that point.

'Oh, and my sweet as honey nails!' She tried to hide her blushes by wiggling her fingers in front of her.

'Sweet,' he said. 'And is that quartz?' He patted his throat.

She nodded, fiddling with her pendant.

'I found some natural quartz once, in the rocks along a secluded beach. Another amazing natural phenomenon.'

'Cool. You know what else is amazing? The dinner I made, if I do say so myself.'

'Oh, please show me. Then I'll show you mine.' He cleared his throat. 'My breakfast, I mean.'

Lacie picked up the phone and turned the camera view around to face the table. 'A hearty chicken casserole, complete with carrots, potato, broccoli, with a hint of garlic and thyme. I can tell this is going to be absolutely delicious, my mouth is watering at the sight of it,' she said in a British accent. 'Do I sound like Nigella?'

Nathan gave a laugh. 'Impressive. And sexy.'

'Why, thank you, I am absolutely delighted to receive your compliment.' She continued speaking in the accent.

'Is that a white wine accompanying your dinner?' Nathan asked.

She moved the camera to her glass. 'Oh no, this is simply the finest sparkling water in Chicago. What is your beverage of choice for this fine day?'

She turned the camera to face her and smiled.

'I am having the finest orange juice in all of Tarrin's Bay.' He showed her his glass of juice, then moved the view to his plate. 'And on the menu we have a mushroom and cheese omelette, fried tomatoes, potato rosti, and... a banana. The only fruit I had. I have to do some shopping today.'

'Is that a cornflower?' She noticed the single blue flower protruding from a jam jar on his table. 'Did you pluck it from Mum's garden?'

'Of course not, after I planted some at your mum's, I had some spare seeds and planted them in mine too.'

'Nice. I like what they symbolise too.'

'Hope, nature's beauty, and love,' he said.

'Oh you already know, I love that.' She smiled. 'Apparently they also used to be worn by young men looking for love.'

'Oh really? I, ah, wasn't aware of that.'

'Flower symbolism is a fun thing to learn.'

'I only know the basics. Mostly, I just like the blue colour of the cornflowers.'

'They are beautiful, like a clear summer sky.'

He smiled, and took hold of his knife and fork. 'Shall we?'

Lacie picked up her spoon. 'Hell yes. I am starving.'

Nathan laughed, and after swallowing a mouthful of food, said, 'I love how you can be talking about the beauty of a summer sky one minute, and exclaiming "hell yes" the next.'

'Haha, I love that you love that.' She ate a spoonful and sighed. 'Oh, this is just as I knew it would be, absolutely delicious. I wish you could taste it.'

'Me too. I bet it beats a boring old omelette.'

'Oh I'd love to taste your omelette too.'

'Actually, it is pretty damn good, I must say.'

They smiled at each other and continued eating and exchanging small talk. When her meal was almost finished, Lacie asked, 'Have you ever had a date like this before?'

'It's been a long time since I've had a *special* date, let alone one as special as this.'

'Really?' Although Lacie knew why Nathan preferred to spend a lot of time on his own, having grown up needing to be independent, she couldn't understand why women weren't lining up to date him. Or maybe they were and he wasn't interested.

'I haven't been interested in dating for a while. Although I am definitely enjoying "hanging out" with you.' He made quotation marks with his fingers.

'No ex-wife or kids?'

Nathan glanced away for a moment. 'Not exactly.' He returned his gaze to her. 'I was in a serious relationship, I thought it might lead to that – marriage and kids – but my thoughts proved wrong.'

'Oh, I'm sorry.'

'Don't be. I'm not. Not now. But she did hurt me, so I guess it's taken me a while to even consider getting out there again. To trust again.'

Curiosity twisted inside her mind like a spreading vine. 'You're such a resilient person. It must've been a big deal then.'

'I am resilient, that's true. And I've learned to be even more resilient now. Life can often throw unexpected things our way, so I try not to expect anything and just go with the flow.'

The vine continued to spread and twist. 'May I be rude and ask, how did she hurt you?'

Nathan rubbed at the stubble on his jawline.

'It's okay, you don't have to tell me anything.'

'No, no, it's fine. It's probably good to get it out, I never really talked to anyone about it, just kind of repressed it and moved on. Took out my hurt on many a garden weed.'

'Except lantana?'

'Except lantana, yes.' He smiled. 'So basically, we – me and Tess – were getting serious. We started talking about the future, which is not something my go with the flow personality was used to, but I found myself getting excited. It was interrupted by some stress in her family life; she had a falling out with her mother, and her brother sided with her mother, so she felt alone. For some reason, she started pushing me away... snapping at the slightest thing, spending more time on her own. As though she didn't want to risk losing me too, maybe she thought it would be easier to not get any closer. Anyway, she took off for a week to have some time out, and came back all refreshed, ready to continue where we left off.'

Lacie narrowed her eyes. 'Hmm, it sounds like this was not as happy an ending as it seems?'

He shook his head. 'A few weeks later, she surprised me with the news that she was pregnant.'

Lacie's stomach flip-flopped. 'Did... something go wrong?' She gulped.

'No, she had a perfectly healthy baby boy. But throughout most of the pregnancy, I thought the baby was mine.'

Lacie's mouth fell open. 'He wasn't yours?'

Nathan shook his head and lowered his gaze, his eyes solemn and distant. 'I went from surprised, to excited, to devastated. She just blurted it all out one day, the truth. That when she'd been going through that stress, she reconnected with an ex briefly, then felt guilty and realised she'd made a mistake and came back home to me, found out she was pregnant, did the maths and realised it couldn't be mine, but pretended it was so we could stay together. For a couple of weeks before she told me, she'd been distant again – that's what she does when things get on top of her. At seven months pregnant the guilt got too much and she not only told me the fact, but that she was leaving to be with her ex, the father of her baby, to try and make it work.'

'Holy moly.' Lacie's heart felt crushed on his behalf.

'So,' he said, sculling the last of the juice, 'I not only lost the relationship, but the idea of being a father. I'd somehow lost something I didn't even really have yet. It's a strange and uncomfortable kind of grief.'

'Nathan, that's awful. I'm sorry you went through that.'

'I asked for a photo when he was born, out of curiosity. The little fella looked just like his dad: dark hair and long nose. I think I would have known he wasn't mine even if she hadn't told me.' He released a long exhale. 'I had been getting used to the idea of being a father, you know? Getting excited, thinking of names, and telling people.' He shook his head in defeat. 'And then that happened. I've never been able to get close to anyone else since.'

'Thank you for telling me all that. No wonder. It wasn't just a relationship, but a whole potential future you lost. That's a lot to deal with.'

'Thanks for your compassion.' He looked her in the eye. 'You're really the closest I've come to... getting close with anyone. For some reason when I'm with you, in person or virtually, words just sort of topple out of my mouth!'

Lacie smiled. 'I'm glad you feel comfortable with me. I do too, with you.'

An uncomfortable, unsettling sensation twisted inside her to replace the curiosity. Maybe it was time to–

'Lace... I feel like I've known you my whole life,' he said, interrupting her chain of thought.

Me too. Her breath caught high in her throat.

'Crazy huh, how you can know someone for years but never *really* know them, and yet you can meet someone new and feel like you know them instantly.'

'Yes,' he said. 'Like a... soul connection, or something. It's like with animals, they know their own kind, they don't have to talk or get to know each other, they just know.'

'True. Although I do love talking and getting to know you.'

'Ditto.'

'And what do you know about me so far?' Lacie resumed a lighter, chattier, flirtier tone, the seriousness of the recent discussion having tensed her muscles and they desperately needed relief.

'You help people with scars and disabilities feel beautiful inside and out. You almost became a florist, and you know *all* about flower symbolism.' He took the cornflower from its vase and popped it into his shirt pocket. He cleared his throat and continued. 'You have a wonderful family, you used to work in Hollywood, you dated Xavier Black, you love putting flowers in jam jars, and, and...'

'And my favourite movie is?'

'Your favourite movie is... the, um, Potato Literary Peel Society Gurney Pie Club thing.'

Laughter burst out of Lacie's mouth. 'Close!' She laughed again. 'Actually, not close, but points for trying. It's *The Guernsey Literary and Potato Peel Pie Society*.'

Nathan pointed at the screen. 'That's it! It was on the tip of my tongue.'

'More like the words toppled off the tip of your tongue and got all twisted up!'

He laughed, and his whole face lit up with a natural glow.

This is what she loved and didn't want to lose. This pure, easy, effortless and fun connection with him. Her heart was swelling with emotions she didn't expect, and also things she hadn't expressed.

'So, Lace, how long till you visit Australia again?' He leaned closer to the screen.

'Not for quite a while,' she said softly, not knowing if she'd even be able to make next year's reunion, or if her family would visit her like her mother had suggested.

'Hmm. Maybe...' He glanced upwards.

'Maybe what?' She leaned closer.

He waved his hand. 'Ah, nothing. So, what's on for the weekend?'

Lacie lowered her head, and one hand gently touched the small mound on her belly. 'Nath, I need to... I should...' *Why were the words so hard to say?* 'Maybe we should talk about... this, us, and the finer details of... this, and us, and...'

Starting with... I'm pregnant.

Nathan held up his hand, palm facing her. 'Stop right there. I know that this, *us*, is... unconventional to say the least, and uncertain, but let's just keep enjoying this, whatever this is, the way it is, which is absolutely awesome and something I look forward to every day. I don't want to change anything about what we have, I mean, I know we're in different countries, and therefore the future is uncertain, but right now it feels great, doesn't it?'

She gave a small nod.

'Let's not get bogged down with the details and the what ifs and the shoulds and all the serious stuff, let's make the most of every moment, go with the flow, and live in the present. One thing nature's taught me is that beauty can be fleeting. One day there's a rose bud, next day it's in full bloom, and then it's gone. Let's enjoy the flowers while they're blooming,' he said. 'I would have said that with a David impersonation but it didn't seem appropriate!'

Lacie smiled. He always knew how to explain things, make things seem simpler than her mind made them out to be. Their connection certainly was blooming, and why did he have to say exactly what she wanted just when she was about to tell him? She wanted to go with the flow too, she wanted to marvel in the beauty of their connection while it was here, no serious stuff to get in the way.

'I *am* really enjoying the flowers,' she said, twirling a strand of hair.

'Whatever flower is blooming right now, with us, it's my new favourite.'

Lacie widened her eyes. 'Even better than lantana?'

'Ten times better.'

Her heart fluttered. That was it then. She would stick to her original plan of waiting till the twenty-week scan to tell him how her life was about to change big time, and therefore anyone else's she was close to. They both wanted the same thing, to simply enjoy each other's virtual company with no rules or expectations. At least for now.

'It's been a lovely date, thank you,' she said.

'It sure has. The meal was delicious too.' He winked.

'Indeed. Well, your day awaits and my night awaits.'

'Goodnight, Lace.' Nathan blew a kiss her way.

Lacie caught the virtual kiss in her hand, enclosing it with her curled fingers, and smiled as she held it to her heart. 'Goodnight, Nath.' She then blew a kiss of her own too, aiming it at the blue cornflower in his pocket.

CHAPTER TWENTY-THREE

Dear Baby,

I am now 17 weeks pregnant and you are the size of a pear. I have had to buy some new clothes to fit my growing belly. In only three weeks I'll get to see you again, make sure you are growing well and that all your organs look healthy.

Something funny happened yesterday. I was on the phone to Penny, your aunt, and telling her... how can I say it? How 'gassy' I was feeling. That I kept feeling these little bubbles inside like gas and it was starting to increase. 'That's not gas, Lacie, that's your baby moving around!' she said. 'What?' I replied. But it feels like gas bubbles.' 'That's how it feels at first,' she told me. I couldn't believe it. I thought I had gas but it's just been you! LOL. That means laugh out loud. And now that I know, I've been paying more attention, and today, there was a definite movement, like a kick or a roll or something, that felt different to gas, and it made me smile so much. To know you're in there, moving about, growing bigger. What an amazing sensation it is. I wanted to write it down so I wouldn't forget. One day you might read this and have a giggle.

So as I lay here in bed, I'm on the alert waiting for more movements. I know they'll start increasing and maybe down the track they might even wake me up, but that's okay. It's all okay. I'm going with the flow and enjoying every moment as it comes lately. The future will unfold how it will, but now, the present, is a real gift to be enjoyed.

Love, Mum xo

CHAPTER TWENTY-FOUR

Three weeks later, when Nathan got into his Ute, ready to finish up the memorial garden at Gloria's that he'd done most of yesterday, his phone pinged. He picked it up and smiled. He hadn't texted her this morning, having been anxious to get to Gloria's and finish early as he didn't normally do garden work on Saturdays, and he was doing a lifeguard shift tomorrow.

> Hey, hoping to talk to you in the morning (my morning, your night), are you free?

He turned the key in the ignition then typed a reply:

> Sure, call me when you're up. Finishing Gloria's garden today, she's so excited.

And so was he. It was nice to help her create something to remember her departed husband.

> Oh nice! Send me pics (if she's ok with it) x

He sent a thumbs up and got on the road. When he arrived,

Gloria hadn't set up the table with scones this time, she said they could share a treat when he finished. 'Here, I brought you a treat as well.' He handed her a jar of South Haven honey, which Martha had said to give her.

'Oh, I'm looking forward to that! Thank you, and thank Martha for me too.'

'Will do. She also wanted me to invite you over for a high tea in the new garden gazebo sometime. She's not sure when yet but wanted to let you know.'

Gloria's face lit up. 'I'd be delighted. I hope you'll be there too?'

'Oh, I'm not sure, she might want it to be a ladies only event.'

'I'm sure all the ladies would be thrilled to have the pleasure of your company, as am I.'

'You're too kind, Gloria,' he replied. 'I'm going to grab the plaque and the remaining bits and pieces from the car and I'll be right back.'

'Can't wait. I'll leave you to it.' She put the honey jar on the kitchen bench and rubbed her hands together eagerly.

He carried the items from the car to the back garden by going through the side gate, noticing the latch was loose. After placing everything out back, he grabbed his tool kit and repaired the latch, tightening the screws and spraying it with WD-40 to help it open more easily.

He glanced around the garden, surveying the progress in plant growth and blooming flowers and gave a satisfied nod. It looked much better than the plain, basic garden it was before. It now looked more alive, with a nice contrast of colours and shapes, the light breeze gently moving the leaves around as though they were swaying in bliss.

He checked the hole he'd dug in the empty patch of garden bed yesterday and, satisfied it was deep enough for the small tree he'd bought yesterday, got to work planting the Blue Arrow conifer. Being narrow, it was ideal for the small space and its blue-grey foliage made it an interesting focal point for the garden, standing out among all the green. He'd checked with Gloria that she was happy with the species before purchasing, and she'd said it was perfect because blue had been Leonard's favourite colour, and as it was shaped like a kind of rocket, it appeared to be pointing up to him in Heaven. The good thing was it was hardy and low maintenance, and would last the test of time, symbolic of a long life well lived.

He patted the soil and confirmed its stability, then made a shallow ditch a little in front of it to nestle the plaque. He bent his knees, activated his core, and lifted the heavy square-shaped stone, placing it into the ditch and wriggling it carefully into place. Its slightly inclined front surface was engraved with the simple words Gloria had requested:

For Leonard
My love is always with you, as yours is always with me

Below was an engraving of two birds close together, outlined by a heart shape. Nathan took a moment to admire it and to honour the man's life it had been created for. It was like a small gravestone but without the standard details of full name, birth date and death date, and beloved husband attribution.

Who would make a plaque for him if he died? He shook away the morbid thought, and his phone beeped in his pocket. He usually didn't keep his phone in his pocket in case there was truth in the fact that the low dose radiation could be harmful, but lately had found himself wanting to keep it on him in the mornings in case Lacie sent any more messages. He took it out and read the text message:

> I know you probably don't want to hear from me, and it's been a long time, but I just wanted to say sorry again. And let you know that you were right, that things would never work out between me and Dimitri – they didn't. We broke up a few months ago. Me and Neo are doing fine though, he's such a great kid. But I've felt the need to get in touch, to catch up, and explain more about why I did what I did. I understand if you don't want to hear from me, but can't blame a girl for trying. Take care, Tess.

Nathan sighed. Part of him felt sorry for her, after all, he had loved her once, but the other part of him was still angry and bitter about how she'd broken his heart. She probably texted him on a Saturday morning thinking he'd have no reason to say he was busy working, but today was an exception. Still, he decided to send a quick reply, cautious to not invite further interaction.

> Sorry to hear that, I'm glad you're both doing well though.

It wasn't a 'yes we can catch up' or a 'no we can't', but it was all he could manage right now. She sent a heart emoji as a reply, and he put his phone out of reach, leaning against the fence. Now was not the time to ponder a failed relationship, it was time to honour a successful one.

He made another shallow ditch to house the birdbath, lifting it carefully from the trolley and placing it into position next to, but slightly further in front of, the tree. He made sure it was secure and stepped back to check everything looked balanced. Satisfied, he planted some lavender cuttings in a circle around the birdbath, then carefully dragged the bench seat into position against the side fence and at right angles to the end of the garden bed where the plaque sat. Only a couple more things to do and he'd be finished.

Nathan turned on the hose and showered the whole garden with water, the always rewarding final step to signal his work was done and it was now nature's job to do the rest. He also filled the bird bath, and then picked up a tray of pebbles and word stones and walked over to the back deck. Gloria caught his eye through the window and scurried out.

'I thought I'd let you tell me where to put these.' He gestured to the stones.

She smiled. 'Thank you, I'd love to.'

She eagerly walked to the memorial garden with Nathan. 'Oh my, it's absolutely delightful.' She held her palms to her cheeks and took a deep breath. 'Rightio, let's see...' She picked up the first stone that said 'forever' and placed it in front of the plaque. The next one said 'love' and she placed it in front of the bird bath and lavender. The smaller pebbles she instructed Nathan to place in a circle around the base of the lavender, and the remaining three stones which read 'joy', 'peace', and 'friendship' she got him to place in a curve around the base of the pine tree.

They stood back and surveyed the final result in a moment of silence. He asked permission to take a photo which he did from several angles, and quickly sent them through to both Gloria and Lacie. He would put some on his website too. He also had an idea for later on, to create a video series for YouTube on garden features. He could showcase a variety, such as this one, that served as either an attractive focal point or a meaningful display. He could even show young Jessie's pebble garden and family tree at South Haven, if her mother agreed, and perhaps he could interview people like Gloria to talk about the meaning and purpose behind their centrepiece. It wouldn't be appropriate to ask her now, he would wait a while and give her a call sometime to see how she felt about it.

'He really was my best friend, you know,' she said, as they sat on the bench which had 'Always and Forever' embossed on a gold plaque on the top wooden slat. 'When we first got together, I wondered if it was normal to feel like friends most of the time and lovers only a small portion of the time. I'd read grand love stories in my teens and always thought it would be like that, but as I discovered, real love is based on a solid friendship. With a bit of attraction thrown in,' she said with a laugh.

Nathan smiled and nodded.

'I think that's why I thought you and Martha's daughter were together, back at the trivia night. You seemed like such good friends. And you looked at her in that special way.'

'I did?' Nathan's face become warm, and not from being out in the sun.

'Oh yes,' she replied. 'Shame she's gone back overseas. You two would have made a lovely couple.'

Nathan tapped his foot on the grass. 'Can I share a secret with you?'

Gloria looked him in the eye, her eyes lighting up. 'I love a good secret! And what is said in Leonard's garden stays in Leonard's garden.' She winked.

'Good to know,' he said with a grin. 'Lacie and I have been in contact quite often over the past few months. We chat regularly, and... it's like she's my best friend.'

'Oh, wow, well that's lovely,' Gloria replied. 'Do you really chat, like actual talking, not just text messages? Because there's nothing like a real two-way conversation.'

'Oh yes, often. We video chat, mostly. Either early in the morning or late at night... it's tricky with the time difference.'

'That's a good sign.'

'A good sign for?'

'For the beginning of a beautiful relationship.'

Nathan opened his eyes wide. 'But she's all the way over there, and I'm here. How can that possibly work?'

Gloria looked into the distance. 'Gosh, my parents survived being separated by war, dear. My father returned safe and sound and never left my mother's side again. Then I was born. No siblings, unfortunately, but I wouldn't be here if he hadn't survived. Strange to think how many children didn't get to be born because of the loss from war.' She shook her head. 'Anyway, my point is, things aren't as difficult as they may seem. Life is much easier now, in terms of connecting with people. Make the most of it. But don't think it has to be perfect. You two are only a flight away. Yes, it may be a long one, but not as long as waiting for a soldier to return home.'

Nathan froze, as though his perceptions about the limited nature of what was going on between them were about to crumble. But he couldn't quite hold on to hope yet. 'But flights are expensive, and it also means time off work, and then there's jet lag, and we wouldn't get to see each other often, so it would be difficult to maintain, and—'

'Excuses, excuses.' She waved her hand as though flicking away an annoying fly. 'Life is too easy for couples these days, though many young lovers make it difficult for themselves, with all these expectations about how it should be, and the effort one has to make to make it work. In my day, there weren't many options, you either met someone local, or while on holiday, or were introduced or set up by parents or friends... we didn't have internet dating or a way to send messages to each other unless you count actual written letters which took ages to post. And if you dated someone out of town you may only have seen them occasionally anyway.'

'So you're saying that long-distant relationships aren't necessarily doomed to fail?'

'Not at all. I'm no relationship guru, but I do know love and what it takes to keep it going. Friendship, dedication, and commitment. We were lucky, my Leonard and I. I'm not saying it wouldn't be difficult, or a risk, but you have to risk your heart or you risk the pain of regret.'

Nathan nodded and absorbed her words of wisdom, his brows furrowing.

'Life is so fleeting. I thought I'd have many more years with Leonard, but it ended too quickly. We still had things we wanted to do together.' Her voice faltered and she sniffled, dabbing at her eyes.

Nathan swivelled on the seat to face her. 'He'd be so proud of you, and I'm sure he'd love the memorial garden you were inspired to create.'

'Thank you for helping to bring it into reality.'

'Gloria, it's been an absolute honour.' He opened his arms to invite her for a hug, which she eagerly accepted.

'You're like the son I never had,' she whispered, and Nathan bit back a tremble in his bottom lip. If only he'd found Gloria and Leonard when he was young.

A bird tweeted and their hug broke off. Nathan glanced at the birdbath where a small fairywren perched itself on the edge, then dipped its beak quickly in the water.

'Oh, how beautiful,' Gloria said.

Then, a second bird joined the other, taking a sip, before they both flitted around together and off into the sky.

Warmth spread through Nathan's heart. It was these simple pleasures that he loved about being in nature. Watching the birdlife enjoy their surroundings with complete freedom and joy.

'I think that little bird has found its soulmate,' Gloria stated.

She stood and stretched. 'Now, how about some lemon poppyseed cake? I made it especially for you.'

'You did? I am truly spoiled, thank you, Gloria.'

They wandered to the deck where she gestured for Nathan to sit at the outdoor table for two. 'What do you think you'll do, about Lacie?' she asked.

Nathan shrugged with uncertainty. 'I just don't know.'

'If I were young like you, I wouldn't waste a second in indecision.' She shook her head. 'Talk to her, or better yet, why not fly over there, give yourself a much-deserved holiday, and see if there's anything between you two in person now that you've had time to get to know each other.'

'And if there is?'

'Then you make the next best decision, and so forth. Life is really just a sequence of choices. Sometimes we make the right ones, sometimes the wrong ones, but not making one is always the wrong decision, so you might as well take a risk.'

'Huh. You really are insightful, you know that? Growing up I didn't have anyone in my life to talk sense to me like you have.'

She smiled as though it meant the world to her. 'Be gutsy, remember?' She winked and went to the kitchen to prepare the cake.

Was it really as simple and as complicated as booking a flight? He didn't have to have the next five years all planned out, he only had to make the next best decision. He wanted to see Lacie desperately, and couldn't bear waiting till July next year, and then for only two weeks, and then repeating the same thing. By that time she might meet someone closer to her, someone it was easy to have a relationship with. He didn't know how on earth it could work despite Gloria's encouragement, all he knew was that he wanted to find out.

His decision made, he couldn't wait for Lacie's call tonight. He wanted to tell her his idea before he chickened out. He thought of writing it all out in a text so she'd receive it when she woke and would have time to process it, but then he decided a real conversation was best. And she had sounded eager to talk to him about something too... maybe she had similar ideas? The thought made excitement bubble up inside him like he'd drunk a whole can of fizzy soft drink in one hit.

When he returned home, he paced around, kept looking at his watch, and practised the conversation in his mind. He stopped and took a deep breath. Time to stop thinking and relax for a while. He grabbed a packet of salt and vinegar potato chips from his pantry and sat on the couch, turning on the TV. David and Nigella were far from his mind right now, he needed something different. He browsed the movies online and then suddenly remembered. He typed in a search and found what he was looking for, and with a big smile, he pressed play on *The Guernsey Literary and Potato Peel Pie Society*.

CHAPTER TWENTY-FIVE

Today was the day Lacie would tell him. It was like when someone gets your name wrong but you can't bring yourself to correct them, so you let it go on and on until it feels too late to tell them. Or when someone serves you green tea even though you don't like it, and you drink it, and then each time you visit they keep giving it to you thinking you like it, and you can't bring yourself to tell them otherwise. This was one of those awkward moments... she hadn't lied, but she hadn't told the truth either. She had simply not mentioned something. A quite significant something.

The twenty-week scan had been scary at first, then she'd been filled with relief when she was told that all looked great. It was surreal and beautiful, emotional and amazing. Her baby looked quite big on the screen, and was wriggling around, swallowing, and they'd even witnessed a few hiccups. She'd made sure they didn't accidentally reveal the gender to her. Here she was, at the halfway mark... no turning back now.

She ate a quick breakfast and got dressed and ready, then picked up her phone. Unfortunately, or possible fortunately, she would have to be quick, as her hairdresser had called to ask if she could come in earlier for her appointment to replace a cancellation. There was still enough time to talk to Nathan about her situation without rushing, but without having one of their usual long video chats.

She took a deep breath and pressed the video call button.

With barely any chance for it to ring, his bright, smiling face appeared on the screen.

'Hi!'

'Hi yourself,' she replied.

'Been waiting patiently for you to get up. You look nice.'

'Thanks, thought I'd get ready for the day first instead of talking to you in my pyjamas as usual! I have an appointment to get to earlier than planned, so, um...'

'Let's cut to the chase then. I wanted to talk to you about something,' Nathan said. 'But you did too, didn't you? So you go first.'

Lacie cleared her throat. 'It's okay, you go first, since you've been waiting all day.'

His eyes brightened and he looked eager to talk. 'I had a great time doing Gloria's garden,' he said.

'Oh yes, I saw the photos, amazing. Well done. I bet she's over the moon with it.'

'Sure is. Anyway, she's quite the wise woman, that Gloria. She gave me some good advice about life, and... love. And the thing is,' his chest rose with a sharp intake of breath, 'I've been thinking a lot, and I know I said a few weeks ago let's live in the moment, and that's still my motto, but also...' His eyes looked at her with a subtle sparkle and her heart beat faster in anticipation of what he might say. 'I want to see you. Like, really see you, in person.'

Her eyes widened and she went to speak but no words came out.

'There's something special here, between us. I know you feel it too.'

Oh, I do. But...

'And I want a chance to explore that further, see how things feel, when we're together. I don't want to think too far ahead, or make plans or promises right now, I just want to explore it and not let distance get in the way of something that could be amazing.'

Lacie sat at the dining table, a wave of dizziness unsteadying her. 'What are you saying exactly?'

'I want to book a flight to come and see you. No need to put me up, I'll arrange a hotel. I don't know how long for yet, but I can probably reschedule my jobs for another couple of weeks.'

Oh my God. Was this really happening?

'Nathan, I'm... I'm not sure, I mean, it's a big thing for you to do, and...' She ran her hand through her hair and glanced sideways, then returned his gaze. 'I'd love to see you too, it's just...'

Her phone pinged with a message from Ellie and the preview hovered on the screen:

I miss Dad :(

Her mind distracted for a moment, she forgot the words she had been trying to say. 'Sorry, a message came through. Anyway...' She smiled for a moment. 'It sounds wonderful, it really does. I'm amazed you would even consider doing that.'

He smiled too. 'You're worth it. And I think *we're* worth it, to see if there really is anything between us. I don't know what that would mean afterwards but sometimes you've just gotta take a risk, look a few steps ahead but not too far into the distance.'

If only she could. But her situation now required her to look into the distance and plan ahead. It was time to get ready for the baby, gather all the supplies she'd need, organise changes to her business, and–

> I can't stop crying, I don't know what's wrong with me.

Another text from Ellie.

'Hang on, Nath, I'm just getting messages from Ellie.' She minimised the call screen and opened Ellie's message on WhatsApp. Her heart shook. She sent a quick reply:

> Hey, it's okay. It's normal to feel enormous grief sometimes. Love you.

'Sorry, she's having some... emotional trouble.'

'Oh.' Nathan's brow furrowed. 'Actually, we had a good chat not too long ago, before I did the honey harvest. She was sitting out on the back step and she looked sad. After we talked, she seemed a lot better.'

'Oh? I didn't know. Well, thanks for being there for her.'

'She's a great girl. Seems to hold the weight of the world on her shoulders though.'

'Yes, she does.'

'Anyway, you probably need time to process what I've suggested, and you had something you wanted to chat about?'

Ellie texted:

> It's so overwhelming.

Lacie's mind flitted between Nathan's revelation, and Ellie's needs.

'Yeah, it's just that I've got a lot going on and...'

Ellie messaged:

> Feel like I can't cope.

Lacie let out an anxious sigh. 'Sorry, Nath, can we take a raincheck? Ellie needs me right now. I have to get going after that too, so I'll call again when I can?'

He looked slightly disappointed but equally concerned. 'Sure, family comes first. Hope she's okay.'

'Thanks.' She ended the call and realised it was a strange thing for Nathan to say, having no family of his own. Who was there to put him first when he needed it?

> Oh, love, you can cope. It's tough but you're strong.

> I feel so weak.

Lacie's heart wanted to reach out and nurture her sister's.

> Do you want me to call? Are you in bed?

> In bed but don't have energy to talk. Can only text. So tired.

> Maybe just try to get some sleep, I'm sure you'll feel a bit better in the morning.

> Maybe.

> Is there anything else bothering you?

> Everything feels so hard.

> Have you talked to Mum? Is she still awake?

Lacie wished she was back in the guest room at South Haven and could simply pop into her sister's room and give her a hug. She waited a moment for her to reply, but when she didn't, she added to her text:

> Don't worry about disturbing her, she'd rather be there for you.

After a few moments there was still no reply. Hopefully she had fallen asleep.

Lacie exhaled. She had to leave for the hairdresser, so grabbed her bag and put her shoes on. Before putting her phone in her bag, she sent a message to her mum:

> Mum, you awake? Ellie is upset and was crying, but I'm not sure if she's fallen asleep as she hasn't replied to my last message. Can you check on her?

Dots appeared, then:

> Oh, just about to fall asleep but yes, I'll quickly check... hang on.

Lacie waited, and took a swig from her water bottle. After a little while Martha replied:

> She's fast asleep, poor thing. It reminded me of when she was a baby, peering into her cot at her sweet face and watching her chest rise and fall. Thanks for letting me know. I'll talk to her first thing when she wakes. Xx

Lacie released a sigh of relief.

> Thanks, Mum, sweet dreams xx

Right. Time to get on with the day, think about what Nathan said, then call him again later to tell him *her* news, because that may very well change his mind.

As Lacie chose some cute, neutral baby clothes while shopping later that afternoon, she stopped a moment when she passed a full-length mirror in the store. She giggled a little, amazed at the position she was in. Her bump was definitely obvious, not huge, but a beautiful rounded belly that was different than looking bloated or carrying some extra fat. Her bra size had also increased, and she'd had to buy some new ones.

'When are you due?'

Lacie glanced to the side toward the voice, belonging to another woman, also with a pregnant belly, though larger than hers.

'February. And you?'

'February also.' She smiled. Lacie must have looked surprised, as the woman added, 'I'm having twins, hence my hugeness.'

'Oh,' Lacie responded. 'Wow, congratulations.' She glanced in her shopping cart at the baby clothes, many in varying shades of blue. 'Both boys, or one of each?'

'Both boys. Husband is over the moon. I am too of course, but growing up with four brothers, whoa! It's gonna be a crazy ride.'

Lacie smiled. One was enough to think about, she couldn't imagine having two at once.

'Let me guess, you haven't found out, or you're a fan of going gender neutral?'

Lacie glanced briefly at her selection of clothing. 'Not finding out.'

'You're strong, I couldn't hold out till the birth!'

'You're strong, carrying twins,' Lacie said.

'Thanks, but I had no choice in the matter. And we're all strong, us pregnant women, aren't we?'

She nodded. 'I guess we are, though I'm feeling pretty tired and not very strong!'

'Ah, you'll be fine. It's normal. Anyway,' she glanced at the baby equipment aisle, 'gotta keep going before my tenth visit to the bathroom for the day.'

'I hear ya.' Lacie chuckled. 'All the best.'

'You too.' She smiled

Warmth rushed through Lacie's body. It was nice to connect with someone else going through the same thing, although she was sure the woman wasn't indulging in a long-distance romance with a man on the other side of the world.

She eyed the blue newborn clothes, and then the pink. Her heart fluttered at their cuteness. She could hardly believe she would have a tiny baby to hold in her arms next year. She was tempted to buy one of each colour, but kept her resolve to wait. She had a big enough family that they would surely send over cute baby presents as soon as they found out, so the ones she had in her cart were enough for now.

When she walked towards the baby equipment aisle, her phone rang. Being a Saturday afternoon, she thought it must be one of her friends checking what she was doing tonight, though they knew she wasn't up for the usual happenings they'd enjoyed before the pregnancy. She much more preferred a cosy evening on the couch these days, especially now the cooler weather was starting to arrive.

'Huh?' She eyed the caller ID and answered. 'Mum? Is everything okay?'

'Oh, Lacie! I didn't want to wake the others yet, apart from Matt, he's with me.'

'Mum, what is it?' Fear lurched like a slingshot in her chest.

'It's Ellie, she's in hospital, we just arrived with the ambulance, she...'

Dizziness swept through Lacie's entire body and her eyes

searched frantically for a seat. She abandoned the cart and rushed out of the store, sitting on the nearest available seat outside.

'She took too many sleeping pills.' Her mum sobbed through the phone. 'If she hadn't called me from her bed just before passing out, I don't know what... I can't imagine... oh, Lace, I can't believe this is happening!'

In the background her brother said, 'Hey, it's going to be okay, Mum.'

'Oh my God. I didn't realise, I mean, I thought she was...' Lacie's head was spinning and she gripped the edge of the seat. 'Is she okay?'

'They're working on her now. She must've woken after a few hours and couldn't get back to sleep. There were scrunched up tissues next to her pillow, like she'd been crying. The sound of my phone woke me – thank God I had my volume switched on – but all I heard was a faint "help". I rushed to her room and found her barely conscious, but awake enough for her to point to the medication and say "too much".'

'Oh, Mum, I should have known. She wasn't quite right earlier. What did the doctors say?'

'Nothing yet, they're too busy. Matt came straight away, he arrived at the same time as the paramedics and unlocked the door so they could get her into the ambulance. She was still breathing but they gave her oxygen and did some checks and told us to head to Welston hospital emergency department.'

Lacie's hands trembled and her eyes stung. The world seemed to be spinning around her. She felt so helpless and terrified. Her heart raced and she had to take a few sips of water. A passer-by asked if she was okay and she nodded and waved them away.

'We just have to wait. Oh, I'm so scared.' Martha sobbed and Matt's voice came onto the line.

'Lace, are you okay?'

She nodded even though he couldn't see her. 'I don't know, I mean, yes, but no. I'm so worried! What can I do?'

'Nothing, it's okay, I'll stay with Mum and I'll call the others. I'll let you know as soon as there's an update.'

Waiting for an update was unbearable. Lacie stood and took a deep breath to steady herself, then walked as fast as she could back to her car, thankfully she had decided to drive now that she was getting bigger and more tired, instead of walking and using public transport.

'I'm flying over,' she blurted to Matt. She couldn't just wait and hope.

'But, Lace, there's nothing you can do right now, and it'd be a couple of days at least before you'd arrive. Don't put yourself through too much, we've got this.'

'No.' She shook her head. 'No. I'm on my way home and then I'll book the first available flight. I'll let you know the details.'

'Well, if you're sure. You're allowed to travel?'

'Yes. I'll stop by the medical centre first to see if I can get an urgent check up and a doctor's letter for travel just in case. I've made up my mind, I'm coming.'

There was no way she wanted to be overseas when her sister needed her. And no way she was ready to lose another family member.

CHAPTER TWENTY-SIX

A couple of hours later, Lacie had arrived home with a medical letter ensuring she was safe to travel until the third trimester, and while in the waiting room had booked a one-way flight to Sydney, Australia, for 6pm the following day. She had no idea how long she could stay or what would happen next, all she knew was that she had to be there.

She plonked her bag on the bed and collapsed onto it, tears bursting out of her eyes.

Ellie, oh Ellie!

Matt had texted not too long ago that their sister was responding well to the treatment, but as some of the medication had already taken effect in the brain, they'd need a few more hours to encourage the excretion of the drug and determine the residual effects. More waiting.

It's going to be okay, she soothed herself. *She's responding, that's a good sign.*

She sat up and texted Matt, not wanting to further upset her mum:

Did she do it on purpose?

Not sure. The fact that she called Mum means she knew she'd made a mistake, accidentally or otherwise.

True. Please let me know once she's stable, and when someone can talk to her. I wish I was there right now.

You will be soon enough, and Penny and Chris are arriving soon. Please look after yourself. And try to get some sleep on the plane. Have you got an ergonomic travel pillow?

Always helpful and practical, her chiropractor brother, even in times of crisis.

Yep. Don't know if I'll be able to sleep but I'll try.

Well, try to get a good rest tonight at least. Let us know once you've checked in for the flight.

Will do. Tell Mum I'll be there on Tuesday morning and I'll come straight to the hospital.

Matt sent a thumbs up and Lacie's stomach grumbled, and she realised she hadn't eaten in several hours, as she'd been planning on having lunch after her shopping trip. She heaved herself up from the bed and rubbed her belly.

'It's okay, baby. Everything's okay.'

She made herself a peanut butter sandwich and a hot chocolate and devoured it rapidly. The boost in blood sugar must have kicked her brain into gear, as she got a pen and paper and jotted down a list of what she'd need to do before tomorrow:

1. Pack bags — don't forget vitamins, travel pillow, and passport.

2. Contact Madeleine to cancel appointments for the next week, and put those booked in the following week on notice of possible cancellation, if I can't return by then.

3. Throw out perishable food tomorrow morning and empty the trash.

4. Reschedule next week's OBGYN appointment.

And that was all she could think of for now, though she felt like she was forgetting something.

A while later, Penny sent a text:

> Lacie! Matt said you're coming. So glad. Doctors tell us Ellie is responding but it's still critical. She's had her stomach pumped and is on IV fluids and medication and oxygen. Just have to wait it out. I can't believe it.

Lacie's hand flew to her chest.

> Oh man. Me neither. I spoke to her before it happened, she was going to try and get some sleep and that was the last I heard.

> I wish I'd known she was struggling.

> I knew, but I didn't know how bad it was. I wish I'd called her before she went to sleep, made sure she was okay.

> Best thing is to focus on what we can do now.
> Look after yourself and have a safe flight.

Lacie longed to be with her family, have a group hug, and just be in their presence. Most of all, she longed to see her sister's funny facial expressions again and feel her arms around her. How could someone with such a great sense of humour feel so sad?

On Sunday morning, Lacie had surprisingly slept longer than she'd planned, apart from two trips to the bathroom during the night.

Crap! She got up and ate a quick breakfast, got dressed and ready, and opened her suitcase to pack. She'd only been able to sleep thanks to the fact that her mum had called last night and told her Ellie was now stable. The relief was like a warm blanket around her heart. She'd need to stay in hospital a while and recover, and have a psychiatric evaluation when she was up for it. Apparently, when Martha had been able to see her, Ellie had apologised profusely. She'd said she'd felt so depressed and exhausted and couldn't think straight. Desperate for sleep and relief, before she realised what she was doing she'd tipped several tablets into her hand and swallowed them all. It was only a little while after that she'd panicked and called Martha, but by then she was getting drowsy and confused. If Martha hadn't got to her in time...

Lacie's phone pinged.

Hope all is okay? Xo

Nathan! She'd been so preoccupied with her family emergency she hadn't told him what had happened. Or, what she had been planning on telling him, and now wasn't the time.

> Sorry for the delay, something awful happened. Ellie took an overdose of medication and is in hospital, she's stable but will need further treatment and evaluation. It's been an anxious 24 hours!

Oh, Lace, I can't believe it! Do you want to talk? Can I go help your mum with anything? I'll check in with her.

> It's okay, I've gotta get busy packing and preparing, I'm flying over tonight. Can't bear not being there.

You're coming back? Please let me know if there's anything I can do. I hope she'll be okay. And I'm here for you. I can't wait to give you a big hug. Xo

A bittersweet smile softened Lacie's lips. So much for him flying over to the States, and so much for her secret being revealed. No doubt he would find out soon enough, but she would speak to him properly once she'd seen Ellie and knew she was okay.

> Thank you. Once I've seen Ellie and settled in the house, I'll give you a call so we can have a proper chat. And… maybe meet up after that, if you want to that is.

Of course I want! I'll wait for you to make contact. Just be with your family and look after Ellie. I'm here when you're ready.

Anticipation and dread shared space in her heart. She didn't know if he would still want what he wanted once he found out she'd kept something important from him. She'd thought their flirtation wouldn't go anywhere, but suddenly it had morphed into something else before she had even realised. And she'd had no idea he felt that strongly until he'd told her his plan to visit. Everything had happened all at once. Anyway, she couldn't think too much about it now, she could only think about her sister and being there for her.

CHAPTER TWENTY-SEVEN

After doing some late afternoon maintenance at the primary school playground on Monday, Nathan arrived home and tried to relax, but couldn't, knowing that Ellie was going through so much, and that Lacie would be arriving back in Tarrin's Bay. He didn't know when, he'd left her to it so she wouldn't feel overwhelmed, but assumed it would be sometime tomorrow.

He got up from the couch and went to his bedroom, eyeing the bookcase. He scanned the titles and pulled out the one he was looking for, *The Wisdom of Nature*. He read a few passages and nodded in agreement at the insights. It was amazing how a few carefully chosen words strung together in a certain way could bring immediate understanding and convey a message that made you believe someone understood how you felt. The book used nature analogies in relation to human life, providing both education and inspiration. He had only mentioned it to Ellie casually, but maybe it could help her right now. Whether she would be up for reading anytime soon he didn't know, but the book also talked about intuition and trusting nature's perfect timing. His intuition was guiding him to give the book to her. It might not help much, or it might help a lot, but hopefully the act of showing his care and concern would help regardless. He wished he could do more. He didn't want another Cooper on his conscience... he wished he'd talked to him more, made him feel less alone, or happier in life, but he'd been young and naïve and didn't have much emotional awareness back then. Now, if he could support another struggling person, even a little, he would.

He grabbed his phone and sent Martha a message. He'd only sent a short *thinking of you all, let me know if there's anything I can do* message on Sunday, to which Martha had replied with a heart.

> Martha, I have a book I'd like to give Ellie. I spoke to her about it a few weeks ago hoping it might help in some small way. Can I drop it on your doorstep?

He placed the book on the kitchen table and started to prepare dinner; Nigella's slow-roasted garlic and lemon chicken, which he was planning on making extra of and taking to South Haven for Martha and anyone else who may be there.

After putting it in the oven, his phone beeped and he opened the text.

> That would be lovely, I'm sure she'd appreciate it. Actually, if you'd like to give it to her in person, I think that may help too. She always speaks highly of your conversations and says that you 'get her'. If that works, feel free to come between 10am and 12pm tomorrow or the next day. Otherwise, the doorstep is fine.

He didn't want to intrude, but it would be nice to visit her and show his support. He replied:

> I'd love to visit, if you're sure she'd be ok with it. I also have a home-cooked meal for you, I can leave that on the doorstep later tonight if you're coming home?

> Oh, Nathan, you're such a kind soul. I'll be home around 9pm or so. Thanks x

Satisfied he was doing something useful at least, he ran himself a shower and enjoyed the warm pressure of the water washing away the day, while the dinner cooked and the aroma soothed his senses. Surprisingly, heat developed behind his eyes as they moistened with a slight film of tears. He didn't know why, maybe it was the traumatic memory of Cooper's death resurfacing again, plus Ellie's emergency, Lacie's impending arrival, and the feeling of isolation accompanying him throughout his life being replaced with a sense of belonging. Maybe his life was finally starting to fall into place.

'Knock, knock,' Nathan said softly, tapping on the door to Ellie's hospital room the next day. He stepped in cautiously, the book in his hand. 'Hey, stranger.' He stopped by her bed, trying not to show his shock at how depleted and frail she looked: attached to a drip, oxygen prongs in her nose, skin pale. Martha took the opportunity to sit down and drink her coffee, checking her phone.

'Hey,' Ellie whispered in a scratchy voice.

'I've brought you a book. I know you might not feel like reading yet, but it'll be here when you do.'

'Thanks.' She glanced at the front cover as he held it up. 'Oh yeah, I remember you mentioned it.'

'Hope you like it.' He offered a small smile.

Her eyes became glossy and she sniffed. 'Sorry you have to… see me like this.'

'Hey,' he said, stepping closer and gently touching her forearm. 'No apologies. I'm here for you. I'll get your mum to put my number in your phone too. Call or text anytime.'

She nodded a thank you. 'My insides hurt.' She shifted her position as though she couldn't get comfortable. 'My throat, my stomach.' She winced.

'Are you able to eat, can I get you anything?' Nathan asked.

'Big Mac and fries, thanks.' She managed a slight smile.

'I don't think her stomach's quite up for that yet,' Martha said, 'but maybe once we're home.'

'I'd be happy to do a home delivery, just let me know when and I'll make a trip to Welston and hope they keep warm by the time I get back to Tarrin's Bay.' He winked.

'Deal,' she said.

A nurse came in and said hello, and Nathan took that as his cue to leave. He didn't want to overwhelm her, just give her the book and show her he was there as a support person when she needed it.

'Well, I'll get going,' he said. 'So glad you're okay, Ellie. See you when you get home.'

'Thanks for coming, and for the book.' She managed a weak wave until her hand flopped back on the bed.

He gave Martha a hug and whispered, 'I'm here for you too, anytime, anything. Just let me know.'

'Thanks, Nathan, and the roast chicken was delicious, I had it late last night.' She smiled.

He said another goodbye and left the room, pausing for a moment and taking a breath. If only he'd been able to visit Cooper in hospital, instead of attending his funeral. He was beyond grateful that the outcome with Ellie had been different.

He walked down the corridor, went down the lift, and

headed towards the entrance. A swish of strawberry-blonde hair caught his attention near the front door, as a woman wheeled a suitcase through and turned side to side as though wondering where to go.

Lacie! His heart somersaulted. He rushed towards her as she rummaged through her shoulder bag.

'Lacie!' This time he said it out loud as he neared the woman who'd captivated him over the past several months. Before she barely had a chance to register his approach, he held out his arms and wrapped them around her, and after a moment she did the same, but in a stiff kind of way. Her bag was between them and bumped into his body. He glanced down and realised it wasn't a bag, it was her belly.

Nathan froze and his mouth fell open. He released his arms and took a step back. His eyes met the worried gaze of Lacie's, and he stepped back again. 'You're pregnant? How far along?'

'Five months. Almost twenty-one weeks, actually.' She held out her hands feebly as though she was surprising him, which she most certainly was. 'I was going to–'

'You were already pregnant, when we first met?' He recalled the puking incident on the patio.

She nodded. 'But, I–'

'Why didn't you tell me?' He raised his hands in exasperation. 'Are you in a relationship with the father?'

'No, no.' She shook her head. 'He doesn't want anything to do with it. I only just found out when I came here in July, it was... unexpected and, I...' She glanced around as though trying to find the words.

'You didn't tell me, even though we were really hitting it off. I know it was online, but still, I was about to fly overseas for you!'

'I know, I know, and I feel terrible, but it just got out of hand. I didn't think "we" would go anywhere, so I didn't think you needed to know, at least at first. I was still deciding what to do.' Red rims framed her eyes. 'I kept going to tell you and then something would get in the way.'

Realisation dawned on Nathan. 'The other day, you were going to tell me? After I told you my travel hopes?'

'Yes, and then Ellie needed me.'

He thought about this for a moment, softened a little, then stiffened again. 'No, you should have told me much earlier before we got too close. Twenty-one weeks? You're already over halfway. Lacie,' he ran a hand over his head. 'I opened up to you, told you about my past, and even how my pregnant ex deceived me. Now here I am, another pregnant woman deceiving me.' His heart was pounding and he wondered if he really knew her at all. How could she have so many wonderful, fun and deep chats with him about their lives and not reveal such a significant thing?

'I just wanted to enjoy what we had, while we had it. Before you... wouldn't want it anymore.'

'How do you know I wouldn't want it? You didn't give me a chance to find out and process it. I know it was long distance but I thought we had a true, authentic connection. Didn't you think it was important enough to at least give me the heads-up?'

'You told me a few weeks ago to enjoy the moment, not have any serious discussions. Remember?'

He did say that, yes. But still. 'That doesn't mean you needed to avoid telling me something so important about your life.'

'Nathan, I'm sorry, but the right moment kept slipping away and before I knew it, it had got out of hand and I didn't know how to tell you. I liked you so much, still do, and even if it wasn't meant to last, I didn't want to risk spoiling what we had.' She glanced awkwardly at people walking past.

'Well you did, by not telling me.' He shook his head. 'Geez,

Lacie, I mean, I hope you and the baby are well and all, and I'm so glad Ellie is okay, but... trust and honesty is *very* important to me. I don't...' He tried to find the words, his body feeling drained now and worn out. He lowered his voice as a couple walked past them, out the door. 'I feel exposed, like I bared my soul but you didn't. I don't feel like I can trust you.'

His heart sunk and he turned away from her.

'Nathan, please, let's talk properly in private after I've seen Ellie.'

He turned to face her again, his jaw tight. 'No. We've talked enough. I think it's best we keep our distance and don't talk again.'

Her eyes welled with tears but he willed himself to turn around and walk out of the entrance instead of pulling her into his arms. It was time he took a stand against dishonesty in his life. No more.

CHAPTER TWENTY-EIGHT

Lacie was desperate to see Ellie and her mother, but wanted to be strong for her. She found a bathroom, thankfully empty, and allowed a few tears to flow. Not too many, then she'd be all red-faced and they would know something was up. She could contact Nathan later and try to talk to him again, explain in more detail about the past few months and how overwhelmed she was trying to make the right decisions. He was right though, he had bared his soul, and he didn't seem like he had done that with anyone in a long time, if at all. Somehow, he'd trusted her right away, and now that trust was ruined.

Oh, what a mess!

She splashed water on her face even though as a beauty therapist she never did such things, water dried out the skin, and her hydrating face mists were much better. But now was not a time for such minor concerns. She was tired and achy from the flight, and her heart was shaken up. She swiped on some berry tinted lip gloss and pressed her lips together. Dabbed a bit of concealer under her eyes, and took a confident breath and readied herself for seeing her sister.

She texted her mum to let her know she was on her way up to the ward, and when she reached the right level and stepped out of the elevator with her luggage, her mum was there waiting with open arms.

Lacie practically collapsed into her and, so much for freshening up in the bathroom, the tears started flowing again. 'I missed you.'

'Oh, my darling, look at you.' She placed her hands on Lacie's arms and stepped back, admiring her growing belly. 'I could have come down and helped you with your luggage.'

'No need. I'll have to get used to carrying a baby around soon enough.' She smiled. 'How is she? She's not asleep, is she?'

Martha shook her head. 'She's as well as can be, considering. Oh, Nathan was just here, did you happen to see him?'

'Yes, but we had a bit of an… anyway, that's a topic of conversation for another day. Can I see her now?'

Martha led Lacie and her luggage into Ellie's room.

Ellie tried to sit up, her tired grey eyes widening. 'Oh wow, you're really big now.'

'Hey, El, don't get up.' She went straight to her sister's side. 'Oh, Ellie.' She wiped her sister's hair from her forehead. 'I wish I'd called you that night. Wish I'd been able to help you.'

'You did, it's just… it was just too hard all at once. I'm so sorry.' She sobbed. 'And you came all this way! I've made a big mess of things.'

'No, no, you haven't. Family comes first, and I'm here because I want to be.' She sat on the side of the bed and hugged Ellie, whose tears moistened Lacie's cotton top.

'Everyone is being so supportive. Nathan even came and gave me a book he said might be helpful.'

Lacie eyed the book on the nearby table. Her heart rose up then plummeted. He was such a caring person and she'd let him down.

'I'm just so embarrassed,' Ellie whispered. 'I didn't mean, I mean, I didn't know...' Her eyes welled up again, and Martha joined Lacie at the bedside. Ellie looked Lacie and then her mother in the eye. 'I didn't want to die, I just wanted the pain to stop!' Tears burst forth and Lacie held her sister, trying to keep her own tears contained as her heart ached like never before. Martha rubbed Lacie's back with one hand while massaging Ellie's hand with the other.

'It's okay, sweetheart,' Martha said. 'We understand. You don't have to feel embarrassed or ashamed. And we're going to get you the right kind of help so you can find a way through all of this.'

'And we'll be with you every step of the way,' Lacie added.

Ellie nodded in appreciation and her sobs eventually subsided.

'Well,' Lacie said, 'I'm glad you have a book, because I found this at the airport.' She retrieved a bookmark from her bag and handed it to Ellie. It had encouraging words on it for those going through challenges.

'Thanks, Lace.'

Martha popped it inside the book, and told Lacie to sit on the chair next to the bed. 'I'll go get you something, love. Are you drinking coffee? Or tea, hot chocolate?'

'Hot chocolate, thanks, Mum.'

'Me too, Mum,' Ellie said. 'I think I'm allowed, as long as it's not too hot?'

'I'll check with the nurse on the way out. Ellie's on a special diet for a couple of days while she recovers,' she told Lacie.

Lacie felt a glimmer of hope that if her sister felt like a hot chocolate, it might also mean that she felt like she could move forward, heal, and focus on living. It was only now she recalled times when her sister had not seemed excited about certain special foods or drinks, or doing something fun, or seemed disinterested in general. Why hadn't she seen the signs?

'How long are you staying?' Ellie asked.

Lacie shrugged. 'Haven't thought that far ahead. My only focus was getting here. I'll have a think after a few days.'

'Thank you for coming.'

'I couldn't not. And anyway, I think our family reunion wasn't long enough, so I thought I'd fix that and get back on over here!'

'I'm glad you did,' said another voice at the doorway.

'Penny!' Lacie got up and embraced her other sister.

'Ooh!' She patted Lacie's belly. 'How beautiful.' Penny glanced at Ellie. 'You're looking much better than yesterday, El.'

She must have looked pretty bad, then, as Lacie had been pained to see her sister looking so drained today.

They chatted about less serious things for a while, had their hot chocolates when Martha returned, and Lacie yawned.

'I can take you back to South Haven for a rest soon if you like,' Penny said. 'I don't have to pick up the kids till later but happy to drive back whenever you need to, you must be exhausted from the flight.'

'It's okay, I can stay with Ellie.'

'No, you go rest, please,' Ellie said. 'I'll be fine, and I'll still be here tomorrow so you can come back then. You have my unborn niece or nephew to look after too.'

'True. I am tired. Okay then, I'll catch up on sleep and see you again soon.' She kissed her sister's forehead and hugged her mum, and walked out the door with Penny. She was reluctant to leave Ellie's side, but now that she'd seen her and was reassured she'd be all right, she did need to take care of herself too. Ellie wouldn't just bounce back, she knew that, but she hoped by being here she would garner strength from everyone's presence and support, and know that she was very much wanted in this world.

CHAPTER TWENTY-NINE

O n Friday afternoon the Appleby family were together
again at South Haven, barring Matt, Sophia, and Chris
who would arrive later in time for dinner. Ellie, who'd been
discharged from hospital yesterday, was slouching on the couch,
tapping her foot to music through her earbuds and reading *The
Wisdom of Nature* as though the past week had never
happened. Melina was helping Martha in the kitchen, Penny
was preparing the dining table, and Jessie and Dane were
building some kind of Lego creation in the nearby sitting room.
Lacie was seated on the armchair near the couch, feet on a
footstool, rubbing her belly as the baby wriggled and poked
gently beneath her skin, and she marvelled at how normal
everything seemed.

Conscious she'd need to book a flight home soon; her heart
was being pulled in two directions. There'd been such relief at
being back home and Ellie being okay, despite the fact she'd
need close monitoring and regular psychology sessions, as well
as a new sleep plan that didn't require sedatives. But Lacie had
also just started getting her life in order in Chicago, with
Madeleine almost qualified she'd be able to share the workload

at the salon and take over for a while to allow Lacie some maternity leave. The next step had been to get the baby equipment purchased and set up. Though she didn't have a spare room in her apartment, she'd planned on getting a co-sleeper bassinet so she could have the baby close to her, and she'd figure out the rest as time went on.

And then there was Nathan. She'd tried contacting him after visiting the hospital, but he hadn't replied until the next day, when he'd told her he was taking two weeks off and going on a vacation – to where, he didn't say. Sadness filled her heart... his vacation was originally going to be in Chicago, but now things had changed.

A squeal of laughter burst from Jessie as Dane did something funny with the Lego figures, and Lacie smiled. Penny was humming in the dining room, and Melina was talking to Martha about her upcoming fertility specialist appointment and how in preparation she had seen a naturopath, was eating healthier and taking a bucketload of supplements to improve her overall health and egg quality. Lacie was glad Melina seemed better emotionally, excited even, about her impending tests and treatments. Lacie knew she'd done the right thing, committing to being the mother of her own baby and letting Melina and Chris go on the journey that was theirs to take, while she took hers.

Her mum's phone rang and Lacie glanced in her direction. 'Yes, hello, Doctor.'

It must be one of Ellie's doctors, Lacie thought.

'Yes ... Uh-huh ... Oh, that is wonderful news, thanks so much for calling! ... Okay, will do. Bye!'

Martha put down the phone and placed her hand over her heart. Her eyes became red and shiny, and Melina stopped chopping vegetables and placed a hand on Martha's back. 'Are you okay?' she asked.

Martha nodded. Ellie took her earbuds out and straightened up, Penny poked her head through from the dining room, and Lacie got herself up and over to her mother.

'What was that about, Mum?' Lacie asked.

Martha took a deep breath. 'I didn't want to say anything because so much has happened and you're all going through your own things. I didn't want to worry you.'

Now Lacie was worried, although by the sounds of things whatever it was had been good news.

'I had a biopsy done last week for a suspicious breast lump.'

Penny came over to Martha as well. 'Mum, you should have told me. But it's all okay?'

She wiped a tear from her eye and nodded. 'Benign. I'm so grateful, oh my goodness.' She leaned on the kitchen counter and let it take half of her weight, and Melina rubbed her back.

Relief flooded Lacie's body, and she realised how caught up in her own life she'd been. When was the last time she actually asked her mother how she was? Yes, she had a growing baby to think about and care for, but the thought that two of her family members could have had tragic outcomes to their recent challenges made her feel guilty, like she should have been there for them more.

'Oh, Mum. I'm sorry you had to go through that waiting on your own,' Lacie said.

'I probably didn't help matters,' said Ellie, now up and walking over to them in the kitchen.

'Oh, sweetheart, don't you feel guilty or worry yourself.' She gestured for Ellie to come to her for an embrace. Five women standing in comfort and support of each other: a woman who'd been awaiting a potential diagnosis; a woman experiencing infertility; a pregnant single woman deliberating her future and her mistake; a woman juggling work and motherhood and a zillion volunteer roles; and a woman struggling emotionally who'd cheated death. No one should have to struggle on their own.

In that moment, clarity and purpose struck Lacie like lightning. 'That's it,' she said. 'I've made a decision.'

'Oh?' said her mother.

'I don't want to miss another moment of your lives. All of you.' She looked at each of them and cast a glance to Jessie and Dane who were still intensely focused on their Lego world. 'I'm moving back to Tarrin's Bay.' She couldn't help the wide smile that stretched automatically across her face, and she knew with all her heart she was making the right choice, again.

Her mother straightened up with a sudden burst of energy, her eyes wide. 'Oh my goodness! Are you sure? When? And with the pregnancy, how will you manage, I'm sure you can't fly after a certain time? Or will you wait till after the baby's born? But then it'll be harder and more to carry, and–'

'Mum, it's okay, I'll figure it all out! We'll work it out step by step, but for now, I think I should get back to Chicago and sort out my business and apartment, and get back here ASAP, before I reach the third trimester.' The plan was bittersweet, she'd miss her life and friends, but she also had a life and friends, and most importantly, family, here too. She could start again, this time as a mother, and could set up a new salon once the baby was older. The idea of having her family around during this life transition filled her with comfort, and also the fact that she could be there more easily for them, too.

'Are you sure you're not just doing this because of what happened?' Ellie asked. 'I don't want you to give up the life you created over there if you don't have to.'

Lacie draped an arm around her sister. 'I *want* to.'

'It might be hard to do everything on your own,' said Penny. 'I have an idea... if I can wing it, maybe I could come too? Help you sort everything out and carry your luggage and fly back with you?'

Lacie's heart leapt.

'That's a wonderful idea!' Martha beamed. 'I can help with the kids when Steve is working, they can stay here and he can come get them on his days off.'

Penny looked relieved, her shoulders lowering. 'That'd be great. I'll need to run it by him of course, logistically and financially, but I don't think it'll be an issue.'

'I can help with the kids here and there also,' said Melina with a smile. 'And my girls would love to spend some more time with them too.'

'I can help with costs,' Lacie said.

'I can too,' said Martha. 'Whatever's needed, we'll figure it out.'

'Then it's official. I'll have a look at flights for us, Penny, if you can arrange time off work at short notice?'

She nodded. 'I know a relief teacher who will probably be able to take over. I'll contact the school and let them know. Oh, I'm going to miss my kids,' she whispered, 'but hopefully the enticement of them staying here, Mum, will ease any worry.'

'I'll make it worth their while. Lots of ice cream, movies, and Lego of course.' She smiled.

'Can I...' Ellie said softly. 'Can I come too?'

'To Chicago?' Martha said, her brows creasing.

Would she be up for it?

'I've never seen any other part of the world, and I always thought I'd visit Lacie one day but forgot about it when my life got crazy, and now this is the last chance I'll get.'

'Well, it's not the last chance, you can do anything and go anywhere you want in your life, El, but if Mum thinks it's okay, and your doctor, then I can't think of anything better than a girls' trip together.'

Martha twisted her lips to the side. 'Okay. We'll ask the doctor on Monday at your check-up, and the psychologist, and I'm sure knowing you'll be with your sisters and not on your own it shouldn't be a problem. It might be good for you.'

Ellie smiled, properly for the first time in a long while, and Lacie's chin trembled, her baby wriggling beneath as though excited too. 'Oh my God, it's really happening. We're going to the States together, and I'm coming back here to live, and,' she patted her belly, 'I'm having a baby!' It was as though she finally realised, and burst into tears.

The women hugged and a few tears were shed, and Lacie felt more at home here and now, than she'd ever felt before.

CHAPTER THIRTY

Dear Baby,

Guess what? I've decided to move back to Australia and start a new life with you. You'll get to be around family all the time, and play with your cousins. I'm on the plane right now to Chicago so I can pack up my life there and begin anew. Lucky I remembered to bring my journal to Australia. Aunt Penny and Ellie are with me, they're so excited! And can you believe it? You're not even born yet and by the time you are, you'll already have had five international flights under your belt! (My most precious cargo.)

Maybe one day when you're older we'll fly back to Chicago together and you can meet my friends and see where I used to live. We could even organise a trip to Disneyland!

There are so many fun things we'll do. What you'll love about Tarrin's Bay is going to the beach and making sandcastles, visiting the country fair to go on rides and see the baby animals, playing at the playground in Miracle Park, going to the ice-cream shop, getting new books from Mrs May's Bookstore, and so much more. I grew up in the Town of New Beginnings and now I'm coming home to it.

Soon, I'm going to watch a movie on the plane. I can't wait to watch movies with you too. Your Grandma Martha pitched in and got us all premium economy tickets so I can recline my seat a bit more and raise my legs a bit, which is good as last flight my ankles got a bit swollen. I'm also wearing these very attractive support socks to keep my blood circulating!

It's all happening so fast now, and I'm looking forward to getting everything all set up for your arrival. Don't come too soon, okay? I want you to be as healthy as possible.

I can't wait to meet you and give you a name.

Until then, keep growing.

Love, Mum xo (Still getting used to that name!)

CHAPTER THIRTY-ONE

Nathan dumped his backpack on his bed and sighed loudly, rubbing the back of his neck then wincing. He went to the bathroom, took off his T-shirt, and surveyed his sunburn. A red curve ran along his upper back, and he had red sleeves to match. His face wasn't too bad as he'd worn a hat, but he mustn't have reapplied sunscreen as often as he should've. He rummaged through his bathroom cabinet and found an old tube of aloe vera gel that he'd often apply after gardening in the summer months. It had a tiny bit left, so he lathered it on and added it to his shopping list on his phone, along with all the other supplies he'd need after being away for two weeks.

It was good to be home. Queensland had been amazing, though hot. Days at the beach in Surfers Paradise, walks in the rainforest, and feeling away from the world in the Gold Coast hinterland. He'd hiked, biked, swam, scuba dived, camped, and connected to nature, had also enjoyed the magical sight of a glow worm cave. He'd even been hit on by a woman at one of the rainforest camps who'd been holidaying with friends, but romance was not part of his itinerary. It was a bit different to what he would have done had he visited Chicago, but that was a way off thought that was now gradually dissolving.

He'd have to start doing some more work at South Haven soon, though it wasn't as full on as before, and he'd also be balancing that with maintenance on the primary school grounds, a one-off job to create a water feature and barbeque area for one of the teacher's homes, plus a seasonal tidy up at Gloria's which he'd start in December (he'd told her to keep paying the 'young chap down the road' to do the lawn mowing). He'd also confided in Gloria about his failed attempt to visit the States and pursue things with Lacie, but put it down to the fact that she was about to become a mother rather than revealing her omittance of that detail as their 'friendship' had progressed to something more.

At least he wouldn't have to see her at South Haven. It would be awkward if she was there all the time while he worked. He loved the Appleby family, and he'd checked up on Ellie a couple of times after her leaving hospital, but had said he'd be away for two weeks and would check back in when he returned. After three weeks since Ellie's emergency, Lacie would surely have returned back to Chicago by now. The thought filled him with both relief and sadness. Relief that he could move on and focus on his work, and sadness that he didn't get to experience a joyful reunion like he'd hoped for. One quick hug was all they'd shared, and then nothing but an argument.

He knew an unexpected pregnancy must've been a difficult thing for her to comprehend, but she'd had plenty of time to wrap her head around it and tell him, it wasn't that hard to say, 'Hey, I love this close connection that's developed, but thought I'd let you know that I'm pregnant, so if that changes anything, I understand.' That was all she'd had to do. And yes, she may have tried to tell him or been about to, but she didn't, and by the time she was *really* going to, their connection had already grown much deeper. He felt deceived, like he'd just been a simple online flirtation to fill the time before her baby's birth. He didn't feel safe trusting her, especially when a baby was involved.

Nathan heated up a frozen meal for dinner and waited for the microwave to beep. *Sorry, Nigella, my inner chef is off duty.* He scrolled social media mindlessly on his phone, and there it was: Lacie's pregnancy announcement. She was right, she didn't post much, her last post had been 'I'm back in beautiful Australia!' in July, and nothing since. This one was from a week ago and simply had a photo of her rosy cheeked smile, her hands lovingly holding the base of her blooming belly, and the words: 'Baby on the way, due in Feb!' and pink and blue love heart emojis followed by a question mark. Only recently she had kept it a secret, and now she was announcing it to the world.

He ignored how beautiful she looked and reminded himself of how many times they had video chatted and he had not seen it. Presumably she hadn't had much to show until the last few weeks, but she still knew. He recalled their dinner/breakfast date and tipped his head back in realisation at how she'd seemed reluctant to stand up and show him her outfit, after he had shown her his tie and shirt combined with casual shorts. She had been wearing a long flowing scarf which would have covered any evidence of pregnancy. No wonder she'd also seemed a bit taken aback when he'd suggested he fly over to see her. He shook his head. First time in years he'd opened the door to his heart and now he didn't know how to close it. But he wouldn't let it get in the way of the friendship he'd developed with her family.

He scrolled through his text message list and texted Martha:

Hi Martha, I'm back and will be there on
Wednesday, text me what needs to be done.
How's Ellie?

While waiting, he chuckled at all the 'older' ladies he was in contact with: Martha, Gloria, the teacher from school, and the school secretary. His gaze then fell on Tess's name. She hadn't responded any further, maybe she'd given up. He read through their last few messages, mostly from her, and sighed. What had led her to such deception? They had been great together for the most part. He knew she never had the best relationship with her family and so communication and conflict resolution had never been her strong point, but she always tried her best. But her taking some space for herself did not mean they had broken up, at least that's what he'd assumed.

It was a bit Ross and Rachel from *Friends*, but he was sure they had not been on a break. And when she'd returned from her time away as keen and eager as ever as though nothing had happened, his assumptions were proven correct. But she had cheated, and had obviously been trying to make up for it, and perhaps she was in denial that he wasn't the baby's father, which led to all the lies. Maybe there was some protective hormone that caused pregnant women to do whatever was necessary to look after themselves, even if it wasn't honest. Tess had lied to hopefully give her child a happy mother and father in a stable relationship, and Lacie had kept a secret to prolong a budding romance she didn't want to risk losing.

Why did he have to be caught in the middle of such things? If he really wanted to close that door to his heart, he knew that he would probably need to speak to Tess at some point. Not that he had to, but it might be the only way for her to get things off her chest and for him to get closure, otherwise she'd keep contacting him out of the blue and destroying his peace.

A text from Martha came in:

> Welcome back! Sounds good, I'll check what the priorities are and text you tomorrow. Ellie's doing well, it'll be an ongoing journey but she's feeling much better. She's been away but getting back on Wednesday, so you might get to see her.

He sent a thumbs up in reply. He didn't ask where she'd been as she might be at some sort of healing retreat, and he didn't want to pry.

He scrolled back down to Tess's message. And before he could stop himself, he typed:

> Hey, if you still want to, I'm open to having a chat, give you a chance to say what you want to say.

The typing bubbles appeared immediately, and then her message:

> Hey, I thought I'd never hear from you. Thank you, I really appreciate it. Can we meet in person tomorrow? Maybe the playground at Miracle Park, so Neo can play while we talk?

He was free on Sunday and Monday, returning to work at the school on Tuesday.

> Sure. What time suits?

> 2pm?

> See you then.

There, all done. One conversation and then he could move

on for good. As for Lacie, he couldn't imagine talking to her right now would do any good.

The sun beamed through the gaps in the branches of the overhead tree as he took a seat on the bench near the playground. He scanned the area but couldn't see Tess anywhere, but he was a bit early. Children laughed and climbed and slid and ran, all big smiles and wild hair, the refreshing afternoon breeze visiting the park.

He wondered if he would have a child of his own one day, maybe then he could give them the stable home he never had, and it would somehow give him a sense of greater purpose and belonging. Or maybe he was destined to be on his own forever: him, his plants, and... he needed an animal. He loved watching the birds that frequented his garden, but they weren't exactly pets and he didn't like the idea of having a bird in a cage – they were meant to be free. A dog might be more work than he could manage at this stage, but a cat... perhaps that would be the best choice, something that would look after itself most of the time, but would provide some company in the evenings. He opened his phone browser to search for cat rescue shelters. He didn't want a newborn kitten, he wasn't home much and they would be too much work in the early stages, so an older cat or kitten might be best. He scrolled through the options then heard the husky voice that had once captivated him...

'Long time no see.'

He glanced up and pocketed his phone. 'Tess. Hi.' He forced a slight smile, and then eyed the toddler holding her hand. 'Hi there. Neo, I presume?'

'Say hi to Nathan,' Tess said in a high-pitched voice he wasn't used to hearing.

The dark-haired boy simply huddled close to his mum, gripping her leg.

'Look at the fun things on the playground,' she said, pointing. 'How about you go and play while I talk to Nathan, and afterwards, we'll get some ice cream!'

The boy's eyes lit up and he dashed towards the small slippery slide.

Tess reached her hand out briefly then lowered it, as though she wasn't sure how to greet him. She sat next to him, her wavy brown hair wafting loosely in the breeze. 'Thanks for coming.' She looked him briefly in the eye then returned her gaze to the playground. Meeting here was probably much better than having to look each other in the eye over a meal at a restaurant. But he gathered she probably didn't wine and dine much these days if she had no one to babysit.

Nathan nodded and said, 'So, how's motherhood?'

Her posture relaxed a little and she smiled. 'It's great, difficult, but great. I've learned a lot since he was born, it's given me patience I never knew I had. It's also made me realise how fast time goes.' A fly buzzed past and she waved it away.

'It sure does. So, ah, is he still seeing his dad?' Nathan asked, gesturing to Neo who seemed to be enjoying his tenth slide.

'Yeah. We've finally worked out the details, so he's mostly with me since I'm not working at the moment, and he sees him on weekends.'

'That's good. A child needs stability, it doesn't matter if things aren't perfect.'

She turned slightly towards him. 'Like you needed, huh?'

'Yeah.' She knew all about his past and his grief, which had felt good at the start, like someone really knew him, but then it just felt like another abandonment when she'd cheated.

'I really am sorry,' she said gently. 'Part of me wishes I could turn back time but then I wouldn't have Neo, so I wouldn't want to. But if I could,' she exhaled, 'I'd turn back time and tell you the truth from the start. It still would have hurt you, but you could have moved on sooner. I'm sorry for wasting your time and leading you on with my dishonesty.' She lowered her head, then looked up at Neo and waved when he had climbed to the top of a climbing frame.

Nathan's tension softened too. She had done him wrong, and she *had* apologised back then, but more in a state of desperation. For some reason it had never seemed authentic until now. He could feel the regret seeping from her heart, and as a hint of some kind of fruity perfume danced around him, she placed her hand on top of his. He flinched a little but didn't pull his hand away.

'I actually think I had depression for a while, before it all happened,' she confessed. 'The conflicts in my family were overwhelming, and I felt alone, apart from being with you of course. But the more I tried to be happy the more fake it felt, so it was easier to retreat and pull away. Putting a mask on my face every day was exhausting.' She ran her free hand through her hair. 'I'm sorry I didn't open up to you. I thought it would bring you down, so I tried to deal with it in my own way. Unfortunately, that led me to needing comfort somehow, and my ex was there, right place right time kinda thing. It was silly, I know. But here we are now. I regret it, but at the same time it was the best thing that ever happened, as I have Neo.'

Nathan's mind flipped back like a book with its pages going back to the beginning, and he could recognise some of the signs in hindsight... she'd found it hard to get out of bed most days, she'd wanted to stay home instead of going out, and she never wanted to participate in small talk whereas she used to be a chatterbox. Little things that showed her state of mind was altering. But he wasn't a mind reader, and he simply didn't know it'd been that bad for her. And it was no excuse for cheating and lying... but he did understand things a bit more now. Maybe she had learned her lesson and changed, she certainly seemed different, more mature and settled.

'I'm sorry you went through such a difficult time. I really didn't know. I would have been okay if you'd wanted to talk about it, or get some help.'

'I know that now, but with my family cutting me off, I was worried you might do the same. After the pregnancy test I clung to our relationship like a life raft, but it was still sinking. I couldn't live with the guilt, so I had to leave. And by then, my ex had come to terms with the idea of being a father and had wanted to see how things went. I couldn't lose the chance of giving my child a complete family.' Her voice faltered and her eyes became shiny with unshed tears. She gripped his hand a little tighter, and he let her. It was good that she was getting an opportunity to let all this out, and he was glad to finally have more of an explanation. It didn't fix things, but it helped.

'I've missed you,' she confessed. 'I don't expect you to forgive me, but...'

'I forgive you,' he whispered, unsure whether he had even spoken the words aloud. Immediately, his heart became lighter.

Her body jolted a little. 'You do? Oh my God, you don't know what it means to hear that.' She held a hand to her forehead in relief, and she inhaled a sharp and shaky breath as though she was trying to hold back a sob. She looked at the playground as Neo ran around the climbing frame in circles, and laughed. 'Always doing things his own way, that boy.'

Nathan managed a smile. Something softened inside him and he felt something he hadn't felt for years... a connection, a longing. They'd shared a lot of happy times together, and he missed that. Missed having someone to go through the daily ups and downs of life with.

Tess turned to face him on the bench and looked him right

in the eyes. 'I don't know if there's the slightest chance, but if there is, I want nothing more than to try again. To do things right this time. Complete honesty, no holding back. We were great together, and could be again.' She leaned close to him, and her warmth was intoxicating, blurring his vision, making his head feel foggy and out of focus. She'd had that effect on him back then, and he was surprised that a remnant of it was still there.

All he wanted to do was lean towards her too, and he found himself doing so automatically, until their foreheads rested together and his eyes closed at the light touch he'd once known so intimately. She lifted her head slightly and he could feel her lips wanting his, and if only in that moment, he wanted hers too. Before she could kiss him, he pulled away. He drew a deep, steadying breath. Her eyes showed a yearning for him but his foggy vision was clearing, and he knew the nostalgia was not sustainable. He would always remember her deceit, and despite her apology and explanation and his forgiveness, it was more to bring himself peace than to allow them to start again.

Nathan cleared his throat. 'Sorry, Tess. I can't do this.' He glanced at Neo who was now digging in the sandpit with another boy. The boy would be okay. Tess would be okay. He would be okay.

He stood. It was time to be strong in himself and stand his ground. He deserved to be treated fairly, and though he understood how one thing had led to another with Tess and her mistake, he knew they couldn't start again. But *he* could. On his own, like always.

CHAPTER THIRTY-TWO

'Well, I guess that's it,' Lacie said with a sigh, scanning her bare apartment. 'Lucky we've got a hotel booked for tonight before the flight home, I don't fancy sleeping on that skeletal bed frame.' She chuckled. They'd cleared the apartment of everything but the furniture and appliances, and the estate agent had already lined up a renter to move in next week as it was such a popular building that hardly ever had vacancies.

'I'd join you for a farewell dinner at the hotel tonight if I could, but the opening of the new exhibition at the museum is pretty important to my husband, so I better be there with him!' Madeleine smiled but her eyes looked teary. She'd helped Lacie and her sisters pack up the apartment over the past couple of days and take various items to goodwill, not to mention finalising the legal and logistical details of the salon she'd be taking over in the new year. Madeleine had bought the business off Lacie, thanks to the help of her savings, a small loan, and her husband's promotion bonus at work. She'd be able to see Lacie's clients who wanted to stay, and find new clients as well. Maria Elvarez had shed a few tears at her last appointment with Lacie, after she'd booked in a few last-chance appointments for her extra special regulars. She didn't have time to see everyone, but she had sent them all a thank-you letter and small gift in the mail, also thanks to Madeleine's assistance.

'Thanks, Maddy, I don't know what I would have done without you.' Lacie embraced her ex-employee and her eyes welled up. 'I'm going to miss working with you.' She sniffled. 'Make sure you send me updates and keep me posted on your new beauty menu when you're ready to start.'

'I will. And I want all the baby spam, please.'

Lacie smiled. 'Thanks for everything. And good luck!'

Maddy gave her a kiss on the cheek then turned to Ellie and Penny. 'Nice to meet you!' She hugged them both, and blew a kiss as she exited the apartment.

Lacie sighed. She'd said all her goodbyes now. She'd seen Rosie this morning and Lulu yesterday, plus some other friends she knew from the industry. Now it was just her and her sisters, then back home to her family, and the new member yet to arrive.

Apart from the chaos of packing up her life in two weeks, they'd also found time to enjoy Chicago's best offerings together, making many happy memories. Penny had loved the art gallery and Ellie the library. Each of them had also had to buy a coat as the chilly air had reared its head now they were in November, and one wasn't usually needed in Tarrin's Bay. Lacie had enjoyed playing tourist with her sisters, it had been a while since she'd first explored the city.

'I can't believe I've reduced my life to this one suitcase, plus the few extra things I squeezed into both of yours!' She grasped her large pink suitcase by the handle.

'Goes to show we don't need much in life,' Ellie said. 'There was something in that *Wisdom of Nature* book about that, like getting back to basics, simplicity, that sort of thing.'

'It'll be good to start again. Think of all the new clothes and beauty supplies I can buy once I'm back. After I've made use of my maternity fashion collection that is!'

'Speaking of buying things,' Penny interjected. 'We need to go shopping back home for all the baby things you'll need. I wish I hadn't sold all of my kids' things!'

'Let's all go together,' Ellie suggested.

'Great idea. And maybe we should have a regular "sisters only" outing every month or so. We need to keep connected, all of us.' Lacie eyed Ellie mostly. 'And no keeping secrets. If something's bothering us, we talk about it. Yeah?'

Ellie nodded. She'd had a psychology session via Zoom while she'd been in Chicago. Penny and Lacie had left her in the apartment for some privacy while they grabbed a coffee at a local café. 'Well, you know all my secrets now, but what about yours?' Ellie placed her hands on her hips.

'Me?' Lacie placed her hand on her heart as if she didn't have any. 'You obviously know I'm pregnant, so...'

'C'mon. Anything else?'

She gulped. 'With everything that happened I didn't want to talk about my own stuff. But Nathan is really upset with me. And so I've been upset about that.' Lacie sat at the dining table chair. 'After I went back in July, we stayed in contact and ended up texting and chatting almost every day. It was a welcome distraction from all the uncertainty I was going through. Anyway, I don't know how it happened but we got really close, probably because we'd already kissed back in Tarrin's Bay before I left, and—'

'Wait, you kissed?' Penny's eyes widened.

'Yeah, yeah, anyway...' She dismissed it with a wave of her hand. 'Obviously it couldn't go anywhere, so we kinda went with the flow and enjoyed some harmless flirtation, even a dinner-slash-breakfast video date complete with bling. We also talked serious stuff, about his past and his ex, and the family he never had, that sort of thing. But every time I went to tell him I was pregnant something stopped me. At first it was because I wasn't yet twelve weeks and we all know it's usual to wait till the second trimester to share the news, but then when that had passed, I thought I'd wait till twenty weeks to make sure everything was okay with the baby, and then tell everyone basically. But that was when...' she glanced at Ellie, 'and it wasn't appropriate, and I had to book an urgent flight, and he'd only just told me he wanted to fly to Chicago to see me and find out if anything was worth pursuing.'

Penny and Ellie stood frozen to the spot, mouths agape.

'You both okay?' Lacie asked.

'You've been holding that in quite a while, haven't you?' Penny said.

'I feel so bad, it's just I didn't think it would keep going, and with my impending motherhood I wanted to enjoy what I had while I had it, before he disappeared, like Xavier.' She lowered her head. 'Selfish, I know. I don't know if he'll ever forgive me.'

'Did he find out at the hospital?' Penny asked.

Lacie nodded. 'I bumped into him on the way in, and he, well, noticed my bump. I had already asked him if we could meet up after I settled in, so I could tell him and explain, but didn't expect to see him like that without warning.'

'Guess you both got a bit of a shock,' Ellie mused. 'I can understand why you hesitated to tell him, but he's a great guy, and if you were getting closer, you should have just told him, sis.'

Lacie's cheeks warmed. 'I know. How can I fix it?'

'You can't,' said Penny. 'You can only apologise and wait for him to process it all, see how he feels after a while.'

'Thing is, he already had trust issues, when...' She bit her lip, not sure if she should reveal Nathan's past. Oh, what the hell. 'When his ex lied to him, saying he was the father of her baby, when he wasn't.'

'Oh man,' said Penny. I'd sensed he was a bit of a lone wolf, always out and about on his own, but didn't know the reason why. He's obviously been holding back in the love department. Until he met you.'

Lacie nodded. 'He was so open with me, and I was too in some ways, but I left out this one little detail.' She pinched her thumb and forefinger together. 'Now he's probably closed himself off completely and will never trust a woman ever again, let alone me.'

'Silver lining,' Ellie said, 'if he does forgive you, and does want to pursue something more than friendship, there's no longer the Pacific Ocean between you.'

Lacie smiled. 'True. But I won't hold my breath.'

'Just focus on the baby right now, that's going to keep you busy for about the next...' Penny tapped her temple. 'Oh, eighteen years or so!'

Lacie stood and embraced her sisters. Penny was right. This was what was most important right now – her baby, and her sisters, her family. They would be closer now than ever before, in more than just locality. 'Oh, Penny, you haven't shared one of your secrets with us.'

Penny shook her head. 'I don't think I have any.'

'There must be something,' Ellie probed with a nudge in her ribs.

Penny glanced up at the ceiling, umming and ahhing. 'Well,' she gathered them close, 'there is one thing... when Steve is on night shift and the kids are in bed, sometimes I dance around naked in my bedroom and sing karaoke to eighties music.'

Lacie went to speak but nothing came out.

'What the?' Ellie said.

Penny burst out laughing. 'I'm joking!'

'Oh,' Lacie said, 'had me worried for a minute. That's a sure sign of needing more fun in your life!'

'But,' Penny said, 'you know what? As much as I love my husband, and I'd be happy to dance around naked in the bedroom with him if he so desired, I actually love it when he's not home! I can watch a movie without him channel surfing, I can eat the whole block of chocolate without having to share, and I can get a good night's sleep without hearing him snore or kicking me with his restless legs.'

Lacie and Ellie laughed. 'That's hilarious, enjoy those nights when you can! I don't need a husband for the kicking part, I've got a little kicker right here!' Lacie patted her belly. 'Oh look...' She grabbed Penny's hand to feel the baby moving.

Ellie placed her hand there too. Slight rolls and movements rippled in her belly, and Ellie blinked out a few tears. 'This little one is going to help keep me going,' she whispered.

Lacie placed her hand on top of Ellie's and bit back a sob. Having this baby was going to be a blessing in more ways than one.

CHAPTER THIRTY-THREE

'See you later, my beautiful Lady,' Nathan said as he walked out his front door on Wednesday, ready to head to South Haven to start preparing the space for the gazebo that would be delivered and constructed on Friday. His new cat, a one-year-old tortoiseshell tabby, eyed him with a suspicious glare. He'd spent yesterday evening curled up with Lady on the couch, and now she was having to get used to being at home by herself on weekdays. He'd picked her up from the shelter on Monday, after knowing instantly she was the one for him – his petmate. Pets were so much easier than humans. She would be exactly what he needed for some company at home without the drama. He'd also suggested to Gloria that she get one, after sending her a photo and asking her when would suit for him to do an interview about her memorial garden.

His steering wheel hot on his hands from the sun, he decided he'd have to start using the windscreen shade, as he tried to steer with only minimal grip on the wheel. The air con blasting, it soon cooled down, and when he got to South Haven he covered the windscreen and unloaded his supplies for the day. Before getting started, he'd be checking around the yard for any bee swarms that sometimes happened at this time of year, since he hadn't been here for a while, he wanted to make sure.

After surveying the property and wondering if or when Martha would pop out to say hello, he noticed the step out the back where Ellie had sat, and had an idea. He gathered some small pebbles from around the firepit and took them to the step. He arranged them into a small heart shape and smiled. Next time she sat in her father's thinking spot, she'd see it and it'd hopefully bring a smile to her face. It reminded him too that he would have to ask Penny's permission to interview Jessie about her pebble family tree garden to add to his YouTube channel. There were so many fun things on his to-do list that he wouldn't have time to feel down about his recent disappointments. Life was going to be even greater, starting now.

When he went to the small storage shed at the front of the house to get the mower, the crunch of pebbles sounded on the driveway and he peeked through the wrought-iron gate. A shiny black vehicle approached. The side panel said Bay Airport Transfers. *It must be Ellie!* Hopefully being away had helped her in some way.

Martha appeared as she stepped off the front steps, her arms outstretched. The driver, then Ellie, hopped out of the car. Ellie ran into her mother's arms, and then Penny got out. Of course, they wouldn't have let Ellie travel on her own after her recent hospital admission. She turned and leaned into the car, helping someone else out. Lacie. With a bulging belly that looked larger than before.

Nathan's heart sank. Just when he'd got his head straight. He thought she would have returned home by now, but maybe they'd had a little interstate trip together and then she'd be heading back overseas before she got too far along.

Ellie noticed him peeking through the gate and she glanced

briefly at Lacie before coming over. She must know what had happened between him and Lacie.

'Nathan! Hey, dude.' She opened the gate, high-fiving him, and he gave her a quick hug.

'You're looking so much better,' he said.

'Thanks. I'll probably be feeling the jet lag later though, an international flight is no easy thing! But I've finished the book you gave me, it was awesome.'

'Oh great. Did you say international flight?'

'Yeah, was amazeballs. Chicago's getting cold now so lucky we didn't go in December.'

Chicago. So why did Lacie come back?

Lacie eyed him and gave a curt nod, and Martha waved to him and turned back to her daughter to help with her luggage.

'Must've been a great experience for you.' He kept eyeing the front of the house. Ellie turned around.

'Oh, Lacie is moving back here. Permanently. So we went to help her sell her business and pack up her entire life and fit it into one suitcase. Was chaotic but we managed to do it in time.'

'Wow, okay. It'll be good for you to have her around.'

'Yeah, can't wait to have a sibling back in the house again. We'll probably stay up way too late watching movies and eating ice cream. She has that effect on me!'

Nathan gave a small smile. He understood how that would be true, with Lacie's playful nature. But... he wouldn't allow himself to think of her like that, he wouldn't let her climb back into his mind and heart. He felt like he'd just been an amusing way for her to pass the time while her baby grew. And he wouldn't let himself get sucked into the uncertainties of romance again anytime soon.

Lacie had wanted to run over and wrap her arms around him (as best as she could with her cumbersome load). It was agonising to see him and not be able to touch him, talk to him, laugh with him. If she'd told him from the start, she could have been giving him a friendly hello and high five like Ellie had. She'd seen the surprise in his eyes, and sadly, the hurt. He probably thought she had flown back to Chicago by now.

Lacie flopped on the couch in the lounge room as her mum set down a tray of tea and biscuits. 'Can I have a cold drink, please, Mum, I'm boiling.' Lacie flapped the neckline of her top to fan her skin.

'Of course.' Martha brought her an orange juice.

'Oh my God, it's so good to lay back.' Lacie leaned back into the corner of the couch and peeled off her circulation stockings. 'So glad to get these things off. Ew!' Her feet were hot and sweaty, slightly swollen from the flight though not as much as when she'd flown without them.

Martha grasped them. 'Into the wash they go.' She disappeared into the laundry then returned.

'Sorry, Mum, I would have done that, but it might take me several hours to get up.' She smiled. Being around her family would help take her mind off Nathan, except when she could see him outside.

Ellie flopped next to Lacie and Penny helped her mother wheel the luggage into the hallway to take to the rooms later. 'Thanks, everyone, for the trip,' Ellie said.

'Did you have fun?' asked Martha.

'The best. I even tried putting on an American accent when I went into some of the stores downtown, it was hilarious.'

'Especially when you forgot for a moment and went back to your Aussie accent and then to American again.' Lacie laughed.

'It's good to see your sense of humour thriving.' Martha sat on the armchair.

'I wish I could pick up the kids from school and preschool now!' Penny stood as though too excited to sit.

'They missed you, let me tell you,' Martha said. 'But they had a ball here too. I'm going to miss having them around so much!'

'Did you miss Steve too, Pen, or are you looking forward to a little... *karaoke* tonight?' Ellie said in a sing-song voice, and Penny's cheeks went pink.

'Oh, stop,' Penny said.

'What are you two going on about?'

'Nothing,' they both said.

'Anyway,' Martha said, 'your rooms are all clean and fresh, new sheets, and Lacie, I know you'll probably want the baby in with you, but I also started clearing out the old office near your room. I thought it might make a good room for the baby? Once he or she is ready for a big cot, that is. No rush, but we might as well get it ready before the big day.'

'Thanks, Mum, sounds like a plan. And I promise I won't live here forever. Just when you thought you were close to an empty nest, and suddenly I'm back and bringing an extra human with me!'

Martha grinned. 'I can't think of anything better.'

'I thought we might go shopping on the weekend for baby things,' said Penny. 'First things first, you'll need a car seat.'

'Oh yes.' She looked at her mum. 'I wasn't sure whether to get my own car or...'

'Use mine. No need to spend even more money just yet. Later on if you get a car we can transfer the car seat. At least living here, you can walk to most places. A good pram will be your best friend.' Martha gave a knowing nod. 'Do you want me to come, or mind the kids?' She looked at Penny.

'It's okay, Steve is off on Saturday so we can go then. You probably need a break too.'

Martha shrugged. Lacie realised that her mum had been mothering for quite a number of years now, and babysitting grandchildren, and probably didn't know how to really take a break. 'Yeah, you should go get pampered at a nice salon. Hmm, speaking of which, I wonder if Tarrin's Bay needs a new beauty therapist.' Not that she'd be able to start anything up yet. She would think about options and make a plan to return to some kind of work part time when the right moment came once the baby was a bit older. She thought she could do some mobile wedding make-up on weekends at first, having the weekdays with her baby, before committing to anything more permanent.

As though reading her mind, Martha said, 'Another thing I was thinking... yes, I've done a lot of thinking while you lot have been gallivanting overseas, is that perhaps the old guest cottage could be repurposed into a beauty salon? If you wanted to return to running a business eventually, that is.'

'Wow, you are thinking ahead, Mum,' said Penny. 'But what a great idea!'

'Mum, are you sure you don't want to use it again as guest accommodation, for income?'

Martha shook her head. 'Been there done that. I want all of South Haven to be for our family to enjoy and make use of. No point having an empty cottage. It would make a perfect and discreet little salon with its separate entrance on the side road. I could be your business partner. And I could look after the baby, or toddler by that stage possibly, right here while you work. I may be getting older but I've still got some oomph left in me yet.' She raised her bicep muscle and they all laughed. 'Give me a free facial every month and we're even.' She winked.

Excitement bubbled up inside Lacie. 'I think that might be the best opportunity I could have wished for.' She made herself get up off the couch and went over to her mum, wrapping her in a hug. 'Thank you for welcoming me back. I feel like I never left.'

Relief swept through her body like a cooling ocean breeze. She wouldn't have to worry about how she'd cope as a single mother alone in her Chicago apartment. She'd have her family with her every step of the way. So there was no father around for the baby, but maybe that was easier in some ways. She may have ruined her chance with Nathan, but she wouldn't ruin the chance she'd been given to become a damn good mother.

CHAPTER THIRTY-FOUR

Dear Baby,

Won't be long before I get to call you by your actual name! I have a few ideas, but I'm going to wait until I know whether you're a boy or a girl, and wait till I see you so I can get a feeling for which name suits you. Whatever it is, I hope you like the name I choose. Don't worry, it won't be something horrendously embarrassing when you're at school!

I wanted to write today to say how excited I am that your room is all set up. It took us a few weeks to get everything, put things together, repaint, and decorate. But it looks beautiful. We've also revamped my room, as that's where you'll be for the first six months or so. I want to have you close by me as you sleep so I can keep an eye on you. I hope I don't snore and wake you up!

Here at South Haven, there's a wonderful garden to play in. Someone very clever helped to create it, and I know you're going to love exploring, running around, and maybe setting up little farm animal figurines in the dirt like I did as a kid. Only it's mostly grass now. It's become like a magical wonderland, with trees, colourful flowers, pebbles and fairies, birds and butterflies, and places to sit to relax in the great outdoors. The only thing missing is a pool! Maybe I can persuade Grandma Martha to add one, though there's not much space left. One day we might move into our own place, but for now, South Haven will be our home, as it has always been mine, even when I lived somewhere else for a while.

I'm going to start taking things a bit easier now, to rest my body in preparation for your birth. I've been doing special exercises and meditations. It's like training for a marathon! I've been told motherhood is a bit like one. But in this one, I'll be a winner without fail.

I'm also starting to think about my future career plans, to earn income and look after us for a long time. Your grandma and I are going to create a beauty salon at South Haven where I can work part time when you're a bit older. That way I won't be far away and I can see you on my lunch break! Grandma thinks I should call it Beauty Haven, but I have another idea. I'm not telling anyone though until I'm ready to put the sign up.

Life is always such an adventure, and I want you to know that you can always start afresh anytime you want to. Don't be afraid to take a risk and follow your heart to what feels right. I have, and it led me back home. Family is so important, and I'm so glad you are going to become part of it.

Love, Mum xo

CHAPTER THIRTY-FIVE

'Holy cow, not again!' Lacie heaved herself up from the wicker chair on the patio, creaking under her weight, as she went for yet another trip to the bathroom. She was barely sleeping at all now, needing to get up every two hours, and then not being able to get comfortable in bed despite five pillows in various positions and a fluffy mattress topper. Last night her back had been aching and waking her up too.

When she returned to the patio, she opened her notebook where she was jotting down ideas for the beauty services and packages she'd offer in her new salon. It wouldn't be for quite a while, but she thought she might as well get prepared before she had hardly any spare time. Her phone beeped with Instagram notifications and she smiled at how many likes her latest video tutorial had received. Despite Ellie only being interested in black eye liner when it came to make-up, she had agreed to be Lacie's model for her videos. And she was building followers every day. It had given her something rewarding to do while progressing through her pregnancy, not being used to not working every day.

She added a custom make-up tutorial to her list of services, so she could analyse the client's skin and advise on the best make-up products and colours to suit them, and instruct them on how to easily apply them at home.

She'd be offering all the usual beauty services, and each time she'd get an idea for a great pampering package, she'd add it to her list. She could have standard packages that were always available, as well as seasonal packages and special occasion packages. She'd need to think of names for her treatments too. So far, Ellie had not been the best name-thinker-upperer, preferring to give them silly names like 'Messy Mulch Massage', 'Geriatric Glow Facial', and 'Pimple Popping Perfection'.

She giggled recalling her brainstorming session with her sister, and sighed at how much better she'd been in the last couple of months. Regular mental health appointments and following a healthy eating plan and more consistent sleep routine had helped. She was even getting up earlier than Lacie lately.

Today Lacie was on her own in the house, as Ellie and her mother were out buying baby presents and she wasn't allowed to come. Penny was at work, and they'd invited Melina too of course, but understandably she declined. It was hard for her, having done her first round of IVF with no success, and gearing up for the next one. Chris had visited the weekend prior while she was taking the girls to their father's, and told them how devastated they'd been when they got the negative test.

The creak of the gate opening made her lose her train of thought, and she glanced up and to the front of the yard to see Nathan walking in carrying a heap of garden things. She was about to discreetly pop inside to avoid having to speak to him, as they'd gotten used to doing the past couple of months with not much more than a polite nod or curt smile in greeting to each other. But he noticed her just as she stood, and she acknowledged him with one of those nods again. She pretended she was stretching and then sat again with her notebook.

'Just dropping off some supplies for tomorrow's work,' he said, and he proceeded to deliver the items to their required locations.

She pretended to write in her notebook but was really just doodling, when he approached and stopped near her.

'How are you?' he asked, but not in his usual friendly way, more of a concerned way.

'Good. Well, I'm pretty uncomfortable, and I'm aching all the time, but it's okay. All for a good cause. How are you?'

'Good.'

'I've seen your latest videos on YouTube, looks like you're getting more of a following.'

'Yep.'

The air was tense and she felt like she had to hold her breath.

'Well,' he glanced to the front of the property, 'I better go.'

'Nathan.' She went to stand.

'It's okay, don't get up.' He held his hand out and she surrendered to the chair again.

'I really am sorry,' she said.

Nathan diverted his gaze from her.

'I hate to see you like this. You're such an easy-going, friendly guy, and now you're all tense and serious.'

He crossed his arms. 'I just don't like people being dishonest with me.'

'I know, and I wish I could turn back time and just tell you. I'm annoyed at myself for not doing so.' She lowered her head a moment, her belly obscuring her view of the ground in front of her.

'Why was it so hard?' he asked. 'You didn't feel like I was worthy of knowing your secret, or you didn't think I was important enough in your life to share things with?' He looked her in the eye with a rawness she hadn't seen before.

She gripped the armrests. 'It was *because* I felt such a strong connection to you that I didn't tell you, it was *because* I liked you so much and didn't want to lose what we had that I didn't tell you.' She sighed. 'Okay, so that was selfish of me, I know, and I'm sorry, I just, it just… all got out of hand. I could blame the lack of judgement on the pregnancy hormones, but I know that's a cop out. Honestly, I thought it would just fizzle out and you'd lose interest anyway, with me being so far away.'

'I was becoming *more* interested each day,' he said, his voice slightly louder than before.

'But if you knew I was having a baby, well, I assumed that'd kill the mood and be the end of our amazing chats and special connection, at least in the same form.' She locked her gaze with his, and it was like she could see deep into his heart, and feel the hurt there, but also the connection they'd had. 'I wasn't ready to let go of what we had so soon. It was special, and unique, and easy, and exciting. And honestly, talking to you was like talking to my best friend, but more than that. It felt like… it felt like…' She looked up at the sky, then down at the ground, and rubbed an ache in her lower belly. 'Oh, it doesn't matter.'

Lacie closed her notebook, no longer in the mood for business planning. She pushed on the armrests and lifted herself up. 'Nathan, if you can ever forgive me, please know you can trust me. I promise, I'm not a deceitful person. I am honest and trustworthy. I just… made a mistake, that's all. I'm only human.' She shrugged, and felt like she needed the bathroom yet again, until an unusual warmth spread below and trickled down her legs, a puddle forming on the patio tiles. She gasped. She looked up at Nathan, her mouth open, humiliated that she'd peed herself in front of him.

'Is that… your waters breaking?' he asked, looking as shocked as she felt.

'Oh!' Relieved, she laughed. 'Yes. Phew. It's just my waters breaking.' She placed her hands over her belly, then realisation hit her. 'Oh my God. It's my waters breaking. My waters broke!'

'I thought you weren't due for a while?'

'A few weeks. Oh my God.' She swivelled side to side, disoriented. 'What do I do?'

'Towel?'

'Okay. I'll go get one. And I'll change my clothes.'

'And then you should maybe get to hospital,' he added. 'Your mum's car's not out front, no one home?'

She shook her head. 'No, just me. They've gone shopping in Welston.'

'I'll drive you then,' he said.

'Are you sure? Should I wait till they get home? Labour can take ages to start and even longer to finish. I'm not even in any pain. Although I have been… achy, I guess.'

'Ah…' He scratched his head. 'I think if you're going to have to get there eventually, you might as well go. I can stay in the waiting room, I guess, till your mum comes.'

Lacie's heart rate rose and blood pumped forcefully through her chest, her legs becoming weak and wobbly. 'I'll, ah, go do those things I said.' She gestured to the house. 'And get my hospital bag. And lock up. And I'll meet you at your car.'

'Do you need me to help with anything?'

She shook her head.

Nathan lowered his head a little. 'I should have left you in peace to relax. I hope our conversation didn't set things off somehow.'

Her nerves had been heightened, talking to him, explaining with heartfelt intent why she'd avoided telling him she was pregnant. But she didn't think a bit of stress would trigger labour. 'No, it's okay. Don't worry. See you out front. Oh, would you be able to wheel my hospital bag out?'

She went back inside with him and he took it out the patio doors, then she cleaned herself up, changing into a loose-fitting, knee-length maternity dress so that if anything happened, well, she wouldn't have to deal with a pair of pants. She grabbed her phone from its charger and packed them both in her handbag, then took a towel from the bathroom, and made her way to his Ute out front.

'I better call the hospital too, let them know I'm coming.' She called and they said if the waters had broken it was a good idea that she come straight in, even if she wasn't having regular contractions. Then she called her mum and told her not to rush, but whenever they finished their shopping they should come to the hospital. She texted Penny who was still at work, and Chris and Matt, to let them know their niece or nephew would probably be arriving soon. 'Am I forgetting anything?' Lacie asked, her nerves jittery and her voice shaky.

'To take a breath?' he suggested, and she thought she saw a hint of a smile on his face. She had no idea if her words had gotten through to him and if they meant anything, they hadn't been able to continue and now the moment was gone. All she could think about was getting to hospital and trying to remember all she'd learned about breathing and movement and affirmations and helping labour to progress as well as possible.

Lacie practised some breathing techniques she'd learned, and her muscles relaxed a little. The ache in her lower belly and back appeared every so often, and she rubbed her abdomen.

Nathan drove carefully and kept to the left lane on the highway, allowing people to overtake. He pushed the radio button and changed the station to classical music. 'Will this do?'

'Yeah, thanks.'

On arrival, Lacie gave her details and situation, and the nurse tried to usher Nathan through as well.

'Oh, I'm not the father,' he said. 'I'll just wait here until your mum comes.' He took a seat in the waiting area. 'Good luck, Lacie.'

She smiled a nervous thank you and entered the room, hopping onto the bed. This was it. She didn't know how long it would take, but soon a real, live baby would be in her arms. Her heart fluttered and her hands shook a little.

She was asked a series of questions and then a cuff was inflated around her arm. 'Blood pressure is good,' the midwife said, 'pulse is a little racy but I guess that's just nerves.' She offered a smile. 'It'll be okay. You're in the right place.' She checked her cervix and was told she was two centimetres dilated, then attached a thick, wide strap with some kind of device on it to her abdomen. 'The CTG will record the baby's heart rate and we'll be able to see if there are any contractions,' the midwife said.

Lacie nodded. It was all a blur. Surreal and a little scary. Her belly continued to feel achy but nothing major yet.

'No pain?' the midwife asked.

'Nope. If it stays like this, it'll be a breeze!' she joked, and the midwife gave an... *interesting* smile.

'Agghhhhh! Ohhhhh my Godddd,' Lacie exclaimed several hours later, another contraction gripping her abdomen like a vice.

'Breathe through it, in and out,' the midwife encouraged.

She exaggerated an inhalation and exhalation, trying to push away the pain.

'Work with the pain, not against it, sweetheart,' her mother said, holding her hand, while Ellie stood behind, rubbing her back.

'Owwwwww, ohhhhhh,' she moaned. Her belly felt like it had a giant rock inside it, pushing against her skin. Heat overtook her body with each contraction, and she begged for another cold cloth for her forehead and an ice cube to suck on as the contraction subsided. She knew she'd only have seconds until the next one hit, and the anticipation was daunting.

She took some slower breaths in preparation as the next wave of pain rolled through her, verbalising her pain with primal sounds as it increased in intensity. She felt like an animal in the wild, her body doing this enormous feat all by itself and all she could do was go through it.

At the next break between contractions, she vaguely heard the midwife say she was fully dilated. Soon enough, a pressure she could not resist weighed down on her pelvis, and an unstoppable urge to push had her clenching her jaw.

'With the next contraction, bear down and push but slowly, allow time for everything to stretch.'

The pain overtook her and she focused all her energy downwards, pushing, taking a breath, then pushing some more. A stinging sensation intensified and she tried to stop pushing from the pain, but the urge persisted.

'I know this part hurts, but it means your baby is on its way out. Keep going!'

She pushed again and again, the stinging, burning pain getting worse, but the urge getting stronger each time. She felt like she was pushing for hours, and she had no awareness of how much time had gone past. Push after push, she thought she'd have to keep going for much longer, until with the next push, her mother gasped and said, 'Almost there, sweetheart!'

More pain and another push. 'The head is out,' the midwife

exclaimed. 'One more big, gradual push to get the shoulders out carefully, okay?'

Lacie followed the instructions as best she could, trying to control the urge not to push too hard and fast all at once, letting it build so she could reduce the risk of tearing.

She took a breath as though she was getting ready to dive underwater, then scrunched up her face and with an almighty effort gave a massive but controlled push. She felt a sudden pop and a release of pressure, a slippery sensation easing her pain.

'Baby's out!' her mum exclaimed.

A second later, a beautiful, high-pitched cry filled the room, and Ellie said, 'Ohh!'

Before she could process it all, the midwife placed the baby on her chest and Lacie's mouth opened wide in awe, her heart swelling with love at the sweet little scrunched-up face. She held out her finger and the baby gripped it with tiny fingers.

'Oh my, it's a beautiful baby girl,' Martha said, leaning in close and giving Lacie a kiss on the cheek, Ellie leaning over her shoulder.

Lacie's heart melted in an instant, all memory of pain forgotten, the angelic little face of her daughter right in front of her. The love was immediate and immense, filling her whole body. She held her baby close to her skin, chest to chest, the midwife placing a blanket over them. She traced the outline of her baby's lips with a gentle finger, then her cheek, her head with a soft coating of blonde hair, and returned it to her baby's hand and surprisingly strong grip. Lacie's eyes welled with happy tears. If this moment lasted forever, it still wouldn't be long enough.

CHAPTER THIRTY-SIX

Six days later, Lacie was sitting on the wicker chair on the patio outside her bedroom at South Haven, one hand supporting her baby while she breastfed, and the other hand trying to type on her phone. She was surprised how full-on her time in hospital had been: nurses doing regular obs, lots of different health professionals visiting at random times, and every free moment spent trying to catch up on sleep. She was finally writing her birth announcement on Facebook, complete with her favourite newborn photo out of the hundred or so she'd already taken. With a smile, she pressed post, then opened a text message and sent a brief message to Xavier, informing him of their daughter's birth. She knew he didn't want to play a role in her life but he'd offered to help financially, and she wanted him to at least see her photo if not meet her in person.

She lifted the baby up to her shoulder for a burp, and heard footsteps approaching. She glanced to the right to see Nathan walking along the curved pathway he'd created from the gate entrance to the firepit area. He slowed and gave a wave, and she gestured that it was okay for him to come over.

'Gotta get used to doing things one-handed,' she said,

putting her phone on the table. She'd sent him a photo after the birth and thanked him for driving her to hospital, and he'd said he'd let her get some rest and meet the baby sometime when she was back home.

Lacie tilted her shoulder forward so Nathan could see her baby's little face. 'This is Elliana Rose Appleby,' she said softly.

'Oh hey there, little one.' Nathan gently touched her cheek with the back of his curved finger. 'She's beautiful.' He smiled. 'Beautiful name too.'

'Ellie was pleased I half named her after her,' she said.

'I bet. And how are you feeling?'

'I'm good. It was the hardest thing I've ever done, but what a reward huh?' She patted Elliana's back and a burp came out. 'Oh, taking after uncle Chris there, bub.' She chuckled.

'How tiny are those fingers. And fingernails! So cute.' Nathan smiled in awe.

'Do you want a hold? Here.' She held her daughter out to him and his eyebrows rose as if to say 'you sure?'.

He positioned his arms and gently took hold.

'Just have to support the head,' she instructed, allowing his hand to replace hers. Her protective instinct was on high alert.

'Oh wow,' he said. 'She's so light.'

'Felt a lot heavier in my belly!' Lacie laughed. 'Have you... held a baby before?'

Nathan looked up from the baby and into Lacie's eyes. He shook his head, and smiled. 'Thank you for this milestone moment in my life.'

'My pleasure,' she replied. She let him sway her gently for a while, then as she grizzled he handed her back, and she lovingly took hold. 'I'll just put her in the bassinet, one moment.' She opened the screen door to her room and after swaddling her in a muslin wrap, placed Elliana on her back in the co-sleeper that sat next to her bed.

She watched her for a moment, never able to get enough of looking at her, then returned to the patio where she could still see and hear her daughter.

'I guess you should take this chance to have a nap?' he asked.

'I'll actually get some breakfast first, I've only had the banana I kept by my bed last night. Mum is making scrambled eggs. I'm so lucky she's here to help.'

'I won't hold you up. I just wanted to ask, when would it be suitable to mow the lawn? I won't do it now while Elliana's sleeping. I've got some other things I can do in the meantime.'

'She probably wouldn't wake anyway, but just in case, how about I text you when she's up again?'

'Sounds good, I'll keep my phone on me.' He scratched his head, and a moment of silence hung in the air.

Lacie didn't know whether to end the conversation there or continue talking, but thankfully he spoke.

'I've been thinking about all you said, before you went into labour.' He took a seat on one of the chairs and gestured for her to do the same. 'I know I was still upset, and we didn't get to continue or resolve anything, but...' He exhaled. 'I can understand why you withheld it from me.'

He did?

'Of course I would have liked to have known, but I know it was your private situation to share or not share as you wish, and I respect that. Once we started getting closer though, and things felt... different, special, like there was definitely something between us regardless of the distance, I guess knowing that you still kept it from me then was what upset me. I wouldn't have just disappeared, Lacie. I can't say for sure how it may have impacted things, but I'm sad you didn't feel you could tell me.'

She nodded and sighed. 'I understand your side of things too and I'm sad I upset you. You weren't just a temporary flirtation to me, Nathan, and I don't want you to feel like you weren't – aren't – an important part of my life.'

'I know, I get that now. I know you weren't deceitful, just cautious, and that's a good trait to have in life. I think I may have overreacted a bit due to my past experience with Tess. She *was* deceitful, so it kind of triggered all that again.'

Lacie felt bad for him. 'I'm sorry how it all happened. I definitely would never do anything like that.'

'I know you wouldn't.' He took her hand. 'I forgive you. And I hope you'll forgive me for being angrier about it than I should have been.'

'Thank you. But there's nothing for me to forgive because you didn't do anything wrong. You felt minimised, and you had every right to be upset.'

He stroked her hand. 'It hasn't changed my connection with you, but it did change the dynamics. I wish we could go back to the way it was, but you've just had a baby, and I think it's best if I let you focus on that... it's going to be full on, I'm sure. And I don't want to get in the way of your special experience or confuse things.'

Part of her wanted to resume where they left off with some slight adjustments, her being the mother of a newborn, but he was right. What she needed most right now was to focus on this new stage of her life, and cherish every moment with her daughter, shower her with love and look after herself while she recovered. She was exhausted from everything – the pregnancy, the birth, the emotional upheavals from what happened with him, and Ellie's issues.

'I'm really glad you moved back though,' he said. 'I didn't expect that, so it'll be nice to see you and Elliana around.' He stood, and she followed suit.

'Don't be a stranger,' she said. 'I might even need your help with landscaping around the cottage for my new salon I'm going to open next year sometime.'

'I'd love that. And keep an eye on YouTube for my special video about feature gardens, uploading tomorrow, featuring none other than Tarrin's Bay's best pebble artist, Jessie.'

'Oh, I was wondering if she'd had her interview yet! She showed me Elliana's special pebble in the garden when I got home. Can't wait to see the video. And Gloria's in it too?'

'She sure is. Her interview brought a tear to my eye, so you have been warned.'

'Thanks for the heads-up.' She smiled.

Nathan held out his hand. 'Friends?'

She grasped his hand and shook it. 'Friends.' And instead of letting go and walking back inside, she pulled him close, and he enveloped her in the long awaited, loving embrace she thought she'd never get.

CHAPTER THIRTY-SEVEN

Dear Elliana,

Tomorrow is your first birthday! I can't believe you are one year old already. The year has flown by in a flurry of sleep deprivation, feeds galore, nappy changes, giggles, cuddles, milestones, laughter, and a few tears. It has been the best year of my life. Every day I love seeing you in the morning, and the way you smile at me when I pick you up from your cot like I'm the best person in the world, is humbling to say the least. Thank you for coming in to my life. You are the surprise gift I never expected, but now I could not imagine life without you.

We have a special party planned for you. I know you won't really understand what's going on and you'll probably just want to play with your toys, eat your favourite vanilla custard, and try your best not to fall asleep at naptime. But all my favourite people will be joining us to celebrate your life. I'll take lots of photos and show you when you're a bit older so you can see the fun we had.

I'm a little emotional writing this letter, because you mean so much to me and I feel so lucky. But I am also sad your grandpa can't be here to meet you. He would have loved you so much, and if he's up there somewhere I hope he is looking down on you and smiling, and writing little inspiring notes to leave on your pillow.

Although it's not yet your birthday, you already have your first gift. It was left on the patio table this afternoon and I noticed it when I closed the blinds and curtains at the end of the day... a small jar with a ribbon tied around it, filled with a posy of tiny little baby's breath flowers. There was a larger jar too, for me, with a single perfect pink tulip. I know who left the secret gift, and I'll tell you one day.

On your first birthday, I want to tell you how much I love you and always will. Keep growing strong, but don't grow too fast! I plan to make the most of every moment, every day, and every year of your life. These younger years will go fast, and it'll be nice to sit back one day in the future and read these letters together. You can always write letters to me too, even though you'll be with me and will be able to talk at any time. What I've discovered is that through writing to a loved one, words are said that might otherwise not be said, and it's a way for us to make sense of what we are thinking and feeling, and hopefully bring a smile to our loved one's face. So I am going to write you a letter like this every year on your birthday until you are eighteen. One down, seventeen to go! I wonder what the last one will say... it's surreal to think about! But I won't get ahead of myself. Right now, I am grateful for my healthy, happy one-year-old; the light of my life.

Love, Mum xo

CHAPTER THIRTY-EIGHT

Nathan walked through the gate at South Haven for what could be the last time. The landscaped gardens were now complete as of two weeks ago, and would only require casual maintenance here and there, which any gardener could do. New opportunities awaited him, and he was excited to see which path his life led him on next.

'Hey, mate, how's things?' Lacie's brother Chris welcomed him and offered him a drink in a plastic flute with... he took a sip... lemonade.

'Good. Thanks, man. Yourself?'

'Yeah good. Come on in and enjoy the best party of the year!' He smiled. He certainly looked less stressed than he remembered. Maybe he had more than lemonade in his flute.

Nathan walked along the pathway, towards the barbeque area he had created, admiring the plants and blooms he had planted and nurtured, and merged in with the small crowd, some he recognised, others he didn't. 'Gloria, nice to see you!' He gave the lady a peck on the cheek. 'I look forward to doing your autumn garden refresh on the first of next month.'

'Can't wait. And most importantly, would you like me to serve scones, lemon poppyseed cake, or chocolate slice?'

'Hmm,' Nathan said, stroking his jaw with his thumb and forefinger. 'Let's go for the chocolate slice this time.'

'Deal.' She gave a nod. 'Oh, and I'd like you to meet my friend Nancy Dillinger... Nancy this is Nathan, the chap who does the videos online.'

'Oh my, you're the famous Nature Nathan!'

Nathan hooked the handle of the gift bag he was holding onto his left little finger as he held his flute, and held out his free hand to Nancy. She shook it with more enthusiasm than he expected for a lady of a certain age, her spindly fingers bony and slightly out of shape. 'I love your videos, and I was inspired to meet Gloria after watching your interview. We're now the best of friends.' She grinned.

'That's made my day,' he said. 'Thank you so much.'

He left the ladies to admire the flowers and waved to Matt and Sophia who were chatting to Penny's husband, Steve, then caught the eye of Penny and her kids who she was trying to wrangle and keep from climbing onto one of the tall trees. 'Not while we have guests!' she said. Jessie skipped off towards Ellie, and he waved to get her attention.

'Hi!' Ellie came up and gave him a hug. 'Thank you for my surprise on the step a couple of weeks ago, I'm going to miss our weekly talks out back if you're not here so often.'

'It's been great. And I'm glad you liked the pine-cone dude I made.'

'He is awesome, love the black beanie and his googly eyes. I'm guessing it wasn't something you found in the garden though, like all the other "step surprises".'

'Haha, no. I did have to make an extra effort for that one.'

'I'll always remember the heart shape made out of pebbles

you left for me when I got out of hospital way back when. Meant so much to me.'

He hugged her again. 'You're doing great. I'm proud of you.'

She smiled. 'Hey, you haven't had an official tour of Lacie's salon yet, have you? We finished decorating last week. Come!' She grasped his elbow and led him to the most beautiful woman in the garden; her bright floral dress billowing, and strawberry-blonde waves wafting in the breeze, pink highlights back again.

'Hello there,' he said.

'Hi, so glad you could make it.' She gave him a brief hug and took the present from him with thanks, placing it on the nearby gift table. It was a child's windchime, made with natural materials including wood and bamboo, that produced a soothing melodic sound. She probably couldn't play with it but it could hang in her room and she could listen to the sounds.

'Happy birthday, Elliana,' he said, giving the girl a light pat on her arm.

'She's very excited by all the attention, as you can see!' Lacie said, as Elliana chewed on the collar of her dress and looked up at the trees. 'A true nature girl, she is, absolutely loves being out here.'

'Shall we show Nathan a sneak peek inside the salon?' Ellie asked. 'Now that he's finished with all the external design work?'

'Yes, come have a look.'

Martha came over and welcomed Nathan. 'Let me hold my gorgeous granddaughter while you take a tour,' she said, lifting the baby from her mother's arms.

Jessie ran over when they reached the separate gate to the private yard that housed the cottage. 'Can I visit the salon too?' she enquired.

'Of course.' Lacie held her niece's hand and they walked to

the front door. A bright wooden hand-painted sign above the door read: *In Bloom.*

'I love the name you chose,' he said.

'Yes, it pays homage to my love of flowers, and represents each client feeling like their best blooming self,' she replied with a smile.

They walked through the white and pale pink painted weatherboard cottage with subtle yellow and fuchsia accents, which Lacie said was based on the colours of the Love and Peace rose. Inside, a reception desk stood against the side wall, a vase of mixed flowers on display – gerberas, carnations, daffodils, and lush green leaves.

'I got these for the photoshoot we did a few days ago. The website is looking fab now with all the photos of the salon and the rooms.'

'When do you open?'

'Valentine's Day.' She smiled.

'Everything looks amazing. Different to your Chicago salon from what I remember from the photos.'

She nodded. 'Yes, that had richer colours and was more glam, this is more organic and lighter, airier and colourful.'

'I chose this wall print,' Ellie said, leading him into one of the beauty rooms with flower-shaped wall sconces and titled The Rose Room.

On the wall was a photo of a calming nature scene and a quote from Vincent van Gogh: *If you truly love nature, you will find beauty everywhere.*

He nodded in understanding. 'I love it. And the salon is beautiful, well done.'

'The flowers you planted in pots either side of the entrance really give it a welcoming vibe,' Lacie said. 'And the stepping stones leading around the side of the cottage to the back garden for clients to sip their post-pampering teas are such a unique addition to the space. I'm going to love working here three days a week, though I'm going to miss being with my girl twenty-four seven.' She led him into the second room, The Tulip Room, which was equally as beautiful, even the bathroom and storage room were decorated perfectly with a floral theme.

'I love this chair,' Jessie said, plonking herself on the pale pink curved armchair that looked like tulip petals embracing her.

'Will you be offering men's services too?' he enquired.

'Of course. Everyone is welcome.' She smiled. 'In need of some pampering?' She eyed him with a curious glance he hadn't seen for quite a while.

'Hmm, maybe.' He returned her curious glance with one of his own.

'C'mon, you two,' Ellie said. 'We better get back to the party.' He thought he saw some kind of questioning exchange between Ellie and Lacie but couldn't be sure.

They walked out the door and Lacie leaned towards him and whispered, 'Thank you for the flower jars.'

Nathan smiled and offered a nod. He had forgotten until she'd mentioned it. He'd asked Martha permission to visit and sneak round the side of the house yesterday to place them on the table when Lacie had been out for a walk to the park.

Jessie jumped on the first few stepping stones next to the cottage, then turned around and looked at her aunt suddenly. 'Oh, I just remembered something!'

'What is it, Jess?'

'Remember when Nathan made us that new firepit millions of years ago and we all made wishes and threw them in?'

Nathan laughed, and recalled he'd made one too.

'Yes,' Lacie said, tipping her head back as though recalling her wish too.

'Mine came true! I forgot to remember and then I forgot that I forgot.'

'What was it?' Lacie crouched to her niece's height.

'I wished that you would come back and live in Tarrin's Bay again.' She hugged Lacie, and Lacie's eyes became glossy.

'Oh, sweetie, that's so nice of you to wish that. Thank you.' She stroked Jessie's hair and squeezed her tight. 'Mine came true too. I wished for my baby to be healthy and happy.'

Nathan smiled, still amazed she had known about the baby right when they'd met.

'I wished to feel happier one day,' Ellie said. 'And I definitely do.'

Lacie draped an arm around her sister.

'What about yours, Nathan?' Jessie asked.

He pondered this. It had partly come true, but he was yet to see if it would come to full bloom. But technically, he had found what he'd wished for, even though a year ago he may have thought otherwise. 'I think it has actually, but it's a secret.' He winked, then pointed to the white gazebo he had erected in the back garden, which they could see the top of over the fence and hedging. 'Do you think it's time for birthday cake soon?'

'Is it, Aunty Lacie?' Jessie jumped up and down on the spot.

'I reckon we can have the cake now before my bub needs to have her nap, then all the guests can eat lunch. No harm in doing things out of order!'

'Nature knows best,' he said.

They returned to the party and Martha helped gather everyone around the gazebo. Lacie stood behind the table with the double-decker flower-shaped cake, holding Elliana who was still gazing upwards. Once they lit the candles, the girl focused intently on them and tried to reach down to grab them, but her mother held her back, as everyone sang 'Happy Birthday'. Lacie modelled to her daughter how to blow out the candles, and although she made the right shape with her mouth, Lacie blew them out for her.

I wonder if she's made a second wish, Nathan thought.

After Lacie had cut the cake and placed a few small morsels into Elliana's mouth, Chris went up to the gazebo and gave her a hug. He whispered something in her ear and she nodded. He stood tall and proud and said, 'If I can have your attention, please.'

Everyone went quiet and he spoke again. 'I want to say how proud we are of Lacie having survived her first year of motherhood. She's done an amazing job, and we're glad to have another little Appleby in the family.' He pecked both Lacie and Elliana on the cheek. 'And on that note, I'd like to announce that there will be *another* little Appleby joining the family as well.' He gestured for Melina to step up to the gazebo stage. She obliged but her face was glowing pink. 'Some of you may know we've been going through IVF for over a year now. We were just about ready to call it quits, but we got lucky. And we've received the all clear at the twelve-week ultrasound and blood test. We are having a boy!'

Nathan smiled wide with happiness for the couple and clapped. By the looks of things, Lacie and Martha had already known, but it was news to the others, as they called out 'congratulations' and cheered, and Penny had tears in her eyes. He understood now that many preferred to wait until they were more confident of the baby's health before telling anyone, even those close to them.

'I'm so happy for you guys,' Lacie said, then turned to the crowd. 'It's time to feed this little one her milk and put her to bed, but I'll see you for lunch once she's settled. Thanks so much, everyone!'

She stepped off the gazebo and after a few hugs, she wandered around to the front of the house. Nathan chatted to a few people, received compliments on the garden design, and gradually made his way to the side gate. He hesitated a moment, then went through to the front of the house and waited at the door for Lacie to come out.

Lacie kissed Elliana gently on the forehead then placed her in the cot. She waited a moment at the door to make sure she stayed settled, and popped the baby monitor into her pocket. Satisfied, she scurried down the hallway and through the kitchen, and on reaching the entryway she stopped. 'Oh, hi,' she said, Nathan standing at the door.

'Hi. Sorry to surprise you, I was just hoping to catch you alone for a few minutes.'

'Sure, what is it?' she asked, gesturing for him to come inside.

They stood in the entry way and he took her hands in his. The warmth as enticing as soft sand on a summer's day. 'I have a couple of work opportunities I'm considering,' he revealed.

'Oh?'

'One is over the next six to nine months, being part of the garden landscaping team at the new resort that's being built up in the hills.'

'Oh yes, I saw the construction plans online, it'll be an amazing place and bring lots of tourism.'

'I've been offered the position and I need to decide soon. It won't be long term, but they will have maintenance roles part time afterwards, so I could work there as well as continue my local casual jobs and my YouTube videos. But I've also been offered another job, a full-time position starting in six weeks doing gardening, walking track construction, tour groups, and general maintenance at a beautiful rainforest I visited a while back.'

'Wow, that sounds amazing, a bit different to the usual backyard makeovers,' she mused.

'True. But it's in Queensland. Gold Coast hinterland.'

Her heart dropped. 'Oh.'

'I don't know what to do,' he said, his eyes searching hers for answers.

She took a breath and her heart rose, filling with peace and acceptance. 'They both sound great, and you'd be awesome at either, but... you should do what excites you. Do what your heart wants the most.'

He held her gaze, and, his voice filled with authentic intent, said, 'What my heart wants most is you.'

Her breath caught in her throat, and her heartbeat intensified. She kept holding his gaze as he spoke again.

'If there's any hint left of what you felt before, what we had before, then tell me now and I'll take the job in the hills and be with you. But if there's any hesitation, if you're not sure, or too much time has passed and it'd spoil our friendship, then tell me that and I'll move on to Queensland.' He grasped her hands more tightly, as though tensely awaiting a verdict on his future.

'Nathan, I...' she began, her heart and mind in conflict. 'I don't want to be responsible for making this decision for you. It should be yours to make. Don't let me hold you back from what you want, if you want the rainforest job then go for it.' She said the right words but what she really wanted to say was 'don't go'.

He smiled. 'Lacie, as I said, I want you. But if it isn't mutual, then I'll go. I'm not making this decision without you. I don't want to be far away from you again if we both want the same thing. But if you've moved on in your heart, please tell me so that I know. I'll be okay.'

Was he really, finally, declaring his feelings for her, despite the trouble she'd caused him? She knew what her heart wanted too, but if he made the wrong choice on her account, would he regret it?

She glanced towards the kitchen, towards the dining room where he'd shared their Christmas in July family reunion, and smiled at the memories. He had somehow become part of not only her life, but her whole family's life. She couldn't imagine not having him in it. She would be okay if he left, but she would be much more than okay if he stayed.

'You really want to base this decision around me?'

He nodded. 'You first, job second.'

In that case… 'Then stay.' She gripped his arms. 'Nathan, I never stopped having feelings for you. I meant it back when I was apologising and I said that talking to you was like talking to my best friend. And what I also wanted to say was that it felt like… like I was talking to my soulmate.' She smiled and her heart fluttered with eager anticipation on what was starting to unfold between them, finally.

His eyes became soft and it was as though they were smiling too. 'I know exactly what you mean. I know without a doubt that you are my soulmate, and I don't want to live another day without you.' He slid his arms around her waist.

'Let's do this,' she said. 'No secrets, no fears. I'm ready.'

'Me too.' He leaned closer to her.

'Oh wait,' she said, placing her finger on his lips that were about to kiss her. 'What was your firepit wish?'

'To find a woman I could trust.'

She stiffened slightly, her past mistake weighing on her mind, but he only held her more closely.

'And I know without a doubt, that I've found her.' He leaned his forehead on hers a moment, and long-held regret seeped out of her body for good. 'Now, can I finally kiss you? I've waited about eighteen months for another kiss, you know.'

'Hey, I waited too,' she said.

'Then let's make it worth the wait, for both of us.' He slowly inched his lips closer to hers until they touched, light as a feather at first, then he grasped her face with his hands and invited her lips to his with pure hunger and intensity. Her insides melted in a state of bliss. If this moment lasted forever, it too, would not be long enough.

THE END

IN BLOOM
OPENING SPECIALS

Treatments performed by Hollywood-trained Lacie Appleby

Rose Indulgence Ritual
A rose petal footbath begins your indulgence, followed by a luxurious back massage with rose infused oil, and a nurturing hydration facial with rose quartz roller massage to bring your skin back to its natural radiance.

Jasmine Joy
A coconut and Himalayan salt full body scrub followed by a moisturising jasmine oil full body massage and facial acupressure to boost circulation and lift your mood.

Tulip Tune-Up
A revitalising foot reflexology massage with pedicure and manicure, followed by professional make-up application to your needs. Take home a bonus tulip to brighten your day.

Lavender Luxury

Pure relaxation awaits with this ninety-minute hot stone massage with lavender infused oil followed by a mini facial with soothing mask and a decadent scalp massage to complete your self-care journey. Bonus lavender eye pillow.

Baby's Breath Bliss

For expectant mothers, take some time to unwind with a half hour pregnancy massage, guided meditation, and half hour organic facial, with your choice of pedicure or make-up application to look and feel your best during this special time.

ALSO BY JULIET MADISON

ACKNOWLEDGEMENTS

Thank you to my loyal readers who waited a long time for this next instalment of the Tarrin's Bay series, I hope you enjoy Lacie and Nathan's story. And to my new readers who've just discovered this series, thank you for reading these books and welcoming the characters into your heart.

To my editor, Abbie Rutherford, thank you for your thorough and helpful editing to help make this book shine, and to Tara and the proofreading team at Bloodhound Books for producing great-looking books, also to Betsy and the Bloodhound team for supporting my work.

To my writer friends around the globe, your virtual presence is always an inspiration and support, thank you for all your encouragement. To my partner, Zeynel, thank you for helping me with both the gardening and nature facts for this story, and for supporting me with the extra time off I needed from motherhood duties so I could finish this book in time. Also a big thanks for help with babysitting goes to my parents, and to Nigar and Remziye; the best aunties a baby could have.

ABOUT THE AUTHOR

Juliet Madison is a bestselling and award-nominated author of books with humour, heart, and serendipity. Writing both fiction and self-help, she is also an artist and colouring book illustrator, and an intuitive life coach who loves creating online courses for writers and those wanting to live an empowered life.

With her background as a naturopath and a dancer, Juliet is passionate about living a healthy and positive life. She likes to combine her love of words, art, and self-empowerment to create books that entertain and inspire readers to find the magic in everyday life.

Juliet lives on the picturesque south coast of NSW, Australia, where she spends as much time as possible dreaming up new stories, following her passions, being with her family, and as little time as possible doing housework.

You can find out more about Juliet, her books, and her courses at http://www.julietmadison.com and connect with her on social media at Facebook http://www.facebook.com/julietmadisonauthor and Instagram http://www.instagram.com/julietmadisonauthorartist

A NOTE FROM THE PUBLISHER

Thank you for reading this book. If you enjoyed it please do consider leaving a review on Amazon to help others find it too.

We hate typos. All of our books have been rigorously edited and proofread, but sometimes mistakes do slip through. If you have spotted a typo, please do let us know and we can get it amended within hours.

info@bloodhoundbooks.com

Printed in Great Britain
by Amazon

46519761R00189